CW00506194

About the Author

Nigel Milliner grew up in Jamaica during his formative years but spent most of his business career working in London. He has lived for over twenty years in Cornwall, with his wife and a variety of dogs. *The Mango Hand* is his sixth novel.

The Mango Hand

Nigel Milliner

The Mango Hand

Olympia Publishers
London

www.olympiapublishers.com
OLYMPIA PAPERBACK EDITION

Copyright © Nigel Milliner 2021

The right of Nigel Milliner to be identified as author of
this work has been asserted in accordance with sections 77 and 78
of the Copyright, Designs and Patents Act 1988.

All Rights Reserved

No reproduction, copy or transmission of this publication
may be made without written permission.
No paragraph of this publication may be reproduced,
copied or transmitted save with the written permission of the
publisher, or in accordance with the provisions
of the Copyright Act 1956 (as amended).

Any person who commits any unauthorised act in relation to
this publication may be liable to criminal
prosecution and civil claims for damage.

A CIP catalogue record for this title is
available from the British Library.

ISBN: 978-1-80074-160-7

This is a work of fiction.
Names, characters, places and incidents originate from the writer's
imagination. Any resemblance to actual persons, living or dead, is
purely coincidental.

First Published in 2021

Olympia Publishers
Tallis House
2 Tallis Street
London
EC4Y 0AB

Printed in Great Britain

Dedication

To Suzy, Alayne and Jessamy.

CHAPTER 1

I come from the land of wood and water.

These were his introductory words to me when first we met. As I soon discovered it was his enigmatic way of identifying himself, or of opening a topic of conversation. In adulthood I have met many West Indians over the years in such places as the Commonwealth Institute, in Brixton Market, at sporting events and even in a police station. I also spent many of the formative years of my childhood in Jamaica. However, the Jamaican in this narrative I met on his doorstep on Clapham High Street. We were introduced by my son, at the time a sergeant in the Metropolitan Police force.

Then there was Sonia, who helped this meeting come about. It was through her innate curiosity, drawn by the man's extraordinary magnetism mixed with the innocence of an ingenue, that much of his story came my way. It was largely through her research and her enquiring mind that a result came about which almost defies belief.

To describe him physically might offer a clue as to the nature of the individual I am writing about. He stood a little over six feet in height, probably even taller when fully erect in his youth. He wore his hair in shoulder-length dreadlocks, greying when we met, sometimes swallowed up under an outsized woolly bonnet and on special occasions hanging lank beneath a shiny bowler hat. In all seasons he wore what used to be known in his youth as a Tower Isle shirt - a loose multi-coloured, cotton garment named after the eponymous hotel on Jamaica's north coast. The hotel is now only a memory to those who today draw a pension, as it has long been operating under another name; if indeed it is still in business. For all I know Tower Isle might have been demolished in order to make way for multi-million-dollar apartments now owned by wealthy Americans.

In cooler weather, the gaunt and lanky West Indian covered the gaudy shirt with a poncho; a gift from a friend who had spent a fortnight in Peru. This garment had once been woven from many coloured wools but with time and wear, was now a faded blur with many loose plucked strands. His trousers of choice were Lincoln-green corduroy, worn smooth at the knees. And to top — or rather bottom — off this ensemble the trousers were tucked into highly polished cowboy boots. Inside his flat he was normally barefooted. As one can imagine the overall impression was striking and when strutted proudly down any High Street, totally unmissable.

It was only much later that I discovered it was all a disguise; a deflection from the character of the man beneath. Or more accurately, his own deeply ingrained impression of what he perceived his character to be. Whatever his motive, it was a magnificent affectation.

He is still very much alive and active today but as I might never see him again, I will tell his story in the past tense and as closely and accurately as it was told to me, via Sonia's recordings and from my own meetings with Moule.

His full name is Meshach Aloysius Winston Moule.

It was a bright summer day, 6th August, Jamaican

Independence Day, when Meshach Moule strode purposefully along Clapham High Street towards his home. Even though he had left Jamaica before the island's independence in 1962 and he had for many decades been a British citizen, he always recognised this day. It was, in part, an honourable gesture in memory of his late mother as well as being an acknowledgement of the country of his birth. It was not an original statement, but he was keen to impress that although you can take the boy out of Jamaica, you will never take Jamaica out of the boy. So, on this day, because it was a special day, he wore the outsized bonnet woven in the colours of the independent nation.

He carried a brown paper bag containing two mangoes and a bottle of Appleton rum. The mangoes could be bought anywhere but the rum was something rather special. To his taste Appleton was the finest rum, matured for twelve years and, in his opinion, the liquid embodiment of the country of his birth. Juice of the sugar cane, refined and distilled to perfection.

As he passed the shops, restaurants, apartment buildings and galleries on his way home he smiled at all who hailed him, with the occasional high-five for those he regarded as friends. This was his place, his territory, where he had lived for all of his adult life. He could walk proudly down this street with his head high, knowing that he was a respected citizen. He had iconic status. Moule was one who could 'strut real boasy', as they used to say in his youth. If you walked proud, the passers-by would shout, "Ah see you, man." That was respect. Real respect and acceptance.

As a boy, Moule had moved in the late fifties with his parents into a compact flat above an Italian restaurant in High

Street, Clapham. After a few years his mother had managed to buy the lease, which had enough years left to run to see out his lifetime. The restaurant had closed many years ago but the entrance to the flat was still through a side door and from there up a flight of stairs. At the top of the stairs there was a small landing from which there was a right turn, two more risers and then a green painted door.

Moule paused on the pavement by the front door to glad-hand a neighbour before taking a Yale key from his pocket. He turned the key and plodded slowly up the stairs, humming a tune in a bass baritone rumble, while the brown paper bag swung gently from his left hand.

He knew these stairs so well that sometimes he mounted them with his eyes shut, counting out each one as he went. On occasions, when the landing light bulb had blown, which it seemed to do frequently, there was no option other than to do it blindly.

Moule turned onto the top step and the humming stopped abruptly. He stood still for a few seconds and then, very slowly, lowered the paper bag to the floor. The step gave a small squeak as he bent down. He let go of the paper bag and then began to straighten up again.

He never made it to the vertical.

There was a sudden scampering of feet from inside and the door jerked open. Moule was knocked sideway against the wall and his head met the flaking plasterwork as a figure crashed past him. Even then, in his surprised state, he instinctively grabbed at the fugitive. His fingers wrapped briefly around a loose garment but were then wrenched away as the wearer bounded down the stairs.

Moule steadied himself against the handrail and for a

second was considering whether or not to give chase when a second figure appeared at the door. This one hesitated before making a break and that was long enough for him. As the front door slammed closed downstairs, he flung his free arm upwards and grabbed the second intruder by the throat. This one was slighter and shorter than the first and offered little resistance as Moule forced him back into his flat. They both fell to the floor and Moule kicked the door closed behind him.

His full fury exploded as he gathered a fist to smash a blow into the head of the invader, pinned underneath his gangling frame. His space had been invaded. His private world, rarely visited by anyone, had been sullied and at that moment his wrath surged uncontrollably.

But the fist never made contact. It remained suspended above a head of loose brown curls and an ear from which sagged a large gold bangle. They belonged to a girl.

She did not move but Moule sensed the fear as he remained on top of her, breathing heavily and trying to regain his composure.

There was slight whimper. "You're hurting me."

Moule did not reply but after a few more seconds slowly rolled away and, watching the prone figure carefully, rose awkwardly to his feet. His eyes never left the girl as he straightened his headgear and then reaching behind, he felt for the door lock.

"Get up." There was still no movement from the girl. "I said, get up."

She moved slowly and warily as if afraid a further assault might come from the imposing figure looming above her. His dark eyes were still wide with anger, but his body was now calm and still, as he watched the girl rise cautiously from his worn, patterned carpet.

When finally on her feet she stood nearly a foot shorter than Moule. She wore a faded denim jacket over a yellow T-shirt. It had a slogan written on the front, which was partially obscured by the jacket's lapels. Her skirt was also denim with a floral trim around its hem. Her slim brown hands nervously and self-consciously smoothed the skirt. It was a gesture that suggested self-preservation in the face of an imminent attack by a wild animal.

There were no socks between her feet and a pair of dirty trainers.

Moule regarded himself, not quite as a cultured man but one who had raised his status in the face of life's adversities. He read books borrowed from the local library, he watched educational programmes on television and had taught himself to talk in the manner of an educated Englishman. At least to his ear, that was how he sounded. In fact, he believed vocally that he could pass for Trevor McDonald. However, his normal default accent, whether or not speaking with fellow former West Indian colonialists, was the old accent which had little changed in sixty years. And with it, the idioms he had learned as a young boy in Jamaica. This was one of those occasions when all cultivated constraint disappeared.

"What you doin' eena me house, eeh?" He thrust his head forward. "Eeh?"

She recoiled at the second demand and then muttered something.

"What's dat you say? Speak up girl."

"It's not your house." Slightly emboldened, she stared at him defiantly.

"My house, my flat, what's de difference? This is where I

live." He made a sweeping gesture. "This place belongs to me. These are my possessions. What you want in here?"

The defiance faded and her lower lip began to quiver.

Moule shook his head in mock disbelief. "Now you bring on the tears. I am de one dat should be sheddin' tears, not you. Now, what you an' you fren steal, eeh?"

She said nothing but gave a small shake of the head.

Moule's eyes swept the room and then settled on the door to his bedroom. He gave a jerk of the head. "You been in dere?"

She shook her head.

"You not goin' to talk to me?" He came to a sudden decision. This girl was going nowhere until he could be sure that none of his possessions had gone. He gestured to a wicker chair by the window. It was a good distance from the door. "Sit down."

She did not move.

"I said, sit down over dere. You not goin' 'til I have some answers."

She moved then. Slowly and furtively, she sidled across the room and then lowered herself onto the chair, modestly pulling the skirt down as she did so.

Moule followed her until he was alongside the window. She glanced up at him as he pulled back the net curtain and peered into the street below. There was no sign of the other intruder hovering around, waiting for his accomplice to be released.

He turned, frowning and focusing again on the brown girl, now a picture of innocence on the wicker chair.

"How old are you?" He adopted his educated voice.

She opened her eyes very wide and adjusted her posture.

"What's that to you?"

"I don't want none of your lip, missy. You and your fren' broke into my home and I want to know if you are old enough for me to call the police."

A sly sneer spread slowly across her face, and she put a hand up to the gold ear bangle. "You can call them, but they won't come."

"What you mean? If I call the police they will come. You have burgled my house and that is a crime. I pay my Council tax and it's their duty to come if a crime has been committed."

She giggled and put a hand up to her mouth. "They never come. Not for a burglary. Not today anyway. And by then I'll be long gone."

"You think so?" he replied sternly. "You will not go from here until I say you can go."

She blinked a few times and a look of alarm flashed across her eyes. Moule glared at her sternly and was quietly pleased to note her concern. He began pacing the room slowly, whilst holding her in what he regarded as his fiercest gaze.

"Fifteen… sixteen?"

"What?"

"Your age. I asked your age. You need to be put straight and so I need to know what age I am talking to."

"It makes a difference?" A few seconds passed and then she sighed and shrugged her slender shoulders. "Fifteen and a half, if you must know."

Moule stopped pacing, placed his hands on his hips and asked, "And how old was the fellow who came in with you?"

"I don't know. I think he is eighteen," she replied sulkily. "Now can I go?"

Moule threw back his head and laughed. It was a coarse

belly sound of such velocity that it seemed to bounce off the walls of the cluttered room. The girl looked alarmed and gripped the sides of the chair.

"You're not going to let me go?"

"Gal, you mus' take me for a fool. You not leavin' here until I say so. An' I am not yet ready to say so."

There was a long period of silence while they both took in the significance of Moule's ultimatum. He had not yet decided exactly what to do and she had the sinking feeling that there was not going to be a quick release.

"So, you're kidnapping me?" she asked in a small voice.

Moule did not answer. He was still thinking. He began pacing again.

"So, you're kidnapping me?" she repeated, thinking perhaps in which case a call to the police might be a good idea. They would certainly respond to a kidnapping.

Moule stopped suddenly, pursed his lips and frowned at the girl.

"What's your name?" he demanded.

She looked back at him with a little of the earlier defiance returning but did not answer.

"What's wrong with telling me your name, girl?" He smiled suddenly, showing an array of firm white teeth. He was proud of his teeth. In spite of his age, smoking for years and not regularly cleaning them they were in good strong condition. If asked, he would put it down to chewing sugar cane as a boy. "My name is Moule. Meshach Moule."

She surprised him by replying, "I know."

"How you know? You're not from around here." He cocked his head. "Are you?"

"Not from Clapham but I know your name."

"So, I am famous, even outside my parish?" A whimsical expression crept across the brown, craggy features as he stuck his thumbs into two holes in the poncho.

"They call you The Grand Moule of Clapham," she said, with a hint of irony.

"So, I have heard."

Moule turned abruptly to face the window, not wanting the girl to see the expression he wore. It felt wrong to him to be seen as smug or even self-important. He knew he had no right to be regarded as *grand*. It was not an epithet he had earned through achievement, sacrifice or right of birth. Never to his face but he knew he was known as grand, simply by the way he deported himself as he walked down the High Street in Clapham. Or by the eccentric way in which he dressed. Only he could know what this façade was hiding and, as far as he was concerned, that veneer would remain in place until the day he died. And now this girl, whose name he did not even know, had said it to his face. The Grand Moule of Clapham. His alter ego.

He realigned his expression to stern and then turned back from the window.

"So, you know my name. Are you going to tell me yours?"

She returned his insouciant stare, as if wondering whether or not to play her ace in this game of bluff. Then, with a faint shrug she said, "Sonia."

"Sonia," he repeated. "Sonia who and from where?"

"That's all you're getting... Mr Moule. Now, you letting me go?"

Her demeanour appeared to be flipping from defiance to contrition in a manner Moule was finding confusing. He did not reply but turned rapidly, went to the front door, turned the mortice key and then slipped it into a pocket. Facing her again, with the stony expression of a jailer, he asked, "You want a drink of anyt'ing?"

She sprang from the chair so rapidly that it tipped backwards and came to rest against the window ledge.

"You can't hold me here," she cried, stamping a foot.

"Oh yes I can, Miss Sonia. You came uninvited into my flat, for what purpose I have yet to find out and therefore you will only leave at *my* invitation." He jutted his wiry chin for emphasis. "Now, you want a drink? At about this time of the morning I have a strong mug of Blue Mountain coffee. Jamaica's finest."

She looked wildly about her, as if there was some other means of escape besides the door.

"No, I don't want a fucking drink. I just want to get out of here," she shouted, on the verge of panic. The bangles swung wildly from her ears.

"Don't cuss like dat. Where you learn such language? At school? You still at school, eeh?" He paused at the door to his kitchen. "If you don't want coffee dat's your choice. Suit yourself. I am going to boil de kettle."

He disappeared into the small kitchen and filled the kettle.

As she tugged at her hair in desperation, now fighting back tears, she heard his raised voice from the other room. "And don't try jumping out the window. It's a long way down and anyway it's locked."

For a man in his seventies, he was remarkably fast on his feet. She had picked up a large conch shell from a table and was just drawing her arm back to throw it at one of the windowpanes, when he grabbed her from behind. She screamed and the shell fell to the floor.

"Let go, you bastard!" she yelled and twisted her head in attempt to bite his arm.

Moule seized both her arms and almost flung her back into the chair. His chest heaving with the exertion he stared wildly down at the now writhing figure. He pinioned her to the back of the chair in his strong grasp and put his mouth close to her ear.

"No more foolin' around, Miss Sonia. Get that into your head. You are staying here until you tell me why you and your fren' was here in my home. Even if I have to tie you to the chair. Understand? I don't want to rough you up."

She calmed down slowly and was now gently whimpering.

"Understand?"

She nodded and he relaxed his grip on one arm so that she could wipe her eyes.

Moule let go of the other arm and then bent down, still watching her closely, as he picked up the fallen shell. He examined it closely and was relieved to see that it had not chipped in the fall. He replaced it reverently on the table.

"This came with me from Jamaica sixty years ago and I would be very vexed if it was broken now," he explained sternly. "Can I trust you not to do anything like that again? Because I don't want to have to hurt you."

She nodded slowly.

"Then, get up and sit over there where I can see you while I make de coffee." Moule indicated an armchair closer to the front door.

Meekly, she obeyed.

She looked up from the deep chair into which she had sunk, her eyes following the tang of fresh coffee that wafted over from the kitchen. Moule gave her a sly glance. "Won't change your mind?"

"I don't drink coffee. Just some water... please."

Moule ran the tap until the water was cold and then filled a glass.

"Where you from, Sonia?" he asked, as he handed her the glass.

"Just up the road. The other side of the Common." She sipped like a bird, dipping her head up and down from the glass.

"Chuh, man. What I mean is where you originate from? Where were your parents born?"

To his surprise, she laughed, and a few droplets of water spilled over onto her jacket.

"How far back do you want me to go? Africa? I don't know about you, Mr Moule but I was born here, in London. So, that is where I am from. My father was born in Barbados and my mother in Spain, but I am from London. Is that good enough for you?"

He examined her features, as if for the first time and slowly nodded. The dark hair was curly but not what used to be derided in Jamaica as bad hair. And her nose was slender at the bridge, only broadening at the nostrils. The mouth was wide with a prominent lower lip. Her skin was the colour of the coffee in the mug he was now holding. Overall, a proper mulatto.

"What you staring at?" she asked, drawing her legs protectively together.

Moule didn't reply but turned away slightly and slurped at his coffee. He was wondering what to do next but did not want the girl to know he was uncertain as to her fate. One thing he did know was that he was not going to let her get away without answering his questions. He turned back to face her.

"You still have not told me why you broke in here. You know I can't just let you go so you and your fren' can come back and do it again."

"We didn't exactly break in," she said slowly, as if explain to a simpleton. "The door downstairs was not locked. We just turned the handle and it opened."

Moule frowned as he pondered this unexpected statement. He always locked his outer door. Well, nearly always. Had he forgotten to do it this morning? Someone had spoken to him as he left the building, so maybe he had been distracted. It was possible.

"Even if that is so, the door at the top of the stairs was locked for sure."

Sonia gave a slow, lop-sided smile as she said, almost with a hint of pride, "Jason picked the lock."

"Picked de lock!" Moule exploded. "Dis fren' of yours... he's a professional tief?"

"I don't know how he did it, but it looked quite easy," she replied calmly. "Maybe you should get a better lock."

"I have lived here for very many years, girl and no one... no one... has ever picked that lock before. I don't need a new lock. You need a new boyfriend. One who is not a lock-pickin' tief."

"Jason's not my boyfriend." She sounded genuinely incensed.

"Den who is he? Someone you just picked up to... to... go on a burgling spree?"

"I know him from school, but he is not my boyfriend. That is someone else."

"So, you have a real boyfriend but dis guy is just someone you cotch up with to carry out daytime burglary?" Moule spread his arms wide in mock incredulity.

"It just happened, that's all." She shrugged as if that simple statement covered the entire episode.

"No, that is not enough," Moule exclaimed. "I have to know what you wanted in here, what your Jason ran off with and why you thought no one was at home when you came. Before you give me those answers you are goin' nowhere."

She said nothing for several seconds, weighing up her options. Did this imposing and rather fierce-looking Rasta really mean he would release her if she answered those questions? Eventually she decided to chance it.

"We saw you walking off up the road. We were bored. Just come from the Common. We knew who you are." She shrugged and then added lamely, "We just wanted to see how you live."

"How I live?" His voice slipped an octave. "How I live? Do you know that when you find how someone lives you look into his soul? Is that what you wanted to do? Look into my soul?"

This unexpected response frightened her, and he could see it in her eyes.

"You regard me as some kind of freak?" His voice was shrill.

Sonia tried to sink more deeply into the chair as she shook her head. The bangles flashed in the ray of sun that now streaked across from the window.

Moule somehow managed to look angry and puzzled at the same time. He reached up, grabbed the bonnet from his head and flung it across the room where it came to rest precariously on the edge of a gnarled oak sideboard. Different, maybe, because that was the image he had cultivated for himself, but not an object of morbid curiosity to be analysed and examined by a couple of vagrant teenagers. He shook his head in bewilderment and the dreads swayed with the motion.

Sonia continued to stare at him, wide-eyed, with growing concern. Had she said too much? She knew nothing of this man's personality. Was he prone to violence if provoked? He certainly looked capable of aggression if riled. Instinctively, she averted her eyes to seek out the front door, even though she knew it was locked and that the key was in his pocket.

Moule stopped shaking his head. He raised a large, long-fingered hand to his face and began gently tugging his beard. He had come to a sudden conclusion. If this girl and her accomplice had stolen nothing, he would get no help from the police and at most, the perpetrators would simply be given a warning. He ran his tongue along his bottom lip before speaking.

"You can go but on one condition." A look of hope flashed across the girl's face. "I know everything in this flat and everything has its place. While you sit there, I will look around this room, my bedroom, my kitchen and bathroom and if anything is missing I will hold you here until your boyfrien'… accomplice… brings it back and apologises. If he does not then I will have to call the police."

He felt pleased with his judgment. Moule the advocate had weighed up the situation and had decreed.

"You have a mobile?" he asked

She nodded.

"Then, Miss Sonia, call him. Call your Jason and tell him what I said."

"If I do, you really will let me go?"

"You have the word of Meshach Moule." His face cracked wide with a reassuring smile.

"And you won't report this to the police?"

"Not to the police," he stressed. "But you must also promise me that you will never do this again. This is my home and you have violated it by breakin' in uninvited."

Sonia remained seated but raised her right buttock to draw a mobile from her pocket. She scrolled down and then pressed a key. Moule stood with arms folded and waited.

"Hello. Jason?" She closed her eyes. "Yes, it's me."

There was a pause of a few seconds as she listened.

"No, I'm not out. I'm still in the flat. Listen, I'm okay but there's something… no, listen. He wants to know if you nicked anything when… What? What do you mean it's too late?"

Moule cocked his head as if to hear but the voice at the other end was not audible. He made a gesture for her to put it on speaker, but she shook her head.

The call ended and Moule guessed from her expression that it was the boy who had rung off.

"Oh, shit!" She frowned as she looked up at him. "How long have I been in here?"

Moule pursed his lips. He did not wear a watch but there was an old wind-up clock on the mantelpiece. It was now a few minutes after noon.

"Less than an hour. Why? What did he say?"

"Will you still let me out if nothing's missing?" There was desperation in her question.

"What did he say?" Moule repeated. "You know my conditions."

"I can't." She suddenly looked close to tears. "Please,

could we quickly check everything? I didn't nick anything. Honest. But I don't know about him. Please, could you just check now?"

Moule didn't move. "What's the sudden rush? Why won't he tell you if he stole?"

"Mr Moule, please check first, then I'll tell you what he said."

"Okay," Moule said cautiously. "But you stay put."

Moule began his forensic examination of his living room, while the girl sat with her head slumped into her hands.

In the stillness of the room the sound of traffic was now amplified. There was the rumble of a bus passing, a horn blowing, somewhere from the Common a dog barked and then there was a police siren. At that last sound, Sonia's head jerked up.

"Oh, God," she murmured but Moule, intent on his inventory check, did not hear.

"That all looks in order," Moule declared as he dusted his hands together. "Now, the bedroom."

As soon as Moule had left the room, Sonia leapt from the chair and moved swiftly and silently to the window. It was grimy but clear enough to see into the street below. Traffic still moved, people still walked by, and an old man was rummaging in the waste bin attached to a lamp post. But right below, there was a police car.

God, she thought, Jason was right. It *was* too late. At that moment, Moule emerged from the bedroom.

"I told you to stay there," he said, pointing to the chair.

But she appeared to be frozen to the spot.

"What's de matter wid you? I said sit." He took a couple of strides towards her and then suddenly there was a buzz from the corner of the room, and he stopped.

"A visitor?" Moule went across to the intercom mounted on the wall. "Maybe your Jason has come back after all."

He pressed a button. "Yes?"

"Mr Moule?" came the metallic reply from downstairs.

"Yes, it is I," Moule replied in his posh voice.

"Mr Moule, it's the police here. May I come up to talk to you?"

Moule was momentarily flummoxed. He turned abruptly to face the girl, who was still standing by the window and now tugging nervously at her fingers.

"What has happened?" he hissed at her. "Why are they here?"

"I tried to tell you," she wailed.

"Tell me what?"

"Mr Moule, are you still there?" came the voice through the intercom.

"No, you can't come in. Not until I sort something out up here."

He took five strides across the room, brushed Sonia aside and peered through the window. Craning his neck sideways, he could just make out a uniformed WPC and another officer wearing a sergeant's stripes. Both were standing close to his outer door. A number of inquisitive people had stopped and were watching what they clearly hoped would be an unfolding drama.

"So, what's de story?" he demanded of the girl, who was now visibly shaking.

"Jason called the police," she said softly. "He told them I had been kidnapped by a… well, he gave this address."

"He told dem what?" He spun back to look out of the

27

window again. "An' is de lickle rahs clart down dere now? Eeh?"

She didn't look down because she knew he was not there. He had left an anonymous message after dialling 999.

"No, he's not there."

Moule stepped back from the window and clasped both hands to his head.

"So, he stitched me up den?" He put his hand on the sill for support. "I never kidnapped you. You know that. Call down an' tell dem I never kidnap you."

"Well," she began cautiously, "maybe you did. Sort of."

"I never invited you here, girl. You bust into my home and all I did was hold you until I was sure you never steal nothing. And now de tables are turned, and it is I who look like a criminal." He waved his hand at the window. "And look at all those gawpin' people. They all now sayin' look at the police at Moule's door. Moule must be a criminal. What you goin' to do about dat, eeh?"

Before she could say anything, the buzzer went again.

He stamped back across the room, pressed the button and shouted, "I'm not ready for you yet, officer. We still talkin'."

The metallic voice came back immediately. "Who is *we*, Mr Moule? Who have you got in there with you?"

"I don't know who she is, officer. She never say who she is." He knew it was a ludicrous reply but then, to Moule's thinking, it was all a ludicrous situation. He went back to the window and grabbing Sonia by her shoulders, he peered into her wide-open eyes.

"Tell dem I never kidnap you. You don't have to tell dem you broke in. Just tell dem I am not holdin' you against your will. I told you that, you can leave. Tell dem!" he implored.

28

She glanced at a hand that still gripped her shoulder and then into the dark brown eyes of the Rasta.

"Okay," she replied. "But how? On the mobile?"

"No, man. Through the window. Shout down to dem."

"You said the window doesn't open."

"Okay, I lied." Moule reached over her head and undid a catch. "Now, tell the nice policemen that you have not been kidnapped."

Moule slid the sash up and it squealed in protest. It was clear that, in spite of the warm summer weather, that particular window was seldom used. The reason for that soon became clear as Moule kept a retaining hand under the frame. The broken sash cord dangled teasingly from its runner.

Sonia moved alongside him and poked her head out. There was still an audience below, in spite of the fact that the WPC had attempted to disperse the onlookers. Sonia hesitated, somewhat intimidated by the watchers. She felt like a stage actress who had forgotten her lines as soon as the curtain was raised. She was Juliet but there was no Romeo down there.

"Go on," Moule hissed.

The sergeant nodded to the WPC, who stepped forward so that she could more clearly be seen.

"It's okay," Sonia began nervously. "Mr Moule has not kidnapped me. It's my fault. I came in when... when he was not here. I shouldn't have done that."

Moule's head suddenly appeared alongside hers and, as if he were an angry defence lawyer, shouted to the street below. "Dat's not the whole truth. This girl is not at fault. She was led astray by a bad boy by the name of Jason. It is he who broke into me flat and, for all I know, tief some of my possessions." He placed an avuncular hand on Sonia's shoulders. "I will not let dis young lady take de blame."

She looked at him in amazement. This speech should not have been written into the script. He was the one wronged and yet he was suddenly defending her.

The sergeant stepped forward and cleared his throat.

"Mr Moule, that is not what we had reported to us. We were told Sonia has been held against her will since earlier this morning."

"I am from the land of wood and water, officer," Moule replied portentously. "You have my word that what I have said is de truth. If Miss Sonia has been kept in my flat a little longer than she wished it is because I wanted to have the real culprit detained. I assume, officer, that the call you had was anonymous, but it can only have come from the rapscallion, Jason."

Moule turned to Sonia and raised an eyebrow as if seeking her approval.

"Is that true?" the WPC asked.

Sonia just nodded. By now she would have agreed to anything just to leave the stage. Just to depart this whole embarrassing scene. By now, the small group of watchers was dispersing. The drama had not developed as expected. They shuffled off, murmuring their disappointment to each other.

"So, can we come up now, Mr Moule?" The sergeant enquired, politely but with an edge of authority.

"Okay," Moule replied magnanimously. "I'll open de door."

He lowered the window gently and then strode across to the intercom to press the release button. They could hear the click at the bottom of the stairs and then two sets of feet on the uncarpeted steps. Moule took the mortice key from his pocket and turned the lock. As he pulled the door open, he let out an astonished cry.

"Me rum and mangoes! I forgot all about dem." He turned to the girl. "You like mango? This one is what we used to call Bombay. Very juicy an' it should come off de stone without too much mess."

Sonia gave a faint smile at this bizarre non sequitur and nodded, just as the two police officers entered the room. Moule bent at the waist and made a sweeping gesture.

"Come into my parlour, said the spider to de fly," he said, followed by a high-pitched giggle. Then he picked up the paper bag.

The officers removed their caps and visually swept the room with a professional air. The WPC then stepped forward and addressed Sonia.

"You, okay?" she asked, bending forward as if to make sure that the girl was intact.

"Yes, fine," she said and then added defiantly, 'look, he didn't beat me up or rape me or anything. I just want to go home now."

"Of course, you can, Sonia," the sergeant said gently, "but, as we've been called out, we do need a statement from you."

"I made my statement out of the window."

The sergeant could not suppress a smile. "I know but there's also the matter of this chap who was with you, when you broke into Mr Moule's flat. Jason, that was his name, was it?"

Moule melted into the background and began securing the catch on the sash window. Glancing outside, all was back to normal. He saw a man in shorts and sports shirt walking past eating a burger and he suddenly felt hungry. He had only had a mug of coffee and a slice of pawpaw for breakfast and it was now nearing one o'clock.

He turned back to see Sonia and the WPC sitting close together on his sofa, while the latter scribbled notes. The sergeant was examining a map on the wall. Moule came up behind him softly and followed the policemen's gaze.

"You come from Jamaica?" the officer asked over his shoulder.

"Yes, sah. Born and bred but I have lived most of my life in England. In fact, all of my adult life."

"I see you have many mementos of your country around the room."

Moule frowned and stared earnestly at the officer's face. "My former country, officer. This is my country now and has been since I stepped off the boat in 1956."

"Of course. I'm sorry." He looked across at the WPC and then at his watch. "I'm also sorry that you appear to have been inconvenienced."

"It has been an unusual interlude, officer." Moule grinned broadly. "Shall we say, a diversion from my normal daily activities?"

The Rasta stood half a head taller than the sergeant and to some he might have appeared intimidating, maybe even threatening. But Moule's mantra, as with most of those with his former persuasion, was *Peace and Love Brother*. The sergeant smiled.

"So, do I assume you will not be pressing charges?"

"That is correct. I would not like Sonia, at her young age, to get into trouble with the law. But I do not feel the same towards the Jason fellow who led her up to this. And then like some sneaky little rat, callin' the police and sayin' I am a kidnapper. If you ever catch him, I would press charges."

The Officer nodded. "Obviously with so little to go on there is little chance we will find him unless Sonia is prepared to give him away. But, if he offends again and he's caught, at least we'll know his name."

"She said they are at school together," Moule said. "But maybe dat's not much help."

The sergeant shrugged his shoulders. "He'd deny everything, of course."

"Thank you, Sonia." The WPC stood up. "We're done here, Sarge."

"Right." He put his cap on and made for the door. "Come along, Sonia, I'll give you a lift home. You live far from here?"

Sonia stood up and straightened her clothes. "No, about half a mile the other side of the Common."

She walked towards the open door and then paused to look back at Moule.

"I'm sorry," she whispered.

"Is okay," he replied. "Mebbe see you roun' den."

They went out of the door, the sergeant leading the way.

Moule suddenly sprang into action and shouted, "Wait! Sonia, you forget de mango."

The WPC turned, smiled and took the fruit from Moule's outstretched hand. He heard Sonia's faint thanks from the stairway.

He listened to the retreating footsteps, gave a sigh and then closed the door. Now for some warmed-up rice 'n' peas and chicken left over from last night. And maybe a bottle of Red Stripe. It had been a thirsty kind of a morning.

CHAPTER 2

Two weeks had passed since Moule's disturbed morning. There had been some rain but the grass on the Common still wore the tired look of late summer, in patches a straw colour and in others simply worn to the roots. But the plane trees by Long Road were still splendidly festooned in their leafy glory. Only the horse chestnut leaves showed rusty tinges around the edges. It was the first hint of autumn.

Meshach Moule strode purposefully along one of the many paths that criss-crossed the Common, occasionally nodding and smiling at those he passed on his way. The afternoon was warm, with high cloud and a gentle breeze and he had just enjoyed a lunch of salt fish and ackee. He was in a mellow mood.

Moule arrived at a bench by one of the three lakes and stopped to look down at the figure, sprawled across the space that should have accommodated three people. He stretched out a foot and nudged the one leg that dangled to the ground.

"Move up nuh, man. Make room for a weary ole Rasta."

The figure stirred and opened one eye. In spite of the balmy weather, he wore a long, grey coat, beneath which pinstriped trousers overlapped a pair of Doc Martin boots. The grey hair was completely free of any attempt at grooming. He opened the other eye and began to adjust his frame into a sitting position.

"Ah, it's the Grand Moule himself," the man said in a surprisingly cultured voice. "I was beginning to think you were languishing at Her Majesty's pleasure."

"What you talkin' about, Abe?" Moule sat down in the space made available for him. "I am free as a bird."

Abe stretched out both arms and yawned.

"I heard about the kidnapping." He winked. "Can't keep that sort of thing quiet for long in Clapham."

"Den you heard wrong. There never was any kidnappin'. A couple of young people bust into me flat, but I apprehended de girl. De fellow got away."

"But the police…?"

"I explained de situation, de girl left and de cops was happy. End of story. De only trouble is de fellow got away."

"Did they steal anything?"

"No, I don't tink so."

Moule looked earnestly at his companion. He had known Abe for several years on and off but even now did not know his surname. In fact, he was not even sure where he lived. He disappeared in the winter and when the weather was poor but otherwise Clapham Common was his back yard. Moule was certain that Abe had fallen on hard times and probably now lived in sheltered accommodation not far away.

Abe, peering across the lake, straightened his back and sighed.

"Okay," was all he said.

"So, you don't believe me?"

Abe raised a couple of weary eyebrows. "Yes, of course I do. Don't protest so much."

They sat silently side-by-side then for a few minutes, an odd couple of misfits, their unspoken thoughts provoking minute facial twitches. A pigeon swooped down and landed near an outstretched Doc Martin boot. Abe lowered his eyes to look at it abstractly.

Eventually, Moule broke the silence.

"So, what you been doin'?"

Abe turned his head slowly to look at his companion and his lugubrious features took on an expression of great significance.

"I have been immersed in matters of high finance," he began. "It can now be revealed that my consortium has raised the necessary funds through a syndicated loan, to make a bid for Marks and Spencer. If you read the Financial Times tomorrow you will find the whole story there. Meanwhile, I am not at liberty to divulge any more."

His face lapsed into a self-satisfied smile as he stuck his thumbs into the folds of the grubby, old coat.

Moule threw back his head and let rip a high-pitched and raucous laugh. The pigeon took off in fright.

"Man, you tell a good story." He let the laugh rumble on and then stopped suddenly to peer at Abe. "Is dat what you used to do? You know, before... before you hit de road?"

"Hit the road." Abe's features creased into a lazy smile. "I like that. But it's more like the road hit me."

"So, what was it you did? A banker? An industrialist?"

"It pains me to tell you, Moule, I was but an accountant. A very well-paid accountant in a large company but something went wrong, and my train left the tracks."

Abe extended his unshaven jaw as if that was the end of the story, with no more to reveal.

Moule's eyes narrowed slyly as he pursued the matter. "Dem catch you with your fingers in de cookie jar?"

It was Abe's turn to laugh. "Nothing as crude as that, old boy. No, I simply backed the wrong people with a deal that turned out not to be as kosher as it looked on paper. There had to be fall guys. I happened to be one of them, so I fell. You can't have the big cheeses at the top losing face now, can you?"

Moule accepted that this could be leading him out of his depth, so decided to bring the subject back to earth.

"So, you lost your job. That don't mean you had to come this far down the ladder, man."

"In my case, yes, it did. I was sacked not only from my job but also from my professional body and then from my marriage." Abe stroked the five-day stubble on his chin.

"Your wife left you? You never told me this before?"

"You never asked before." Abe leant across and patted the back of the poncho. "Don't worry about it. It happened and now I have chosen a different life."

"You *chose* it?"

"Okay, it chose me. But at least there are no responsibilities any more." Abe beamed broadly. "I live life on my terms."

Moule nodded his shaggy head sagely, but he found it difficult to understand Abe's philosophical approach to his current situation. The man had clearly fallen a very long way but there was no bitterness in his voice.

Once more a deep silence fell over the two men. Again, lost in their respective thoughts they were oblivious of the curious looks from passers-by and not hearing or heeding their muttered comments. Clapham was a relatively up-market area and the sight of a tramp and a Rastafarian together on a Common bench was worthy of passing comment.

"You're Jewish, aren't you, Abe?" Moule asked suddenly.

Abe considered the question before answering. "Sort of. Depending on where you start from. My parents were Jewish and so was I until my bar mitzvah but then I abandoned all that. I went into a Catholic Church one day and was really moved by what is sometimes sneeringly called the *bells and smells*. I was also intrigued by the idolatry and the liturgy. So, I became a Roman Catholic. Of course, my parents were horrified."

Abe chuckled.

"I know it sounds a frivolous reason for such a dramatic change in one's religious belief but that was how it was. After all, they worship the same God. Just by a different name."

"An' you still Catholic?"

"God, no. The lure of bells and smells wore off and when I read of priests buggering small boys in the choir, I thought to hell with all religion. I am now a complete non-believer. I don't even miss the confessional. I ask you, how pretentious to think that a mere man in a smock can forgive a sin." Abe turned to Moule. "And you? Do you believe in God?"

Moule was unaccustomed to being asked such a forthright and personal question and he paused to consider how to reply as he gazed randomly across the lake. It was a question he sometimes asked himself and often, when his inner self replied, he felt ashamed. And, as he grew older, so that shame morphed into a mystic kind of fear. How could he deny The Almighty when very soon he might have to face Him? But now that his companion had been so frank with his own religious beliefs — or lack of them — it was unfair that he should not be equally honest and forthright.

His eyes came back into focus as he half-turned towards Abe.

"You know anything about Rastafari beliefs?" he asked.

"A little but you're the only one I have ever met."

"Den I will give you the full story. Well, as much as I have been taught."

He coughed and straightened his back against the bench.

"The Rasta movement began in Jamaica in the 1930s. I don't know why it was there rather than anywhere else in the world but round about that time it sparked off as a cult form of Christianity, dat still held de belief dat there is one God, who the Rastafari called Jah. And Jah came to Earth in human form as Jesus Christ." Moule stopped and looked at Abe to see his reaction so far. Abe had closed his eyes but was silently nodding, as if absorbing this information, so he continued. "Again, I don't understan' why but the Emperor Haile Selassie of Ethiopia was given a position of considerable importance by the Rastafari in their belief and some even thought that he was God incarnate. As a result of this belief there started a movement for those descended from slaves to be returned to Africa. To them this was their Promised Land of Zion."

Abe opened his eyes and held up a hand.

"Forgive me for interrupting, Moule, but how can that be logical? The slave trade was not focused on one point in Africa but those taken into slavery were rounded up from several different parts of the continent. And certainly not exclusively from Ethiopia, which is right over on the east?"

"Man, don't arks me difficult questions like dat. I never made de rules. All I know is what I've been told or what I read or heard at the meetin's I used to attend. I just know dat the ambition of de Rastafarian movement was to break free from Babylon and to be resettled in Africa." Moule cast a scolding sideways glance before continuing. "One of de problems with these cultural beliefs was dat they clashed with authorities in Jamaica, especially in the late fifties and early sixties."

"You mean there was violence?" Abe enquired.

"Yes, man, violent clashes. My father used to come home with stories of Rastas storing sharpened machetes in caves up in de hills, waiting for de revolution and a return to Africa. I don't know how much of dis was truth, but it was a difficult time." He broke off suddenly to slap his thigh, and let out one of his cane piece laughs. "I mus' tell you dis, Abe. Myself I don't believe a word but I t'ink it was PNP in power at the time…"

"PNP?" Abe interjected.

"Sorry. Jamaica has two main political parties, People's National Party and Jamaica Labour Party: PNP and JLP.

"Anyway, someone in government had a bright idea. If these Rastas want to return to Africa so bad den give dem a boat to take dem there. So, a ship is provided and an invitation to all de Rastafarians to go down to de docks and get on board." Moule's face cracked into a broad grin. "When de day of departure come, no one turn up. Dey like it too much in Jamaica. Anyway, like I say, it cannot have been true, because where was de ship sailin' to? If it was to Ethiopia then as soon as it arrive at Addis Ababa, Haile Selassie would go down to de dock and tell de captain to turn right aroun' and go right back to where you come from."

Moule slapped his thighs. "To me dat is a true Jamaica Nancy story."

"It does seem unlikely," Abe murmured. "But things must have settled down there by now?"

"Oh, yes. I lef' Jamaica long before de eighties but Rastafarianism became respectable about dat time. An' you know how? It was through music. Bob Marley an' de Wailers came out of Trench Town but now their music is known throughout the world."

Moule leant back and peered up at the clear blue sky. A small boy cycled past at a speed, swerving to avoid a young woman pushing a baby buggy. He felt a rumble from his stomach and patted it absentmindedly.

"So," Abe began, "what is a Rasta's lifestyle? I mean, are there dos and donts in their everyday lives?"

"Oh, yes, man." Moule reached up and stroked his hair. "Dreadlocks are a requirement; some food must be avoided, and a true Rasta don't drink alcohol. You must also attend the meetin's. There are other tings, but I forget dem now."

Abe looked at him slyly. "You drink alcohol, Moule."

Moule roared with laughter again. "And dat is why I am not a true Rasta. I confess, man, I am a lapsed member of de faith. In fact, come to t'ink of it maybe I was never a true member."

It was Abe's turn to laugh. "So here we are. One lapsed Rastafarian and one lapsed Jew-turned-Catholic. Are we wiser men for straying, or have we just slipped down the plug hole of life?"

"You are a philosopher, Mr Abe," Moule said admiringly. "Plughole of life, eeh?"

"And, if I remember correctly, you are also a poet, Mr Moule. Have you had anything published recently?"

"Look, man, I'm no Benjamin Zephaniah but it is true, I have had some poetry published from time to time."

"I'm sure you're being modest," Abe said and then repeated, "So, anything recently?"

Moule shrugged and gave a kiddy wave to a little girl who

stared at him as she passed by. "There was a short one in a magazine a couple of months ago."

"How much do they pay you, if I might ask?"

"It depends on de publication but usually about twenty-five pounds." He chuckled. "I surely won't get fat on it anyway."

Children began to appear from the direction of the bandstand, in couples and threes and larger groups. Their shouts and laughter carried across the Common as they made their way home along the asphalt paths. The two men looked up with mild interest as the youths thronged haphazardly down the paths towards them. Even the old men were aware that summer holidays were still ongoing, so the children's arrival clearly signalled the end of some extra mural activity. Neither of the two men on the bench had much need to heed the days of the week, or even months of the year. Only seasonal changes mattered. And Mondays. Monday was when the pension arrived.

Abe stretched and glanced at his wrist where a watch should be if he wore a watch, which he didn't.

"Well, I have an important board meeting to attend. Mustn't be late." He pulled a wry smile. "It was good talking to you, Moule."

"And you, man. Always good to chew de fat."

Moule waved a casual hand and watched his companion rise slowly to his feet. Abe had obviously been on the bench for a long time because the leaving of it proved to be a struggle. Moule had no clue as to Abe's age, but he knew the former accountant now drew a state pension, so he had to be at least sixty-five, maybe going on seventy-five.

"See you, man," Moule called after Abe, as he began his

shuffle off to only God knew where. "Walk good now."

He leaned back and thrust his hands into his trouser pockets. There was no reason why he should not sit there in quiet contemplation until the sun set but some instinct told him not to waste time in idleness. It was something his father had instilled in him, sometimes with the help of a short piece of rubber hosepipe. *Show me you backside and mek de rubber taste de flesh*, was one of his father's sayings before he laid into his son. Sometimes the punishment, although harsh, was justified but on other occasions it was meted out for mere idleness on young Moule's part. It was how things were in those days. A small boy did not analyse the situation and did not think to condemn his parent for being a sadist. Back then there was no such thing as a telephone helpline for a child to call, no political correctness nor victim protection. And few mothers had the courage to step in to prevent the punishment, because they might also suffer from the heat of a father's wrath. So, whenever Moule found himself being idle he almost felt the welt of the rubber hose on his bare backside. He sucked his teeth with a loud rasping noise and stood up.

It was a short walk from the bench to the High Street, but it was a warm afternoon, and he was in no hurry. He smiled as a young cyclist raced past him and shouted, 'Rasta man'. He was the Grand Moule of Clapham, well known in the community and when people shouted things like that, he liked to think it was out of respect. At least, he hoped it was.

His random thoughts were suddenly broken into when from behind, he heard his name being called. He stopped and turned, to see a man walking briskly towards him. The man had swept-back, light brown hair, a blue jacket, and pale trousers. Holding one hand was a girl of about eight years old.

He looked fit.

"Mr Moule, I was hoping to catch you," the man said as he drew alongside. He glanced down at the girl. "This is my daughter, Alice."

The small girl took half a step back at the sight of the large, brightly dressed Rasta looming over her.

"I'm sorry," Moule said with a tilt of the head, "do I know you?"

A pleasant and warm smile creased the man's face. "It's the uniform," he said by way of explanation. "Or lack of it."

Moule cocked his head and peered at the man's features, as if examining an exhibit in a museum. There was a trace of recognition, but he could not place it in any context.

"I visited your flat after the break-in. I was with WPC Sanders."

Moule snapped his fingers. "Of course. The sergeant. So, how come you not in uniform today?"

"I took a day off to talk with one of Alice's teachers." He looked down at his daughter. "She's having a little extra tuition in the summer holiday."

Moule bent his woolly head towards the girl, who by now seemed to have accepted that he was not hostile. "An' did they give you a good report, young miss?"

She looked up at her father for his assessment of her achievements.

"Yes, she's doing fine." The sergeant patted her head and then turned back to Moule.

"Actually, what I wanted to tell you is that we've apprehended the young man, Jason, who broke into your place. I know this is informal, telling you like this but one of our patrols caught him at another break-in. He lives with his

44

mother and when we searched his bedroom, we found a hoard of stolen property. It's going to be difficult to trace most of the owners, but we know that you are one of his victims."

"You sure it's de same Jason who did my place?"

"He admitted it. So, what I would like you to do is go back home, check once more to see if anything is missing and then come to Lavender Hill station for an identification check. Can you do that for me?"

"Sure. I'll have another look."

"You know where the station is?"

Moule grinned. "Of course. Even though I have never been there as a guest of the local constabulary."

"Good. Next week then?" The policeman took his daughter's hand again and prepared to move off.

"Sergeant," Moule halted the policeman with a brief touch of his arm and said awkwardly, "thank you for taking the trouble to tell me this, but... what about the girl? Was Sonia with the rapscallion Jason?"

"No, she wasn't. He was on his own. Why?"

"I jus' would not like to think she got herself into more trouble. I don't think she's a bad girl. She jus' got into bad company."

The policeman looked curiously at Moule for a few seconds, before saying, "I hope you're right, Mr Moule. You have a good day now. What's left of it."

"Thank you, sergeant," he said to the policeman's retreating back. "Oh, you never told me your name."

The policeman stopped and looked back.

"It's Grant. Sergeant Noel Grant."

The policeman, now striding away and in conversation with Alice, did not see Moule's strange reaction to that simple piece of information. For several seconds he stood very still, looking stunned, almost as if he had been stung by an insect. But it was an invisible insect, one that had done its deed and then flown away a very long time ago. Moule's unblinking dark eyes took on an opaque hue, as if an unwelcome ghost had passed across them.

"Grant," he whispered, as he began a slow trudge back to the High Street. "Grant."

CHAPTER 3

Almost another two weeks had passed since Moule had met Sergeant Grant on the Common. As the policeman had suggested he went home and began methodically inspecting every corner of his flat. He had done this once before but at the time there had been so many distractions that he could not be sure he had accounted for everything.

He had been carrying out the inventory for nearly an hour when suddenly he let out a cry. The silver spoon had gone. He chastised himself for not noticing its absence before. For years it had hung from a hook on the wall just to the right of the picture of Sir Alexander Bustamante, the first prime minister of Independent Jamaica.

He had never used the spoon for eating. It was too large and deep to be pushed comfortably into his mouth, so it hung as a memento rather than as a utensil for serving up food. Somehow it seemed to Moule to be too smart a piece to be used for everyday service, such as dishing up his rice 'n' peas, so it hung from his wall, gradually tarnishing to a shade of pale brown.

Moule had stared at the empty hook for a few moments, recollecting how the spoon had come into his possession. When his father had left him and his mother, never to return, there were few personal possessions of his that were of any worth. And of those scant possessions, Moule knew that some were strictly not his at all. The silver serving spoon was one of those things, but his father had valued it highly. Some years after his father's departure, Moule had examined the spoon carefully and from a faded engraving on the handle he saw that it had been the property of the shipping company Elders and Fyffes. From that, he concluded that his father had slipped it into his trousers pocket after a meal on their way across the Atlantic to England.

Moule ran a finger down the stain on the wall where the spoon had hung, and a wry smile crossed his face. How could he walk boldly into Lavender Hill police station and claim something that his father had stolen? But then, he reasoned, that was more than sixty years ago and anyway would the police be that forensic as to the provenance of a mere serving spoon? And anyway, it might not even be there amongst the loot that Jason had lifted.

Bearing in mind those imponderables, Moule had gone along to the station and asked to see the items on display. He also asked if Sergeant Grant was in the station and was quite relieved to be told that he was out for the morning. The desk sergeant asked him if he knew what was missing and, after Moule had described the spoon, he was led into a back room.

It had not taken long for him to spot his missing tarnished object amongst the assorted items spread out on a table. He was handed the spoon, duly signed for it and then left the station, trying to conceal his desire to make haste.

Now he stood in his kitchen, stirring a pot of curried stew while one of Byron Lee's calypso records played from the living room. Like much of his lifestyle, very little had moved forward in terms of his taste in music. Bob Marley, of course, was the very best to come out of Jamaica but he had never grown far away from the rhythms of his youth. Calypso today is musically in deep freeze, revered still but in a niche way by connoisseurs of that genre. Round about the late fifties, calypso had morphed into Jump-Up, then Ska and eventually into Reggae. Byron Lee had led a group that made the early transition from Calypso to Jump-up. He and his band had even appeared briefly in the first Bond film, *Dr No*.

However, Moule did admit to himself that he was not narrow-minded when it came to calypso. It was not all about Jamaica. One of the finest exponents of the art was undoubtedly the Mighty Sparrow and he was from Barbados. His calypsos, which had won many prizes over the years, were based on political issues of the day as well as more vernacular topics, such as infidelity and sexual mores, many of which were probably composed from personal experience.

The record ended and he was just about to put on Tighten Up, Volume 2, with *Long Shot Kick the Bucket* as its first track, when the buzzer sounded on his intercom.

He sucked his teeth, put the record down and checked the stew before going across to the front door and pressing the button.

"Yes, who is it?"

The reply came faintly and indistinctly through the grill.

"Say again?"

"Mr Moule, it's Sonia." The last syllable of her name came over on the rise, as if she was unsure that he would remember her. "Can I come up? I need to talk to you."

Moule stood silent for a while and scratched his head.

"Mr Moule? Remember me?"

His immediate reaction was one of distrust and suspicion

but overcome by curiosity, he flicked the switch to open the outer door. "Okay, come on up, Miss Sonia. But don't bring any of you fren's wid you."

He heard the outer door slam closed, followed by the soft pad of the girl's feet as she mounted the stairs. Moule opened the door and stood back to let her in.

She was wearing the same denim skirt but above that she had on what looked like a school uniform shirt and on her feet were a pair of white socks and smart, leather shoes. She carried a school bag. Moule made an expansive sweeping gesture and she smiled up at him.

"You hear dat they catch your fren' Jason?" he said, by way of opening a conversation. "Or is dat what you come to tell me?"

"I told you, Mr Moule, he was not my friend. And now he's left school I haven't seen him since... since that day."

"That day when he abandoned you in my flat," he said more gently. "So, to what do I owe this pleasure?"

"Can I sit down, please?" She didn't wait for a reply but sat in the large chair in which she had been restrained nearly a month earlier.

Moule made a gesture of resignation with both hands and pursed his lips. This looked as if it would not be a fleeting visit.

"You like a mug of herbal tea, or maybe some coffee?"

She shook her head.

"Mr Moule I've come to ask you a favour. After what I did there's no reason for you to agree but hear me out anyway, please."

"Okay, Sonia but this sounds most mysterious. Back in a minute."

Moule shuffled off to the kitchen and switched on the

kettle. He felt he should be cross with this girl but there was something about her that reminded him of his own spirited daughter: the young woman he had not seen for many years and who now seemed to have disowned her own father.

As he turned off the heat under the stew, he reasoned, that if somehow he could help this girl with whatever favour she sought, then it might go some way towards making amends for being a hopelessly ineffective father. If her request for a favour was not too unreasonable, then maybe by not rejecting it he might help keep her on the path to righteousness. Or at least, on the path of future good behaviour.

He pondered these things as he waited for the kettle to boil. It clicked off and he topped up the percolator.

Coming back into the living room he found Sonia stretching back and staring at a pair of calabash maracas that hung from the wall. He pulled up a wooden chair and sat facing her.

"You've got a lot of interesting things here," she said and then suddenly winced, hoping he would not take the comment in an unintended way. He pretended not to notice but followed her gaze.

"Those came from a short visit to Cuba." Moule took a sip of the coffee and waited for her to talk.

"Mr Moule, I am back at school now. The term began this week."

"I noticed de uniform." He grinned and then added, "Drop de mister. Everyone in Clapham who know me call me Moule. Jus' Moule. Okay?"

"Okay." She looked down at her hands, as if nervous at seeing his reaction to what she had to say. "We, in our year, have been given a project. It's sort of a sociological study."

She stopped, gave a little giggle and raised her head. "That's not an easy word to say."

"What kind of study?"

They both laughed then, and it seemed instantly that a barrier had been broken through. They were on a level plane together, simply over the pronunciation of a six-syllable word.

"Go on," he encouraged.

"We've been asked to talk to someone in the area where we live and to write about that person. To get his or her life story and the more interesting the better." She noted the frown creases beginning slowly to multiply on Moule's brow and she hurried on. "I hoped that you would agree to be the subject of my research. I can tell that you are an interesting person. I mean, just looking around this room I can see you've had much variety in your life. It does not have to be too personal. I mean you don't have to let out anything that would…"

She tailed off and almost bit her tongue in annoyance. She had put this badly and she could see that his reaction was far from positive. There was a long silence and they both sat very still. Eventually Moule shifted in his chair and reached out to put his mug down.

"Young lady, when you said you wanted a favour from me, I was not expecting de kind of request you have just made. I was fully prepared to help you but…" He shook his head and the dreads waved around like Medusa's snakes. "… but this request… is something I cannot agree to. I am truly sorry to disappoint you."

Sonia's disappointment was indeed palpable. She bit her lower lip and clasped her hands tightly together. Clearly, she had not expected instant and unequivocal rejection to her request.

"Oh," she replied eventually in a small voice. "But why? You must have so much to say to young people about where you grew up and stuff like that."

"I am truly sorry, Miss Sonia but that is all too private. I do not wish to… *regurgitate,* if dats' de right word, things from my past for the world to know about. I suggest you find someone else who is more willing to reveal their… their skeletons."

"Skeletons? I wouldn't be asking you tell me anything that would cause you upset or embarrassment." She was leaning forward now and almost pleading with him.

Moule stood up abruptly and moved towards the window, looking out at the street below. He was cross. Cross with himself for causing this girl such disappointment but also cross that he had been placed, quite innocently, in this invidious position. His past was his past and not for publication, even for a scholastic project. He had not spent so many years trying to bury that past for it now to be dug up by a schoolgirl. And yet, with memories of his distant youth, he still recalled the deep feeling of disappointment when faced with rejection by an adult. His own father had been anything but an exemplary role model, so expectation of parental approvals was never high. Nevertheless, there was always a feeling of utter deflation whenever he refused even a simple request. And especially when that refusal was not accompanied by a fair reason for rejection.

As he stared abstractly at the pedestrians and traffic passing his window he wondered if he was now being unfair in not giving this girl a sound reason for his reluctance to cooperate. He turned abruptly to face her and was dismayed to see the expression on her smooth, coffee-coloured face. It reminded him of a puppy that had been scolded.

"Look, Sonia. Let me tell you why I say no to your request. I have had a tough upbringing. Times have been hard, and I have had to fight sometimes just to get out of life what little I have now. I have not always been a good person but now, in my declining years, I want to put it behind me and move on gently and peacefully into the setting sun."

For a second, she looked startled at Moule's poetic language, so unexpected from this grizzled septuagenarian Rastafarian. He noticed the expression but did not feel inclined to offer any further explanation.

"Can you understand that?"

She shrugged. "I guess so. Not if it would be painful for you."

"I'm sorry. But I hope you find a subject who is more willin' to talk about themselves."

"Oh, I might." She stood up. "But they will never be as interesting as you. I just know it. Most of the older people I know are dead boring."

"You flatter me, young lady." He forced a grin as he handed her the school bag.

As she went through the doorway and onto the landing, Moule asked, "How long do you have to complete dis project?"

"I have all term," she replied dejectedly. "Well, goodbye, Moule. I'm sorry to have bothered you."

"Goodbye, Sonia."

Moule closed the door, sucked his teeth loudly, walked across the room and kicked at the chair she had been sitting in. He cursed himself with words he had learnt in the playground of his dirt school in the Jamaican hills.

A few days passed and with it the long spell of fine weather. Moule woke up on a Saturday morning having drunk too much Appleton the night before and shuffled into his kitchen, wearing just a pair of bright, red underpants. He pulled out one of the stools and sat, with his head in his hands.

Ever since he had said goodbye to Sonia his nights had been disturbed by feelings of guilt. Here was a young girl, of whom he knew little but who appeared to wish to improve her life, through learning about the lives of others. For a brief period perhaps, she had fallen in with a bad influence, but she was intelligent and also resourceful. Her school had given them a project and she had had the courage to return to his place and ask him a favour. But, for dark reasons of self-awareness and a desire to keep his secrets unearthed, he had sent her packing. However rational his reasoning, his rejection of her request was continuing to cause him deep feelings of remorse.

He got up to pour out a glass of water, into which he dropped two effervescent tablets. He watched as the bubbles burst to the surface and splashed over the side of the glass. Outside, a fine rain spattered against the kitchen window causing thin, grimy rivulets to run down the panes. The weather seemed to have changed to match his mood. He drank the sparkling liquid and grimaced.

Unable to face any food, Moule put *Calypsos from the Arawak* onto the turntable, lowered the stylus and then returned to the bedroom to dress. In his bemused state of mind, he had finally come to a conclusion. It might solve nothing, but he had to seek advice.

He slipped the poncho over his shirt and at the bottom of

the stairs, picked up an umbrella. Outside the house he raised the umbrella, one with red and white stripes and advertising an insurance company and then turned left. Just down the road he went into the deli and bought a cheese roll and a bottle of cola. The young woman behind the counter commented at how dreadful he looked, and he agreed with a nod. Outside again he turned right and headed for the Common. The person to offer advice should be there. *He had to be there*, thought Moule.

He crossed the road, dodging a number thirty-four bus and scampered ahead of a red mini. The latter hooted at him, and the driver gave him the finger.

"Not a resident of dis parish," Moule said, as he passed an old woman who stood and stared at him. "He don't know to slow down for de Grand Moule."

His exaggerated stride took him along the High Street and past Clapham Common Underground station. There he forked right and proceeded onto Clapham Common North Side until he reached a gate in the iron railings. He stood back to allow a woman with a baby buggy to pass and then went through.

Several runners were exercising at varying paces along the paths that were now shining with a silvery sheen. The early morning rain had eased, and a watery sun was beginning to appear through patchy, grey clouds. A few walkers made their way from various directions, hunched in their rainwear, many carrying shopping bags. Moule paused and took a panoramic scan of the Common. Unsurprisingly, none of the benches that he could see in the triangular park was occupied, so he headed for one of the few places that would be sheltered from the weather.

As he approached the domed Victorian bandstand, Moule

gave a grunt of satisfaction. There, leaning against the rail at the side of the structure, was the person he was looking for.

"How you doin', man?" he hailed Abe as he went up the steps to the platform. "You not bring your trumpet today?"

Abe raised his head and nodded a greeting. "You're lucky to find me here on this shitty morning. That is, if it's me you were looking for?"

"You, Abe, are the very man. My main man." Moule lowered the umbrella, rested against the rail alongside Abe and came directly to the point. "I have a problem."

"*You* have a problem? And you come to me to sort it out?" Abe held open his stained raincoat. "Look at me. One button to hold this together, holes in my socks, a leak in one of my boots and just enough money in my pocket to buy a cheese roll. And you say you have a problem, already?"

Moule laughed and reached into the paper bag he carried. "Fresh dis morning from de deli. You can share my roll. I'm not hungry anyway."

Abe pulled his coat closed and smiled at the Rasta. "You are too good to me, but I will accept your munificent gesture."

Moule tore the roll down the middle and handed one half to Abe, who immediately sank his teeth eagerly into the soft bread.

"So, what's the problem?" he asked through a full mouth.

"You remember from a few weeks back a couple of youths broke into my home?" Abe nodded and took another bite. "Well, de police have caught the fellow and I have retrieved de item he took from me. But maybe I tell you dat already. Anyway, de other one, de girl, she come to my flat a few days ago and surprised me with a request for a favour."

Abe stopped chewing and looked quizzically at Moule.

"Sounds like a bit of a cheek. After what she did?"

"I know but she's not a bad girl. I t'ink she was just led astray by de bad boy. We had a long talk before the police came and I t'ink her heart is in the right place." He paused to look across the park to where a police car was racing along the South Side with its siren wailing. "Now she has come back to my flat and arks me something that has put my head in a spin."

Abe raised his eyebrows enquiringly as Moule hesitated, wondering how best to explain the conundrum.

"Her school," he continued, "has given de pupils a project. This term they are to find a local person and interview them so they can write it up for markin'. This girl, Sonia, has chosen me as her subject, because she t'inks…" he scrunched his face, "… my back story will be interestin'."

"Well, Moule," Abe said expansively, "I'm sure she is right. Yours must surely be a fascinating story. After our talk a couple of weeks ago you certainly gave a hint that there is immense depth to your background. Yes, she chose her subject wisely."

"Shut up nuh, man." Moule sucked his teeth. "You supposed to be helpin' me, because I am in a quandary."

"Oh? In what way."

With some difficulty Moule began trying to explain why he was reluctant to expand to anyone, let alone a stranger, his back story. How there were things that were now painful to talk about and other matters from the past that he would rather forget about completely.

Abe heard him out without comment, just fiddling idly with the remaining button on his coat.

"So, you see why I sent her away?" Moule pleaded.

"Maybe but as you say, you don't want her to go away

with a feeling of rejection," Abe mused. "That way she might lose her faith in adult judgment, which in turn might make her slip back into bad ways. Yes, I can see your quandary."

"You got it exactly."

"So, where do I come into the equation?" Abe asked, licking his fingers.

"I was hopin' you could advise me what I should do to resolve de quandary."

"Look, old boy, I'm no Solomon. I've no experience with this kind of situation."

After a few seconds silent pondering, Moule suddenly snapped his fingers. "I know de answer! Why don't you volunteer to tell her your story? I'm sure it will be just as interestin' as mine. Maybe more so."

Abe threw back his head and laughed. "You mean, like how I fell from grace and kept falling until I hit the bottom of the barrel? That would be a cautionary tale to tell, spiced up with a large dose of reverse schadenfreude."

"No, maybe you're right," Moule mused. "So, you have no suggestions to offer?"

Abe studied his fingers for a few moments before replying.

"Well, I could suggest you steer a middle course. Give her your story but use a heavy redacting pen." Abe raised an eyebrow and grinned mischievously.

"Redacting? What's dat, man?"

"Expurgation. Invite her to hear your story but give her the Readers Digest version. You know, cut out all the bits that you don't want the world to know about."

"I see," Moule said slowly. "Chop it up a bit? Maybe t'row in a Nancy story or two?"

59

"No, no, you don't have to go so far as fabrication. Just the truth, perhaps watered down in places and cut out the heavy stuff you want to keep under wraps. It should still make a good story... certainly for school kids."

The rain had stopped now, and drips fell from all parts of the bandstand roof onto the railings. Two boys appeared along one of the paths, throwing a Frisbee to each other and laughing. A dog, with no obvious owner in control, sidled up to the bandstand and cocked its leg against the bottom step.

Moule gazed out across the Common and then began pacing up and down the boarded platform. Eventually, he stopped and stared at Abe's coat.

"You know, man, with autumn here you should find someone to sew on a couple more buttons."

"Well, there's a non sequitur if ever there was one," Abe laughed. "So, what's your conclusion to my words of wisdom?"

"I t'ink maybe you are right. That is what I will do," he stated decisively. "I knew you were de man I should arks." He snapped his fingers again. "An' maybe I could t'row in some Jamaican poetry too."

"Good idea. A little diversion might make it easier."

"Louise Bennett," Moule announced, as he picked up the umbrella and folded it neatly. "She was an island poet long before Benjamin Zephaniah was born."

"Not heard of her but then I'm not a great one for poetry." Abe said, "I knew about Poet's Day though."

"Poet's Day? When is dat?"

"Friday. *Piss off early, tomorrow's Saturday.*" He gave a dry laugh, which ended in a cough.

"Dat one pass me by," Moule chuckled and then frowned.

"But wait a minute, I have another problem."

"Another one? Isn't one a day enough?"

"No, it's connected with my first problem. How do I find Sonia? She never told me where she live an' I don't know where she is at school."

"Forget the school, old man. Even if you do know which one it is they are hardly going to let an unknown man like you talk to one of their pupils. No, your best bet is the police station. They would have recorded her name and address when they took her statement."

Moule palmed his fist with a loud smack. "Of course. You're right again. I'll go along there this very afternoon. An' t'anks for de very valuable advice, Abe. It is greatly appreciated."

Moule slapped his companion on the back and then turned to go. He had a foot on the top step when he stopped suddenly and reached into the paper bag.

"Here, have de other half of de roll." He took out the bottle of cola and tossed the bag to Abe. "Enjoy!"

Abe waved a hand airily and took a large bite.

In fact, Moule did not go to the police station that afternoon. Instead, he walked back past Clapham Common Underground and settled at a table on the pavement outside one of the cafés he frequented. He ordered a hot pasty and a cup of tea from the young waitress, stretched his legs out and watched the world and its dog pass by. His early hangover had passed, and the freshness of the early autumn air had not only cleared his head but had also given him an appetite. Any action regarding Sonia would have to wait until the next day. He still had some thinking to do.

CHAPTER 4

The constable at the desk studied the tall black man's craggy features and shoulder-length dreadlocks and pondered his request. Apart from the woman with the missing cat, there was no one else waiting, so he nodded, turned and took the door leading to one of the back rooms.

"Wendy," he called out to a WPC who was seated at a table studying a screen, "there's a guy at the front desk wants to speak to you. At least, I think it's you."

"Who is it? Did he give a name?" WPC Sanders came away from her screen.

"Rasta guy, name of Moule. Says you checked on him after a break-in last month," the desk sergeant whispered.

"Oh, yeah, that's me." She peered over his shoulder. "I'll see what he wants."

WPC Wendy Sanders followed the constable back to the front desk and found Moule pacing the floor and frowning deeply.

"Mr Moule, what can I do for you?"

He glanced at the missing cat woman, who was sitting on a chair in one corner and then turned his back on her to afford a bit of privacy.

"It's about de girl Sonia," he began. "I need to find her because I have to tell her something. You have her address, officer?"

WPC Sanders had been trained to handle all kinds of situations with the minimum of fuss, but it took her a few seconds to assess Moule's request. She glanced over his shoulder at the woman, who was pretending not to be remotely interested in what was being said and decided to conduct the conversation in greater privacy. She took his arm.

"Come with me, Mr Moule." She led him over to a side door that opened into an interview room. She opened the door, and he followed her in. She shut the door and invited him to sit down.

"Now, why do you want Sonia's address?"

Moule began the to explain Sonia's request and the fact that he had initially refused to take part but now he had had a change of heart and wanted to help the girl. The policewoman listened patiently but without expression until Moule had finished.

"I did take Sonia's statement and the incident in your flat is now logged in our files. So, yes, I do have her address, but I can't give it to you just like that."

"Why is that?" Moule seemed genuinely surprised. "If I had agreed to do her de favour she asked right away then I would have it now."

"But you didn't," she replied quietly, "so it has become our responsibility to divulge or not divulge this information."

Moule sucked his teeth and looked aggrieved.

"There's another thing to consider, Mr Moule," she continued. "Do you know how old Sonia is?"

"Yes, she said she's nearly sixteen."

"Which means she's still fifteen. Have you heard of the Children's Act?"

Moule gave a small shake of the head.

"Well, basically, it is to protect children from harm and abuse from adults who might take advantage of their vulnerability." She realised that it sounded as if she was explaining to a child and not to a grown man, so she added, "I'm talking about paedophiles, Mr Moule. The Act is to protect children."

Moule's mouth fell open. "What you sain'? You think I am one of those? That I would wish Sonia harm?"

He had raised his voice, so she added hastily, "No, I'm certainly not saying that of you personally. I'm just telling you that the law is there to protect young people who have not yet reached adulthood. It would be wrong of me or of any law officer to hand over a child's address without the appropriate clearance."

"So, what can I do?" Moule wailed as his hands beat a tattoo on his knees.

She assessed the situation, weighing up the strict interpretation of the law against her judgment of Moule's stated motive for making contact.

"If you really need to contact her for genuine reasons there are a couple of things you can do. Strictly, anyone having dealings with minors who are not their own offspring must be CPD certified."

"What is that?"

"You would be checked to see that you have a clean record basically. With the necessary paperwork that would take time though, so the other thing could be by getting the parents' consent to have your interviews with Sonia."

Moule laughed his high-pitched cane cutter's cackle. "But, officer, that can only be achieved if I have the parents' address and that is all I am askin' for now. So, we goin' round in circles."

"No, Mr Moule, *we* would approach the parents and not you," she explained.

"Okay. So, if that is acceptable, how soon can you make contact with them? You see, Sonia only has dis term to complete de project an' because of my foolishness, she is already fallin' behind."

"I'll see what I can do, Mr Moule but I might have to clear this with my inspector first."

She stood up and Moule followed suit.

"Thank you. It's much appreciated. I am just so sorry to have disappointed the poor girl."

As she led the way out of the interview room, WPC Sanders' face wore a faintly bemused look. She could not quite understand the strange link between this wild-looking old West Indian man and his apparently tender consideration for the feelings of a girl who he hardly knew and who had recently broken into his home. It would be a strange tale to have to relate to her superior officer.

Moule pushed open the blue doors and left the station in high spirits. He bounded down the steps in such haste that he almost tripped at the bottom. It had taken him some courage to go up to Lavender Hill again, because he was innately nervous of the police. It was something ingrained in his psyche after the bad old days of random stop and search. Even though he was now a well-known and respectable, local citizen, there was still the residue of uncertainty in the presence of officers of the law. And that residue went way back. All the way back to Jamaica when he was a small boy in ragged clothes.

He was still in high spirits when he arrived home and opened his front door. He bent down to pick up a couple of envelopes and then carried on up the stairs.

If his visit to the police station brought a positive result, then there would be a cause for celebration. In fact, he decided at that instant, he would not wait to hear back from WPC Sanders. He would bring the celebration forward immediately by preparing one of his favourite meals: jerk chicken with rice 'n' peas.

He flung the two envelopes onto a table and went to the kitchen to check that he had all the ingredients. A few minutes later he found that everything he needed was there except for a can of kidney beans. Grabbing a plastic bag and his purse he loped down the stairs and out into the street, heading for the nearest grocer.

Not every grocer stocks kidney beans of the make that Moule favoured, but he found a four-hundred-gram tin and then picked up some Red Stripe as well and made his way to the check-out. It was there, while he was paying and chatting up the girl on the till, that he felt a tap on his back.

"Hello, Moule, how you doing?"

It was a dark-skinned, middle-aged woman with incongruously bottle-blonde hair.

"Hi! Good golly Miss Molly. Long-time no see." Moule glanced at the till girl and took his change. "How's Dwayne?"

"Wait up there, Moule and I'll talk to you in a minute."

She began loading her goods onto the conveyor belt, while Moule waited patiently outside the shop.

"Look, Molly," Moule said, as soon as the woman had squeezed herself and her goods out of the door, "I'm celebrating tonight. If you an' Dwayne not doin' anything else, come an' join me."

"Sounds nice. What you celebrating?"

"Just some good news. Well, I'm hoping it will be good news, so celebratin' early."

"Well," she hesitated and pursed her lips. "It's sort of spur of the moment but we're not doing anything tonight, except perhaps watching an old movie…"

"Good, then you'll come. I'm cooking jerk chicken."

"Wow! Then we will definitely be there. What time?"

"Come about six, then we get some drinkin' in first."

"Right. See you then."

Molly, obviously one who did not follow any of the fashionable diets, rolled off up the High Street, with Moule heading away in the opposite direction.

It turned out to be a night of proper Jamaican celebration, although Moule never did reveal to his friends the full reason for his euphoria. Molly and her husband Dwayne, a long-time employee of Wandsworth District Council, arrived just after six and they all got stuck into the Red Stripe beer. In Moule's youth, before he left Jamaica, the drink had always been referred to as Red Stripe Lager beer and there was a little ditty that went with the RJR advertisement that still jangled in Moule's memory bank. After all his years in England it was still, to his taste, the finest lager available.

The jerk chicken had been prepared over several hours and even the chef had to admit that it was a very fine effort. Maybe not quite up to the standard of his late mother's preparation but worthy of at least four stars. Fortunately, his guests agreed.

"How much rum you put in it, Moule?" Molly asked.

"Four tablespoons of the best Appleton. Why, too much?"

She giggled. "I thought so. I believe the recipe says only

two tablespoons."

"Chuh, man. Two is for cissies," he laughed. "And de only other ingredient I had to change was de hot Scotch bonnet. I couldn't find that, so I used tabasco instead."

Dwayne looked at him and winked. "I would never have noticed but the rice 'n' peas was great too. Just the right amount of coconut."

To follow the main course, Moule produced one of his favourite deserts: potato pone with heavily laced custard. Molly and her husband peered suspiciously at the grey-green and leaden-looking pudding as Moule dispensed it from a basin. As second-generation West Indians who only went there as tourists, this was an alien offering. Moule noted the hesitation.

"Don't worry. It's made of sweet potato and is a bit like de English bread pudding."

With that assurance his friends dug in.

Two hours later he saw the couple out of the front door onto the street. Molly held onto Dwayne with a giggle as she stumbled at the bottom step. They had ended the evening with a generous nightcap of Appleton and the forty-proof effect combined with the sudden blow of night air took her unawares.

He watched them walk unsteadily up the pavement and then peered into the sky. It was only just after ten o'clock and the traffic, as ever, was still going about its business as it made a muddle of the criss-cross shadows cast by the streetlights.

Focussing on the artificial glow of the sky he saw no stars. If he were on a hill in Mandeville now, he knew he would see stars. Countless millions of them. But that was a sight he knew would never again be possible. Because of the event on that afternoon by a crumbling wall near a towering cottonwood tree, he could never return. He could only recall and dream. Tonight, with the meal he had prepared and shared with friends, he had silently remembered and now he prayed to the God whose existence he questioned, that the celebration would not be in vain. He had nailed his hopes on a kind of redemption by agreeing to tell his story to a schoolgirl he hardly knew.

He exhaled loudly, turned and went back inside.

CHAPTER 5

It took a week but at the end of it, Moule had the answer he so wanted.

He never knew exactly what investigation into his background was carried out and by which Authority. He did not care. All he was interested in was the fact that seven days after he had visited the police station, he had a call from WPC Sanders telling him that he would be permitted to visit Sonia's mother to ask her permission for the interview to proceed. He noted the address, but they did not give him a phone number, only saying that the mother was expecting a visit from him.

It was, as he guessed, a modest, semi-detached house in a row of soot-stained brick just over the Clapham District boundary. Somehow it had escaped the ravages of so-called enlightened town planners who had knocked about so much of his own area in the middle of the twentieth century. It also seemed that Hitler's V1 and V2 indiscriminate flying bombs had past it by.

Not knowing exactly what to expect, Moule had taken a bus and walked the remaining four hundred yards to the house. He now stood nervously at the front door and straightened his shirt before ringing the doorbell.

She opened the door promptly, almost as if expecting a visitor. She was short, with wavy, copper-coloured hair framing a round, pale face. However, her expression of astonishment could not be disguised at seeing a tall Rastafarian in a bright, tropical shirt on her doorstep. Moule, who had decided to adopt the *Trevor McDonald* as being more engaging, smiled broadly and held out his hand.

"Good morning, Mrs Benjamin. I am Meshach Moule. You might have been told to expect a visit from me?"

She seemed flustered for a moment but then recovered quickly and said in a strong foreign accent, "Yes, Mr Moule, of course. I just wasn't expecting…"

Sonia's mother took his hand and gave it a peremptory shake, before standing aside and holding the door open.

"Come in." She glanced fleetingly up and down the street and then closed the door firmly after Moule had wiped his feet.

Moule placed his umbrella in a corner and then looked around the entrance hall.

"Would you like a cup of tea, Mr Moule?" she asked, wiping her hands on the stained apron she wore over a floral dress.

"That would be most acceptable, Mrs Benjamin, if it's not too much trouble for you."

She led him into the front room and invited him to sit. "I'll only be five minutes."

He sat down as she bustled out of the room. He looked around. Dull brown carpet, net curtains, striped wallpaper, two armchairs, a sofa and a forty-inch TV. Not much poetry here, he thought.

"Do you take milk and sugar?" she called from the kitchen at the back.

"Milk and two sugars, please."

A few minutes later she was sitting opposite him, holding her tea mug in both hands. He noted that she had given him a cup and saucer for his, which he now cautiously placed on the table beside his chair.

"Did the police officer tell you why I would be coming to see you?"

"Yes, about Sonia doing an interview for a school project?"

He placed the accent now. Sonia had said her mother was Spanish and her father Barbadian.

"I don't know why she chose me, but I suppose because of my background, she thought I would have an interesting story to tell." He had decided not to make any mention of how they had met. Maybe she knew already but he was not going to stir that pot. "I have to admit, I was not too keen at first, but she looked so disappointed that I changed my mind."

He lifted his hands in a compliant gesture and flashed his teeth at her.

At first she just stared at him, not coldly but in an analytical way, as if trying to assess the character beneath the scruffy beard and the dreadlocks. Moule had tried to spruce himself up before setting out that morning, but he was still a Rasta, for all the world to see.

"Mr Moule," she began, "Sonia is fifteen, nearly sixteen and already she does much of what she wants to do. She's a good girl but still quite innocent and sometimes... what is the word...? wilful? Since her father went away, I am on my own to watch over her and sometimes..." she shrugged, "...sometimes a mother and daughter they don't agree. I am working, so when she is out of school I don't know where she goes, or who she sees. It is not easy. So, of course I needed to meet you to know that Sonia will be safe. You understand?"

"Of course, Mrs Benjamin. I understand. I have a daughter

of my own." *Even though I never see her now*, he thought. "You know now where I live, and before I leave here I will give you my mobile number, so if you ever have any worries you must contact me."

She didn't take long to make up her mind.

"Then I will give my consent for Sonia to visit you after school for the purpose of making her interviews."

"Thank you." He reached out for the cup. "Has she said how many times a week she will be coming?"

"We have not yet discussed any detail, but I think it will be about three times in the week. Will that be all right for you?"

"I will make certain that I am free to invite her in." He had a sudden thought. "Sonia's father… you say he is away. Will he agree to this?"

To Moule's surprise, she laughed. It was a coarse and bitter sound, which ended in a rasping smoker's cough. "Benjamin has been away for a very long time and will not be coming back. If he comes back, I would shoot him, if I had a gun."

Moule decided that discretion was required and did not pursue the matter of the errant Benjamin. He just nodded and opened his mouth in an expression of silent understanding. He drained the remains of the now warm tea and then stood up.

He asked Mrs Benjamin for a pen and paper and wrote down his mobile number. Also, for completeness, he added his address. They exchanged a few pleasantries before he collected his umbrella from the entrance hall and then walked out into a bright autumn morning. His face held the grin of a man who had just had a win on the Lottery. His leather boots slapped the pavement eagerly beneath long strides, as he made his way to the bus stop.

Now, it was up to the girl to contact him.

Sonia's first contact did not take long after that. Moule's mobile phone burbled on the kitchen table in the afternoon two days after his visit to her mother and before he even picked it up, he knew who it would be. Very few people had his number and if it rang more than twice a week it was too much for his liking.

She wanted to come round after school that day and he agreed immediately. Moule did not realise it then, but she was as nervous as he was. This was to be the beginning of an unexpected innovation for him and for the girl, an exploratory adventure into an alien era and culture.

Sonia arrived at the flat shortly before four o'clock and, after an awkward greeting, he asked her if she would like some refreshment. She asked for a diet coke. He fetched one from the fridge, opened it and gave her a glass.

"How do you want to do this?" he asked, looking vaguely around the room.

"Shall we sit at your kitchen table?" Having asked advice beforehand she had decided to make it as formal as possible, without being physically uncomfortable. For that purpose, it had been suggested to her that each session should last no more than an hour.

"Okay," Moule agreed, and they went into the small kitchen.

Moule cleared a few items from the table, and they sat opposite each other.

Sonia reached into her school bag. "Do you mind if I use a tape recorder? I'll make a few written notes, but I won't be able to keep up with you when you talk."

"No, I don't mind, Miss Sonia." He straightened himself on the chair, clasped his hands on the table and took on the demeanour of a *Mastermind* contestant.

Sonia smiled at him. "You need to relax, Moule, or you will make me even more nervous."

He chuckled and slumped back in the chair. "Okay, you de boss. Tell me what you want me to say."

"Right, what I am asking you to do is give me, in your own words, your story from the beginning. From your first memories of your life in Jamaica up to the time you arrived in England. I hope you can do that for me."

So, that was how it began.

From the tape that I heard it started in a rather stilted and hesitant way as Moule got his mind into gear. It reminded me of a piece of rusty machinery, long out of use, that desperately needed a good dose of WD40 to get things moving.

And why am I listening to Sonia's tape and reading her notes? That is a question that is better answered later in this narrative but meanwhile, I will set out almost to the word what Moule voiced across the kitchen table to Sonia Benjamin over the course of several late afternoon sessions, during that September and into October.

I have to admit however that, although Moule's strong Jamaican patois was familiar to me, to make it easier for Sonia and for anyone else reading it, I have transcribed it all in more conventional English. In doing so, I hope that I have not lost any of the essence of what he actually said. I have also left out the occasional comment or question raised by his interviewer. But I have retained the first person throughout the transcription. I hope I will have done it justice.

This is Meshach Moule's story as I transcribed it from the beginning:

I was the third child, born in a shack in a small village near Mandeville in the Jamaican Parish of Manchester. The midwife who attended my birth was called Mama Leandro. I don't believe that was her real name and she was no relation of ours, but she had a basic knowledge of how to assist at the birth, of those not privileged enough to go to hospital. I have never seen any registration of my birth, but my belief is that I was born in the year 1944. I have always regarded the fifteenth of March as being my birthday. This was not a good day for Julius Caesar, so maybe I should have chosen another but by the time my mother registered me for school, it was too late. My earliest memories are from the year 1947. This was a bad year for Jamaica as there was a lot of civil unrest, with many strikes at sugar factories and other places of mass employment. Up in the hills round where I lived, we were not much affected, but I learnt about it years later, at my school. Yes indeed, I did go to school.

I don't think my father was ever married to my mother, so she was what is known as a common-law wife. He was not an educated man, being the son of a manual worker and the great grandson of a plantation slave. But I must give him some credit in that he taught himself to read and write and later on learned to drive a truck. This was useful for employment as transport in the island across rough roads was of extreme importance. He began by driving a truck for Bronstoff's Ice Company, delivering large blocks of ice wrapped in hessian sacks — known in Jamaica as crocus bags — to local food stores, eating places and even schools. The sacks were wrapped around the ice blocks and covered also in sawdust, which delayed the melting. You see, not many places in the bush parts in those days had electricity. Our lighting at home was from kerosene lamps and my mother cooked on a wood burning stove. I believe some people called these stoves Smokey Joes, because a lot of the wood they burned was still young.

My mother bore my father four children. I had two sisters, who were three and five years older than me. As I grew up they gave me a rough time, but I think that might be usual for older sisters to be bossy. Then I had a younger brother, but he died when he was only about a year old. I think he died of a bout of dengue fever that was going around the island at the time. As I was so young, the loss of my brother didn't mean a lot to me, but my mother was mourning for a long time. For some reason, I think she blamed my father, but she blamed him for a lot of things. I often heard her say behind his back that *he's a wuttless so and so*.

The first house I remember was, as I said, little more than a shack on the side of a dirt road. Not a lot of traffic passed by, mostly mule carts carrying wood and some trucks from the bauxite mining a few miles away. But sometimes, adventurous tourists would come by and for them she kept a stall with fresh fruit for sale. The stall was made of poles tied together with rope — we called it jackass rope, because it was used to lead and tether the donkeys — and there was a roof of banana leaves strapped down. In high winds these would usually blow off but there was no shortage of banana trees around. Every time a car stopped to look and feel up the produce, my mother ran out to make a sale. It didn't make her much money, but it was her own and she kept it well away from my father.

Although we were poor, my father had a regular job and in our yard at the back we had several fruit-bearing trees. There was a mango, naseberry, banana and breadfruit. Naseberry was my favourite. If you have not seen or eaten one, I will tell you how it looks. It is the shape and size of an egg, with a brown soft and sort of furry outer skin. The fruit inside is a bit like the New Zealand Kiwi and inside there is a shiny seed the size of a prune stone. Our mango tree produced a good crop every year, but it was the type we called a number eleven, very stringy and the fruit did not come easily from the seed. My favourite mango was, and still is, the Bombay. Very juicy, fat and comes away from the seed with ease. The only way I could get one of them was to steal it from someone else's tree (*Moule pauses to chuckle at the memory*). If the tree was too high to climb then I or a friend found a suitable stone and threw it at a ripe one to knock it off. The real skill was to hit the stem and not the fruit, because you didn't want to bruise it before eating. Boys who had this skill were said to possess a mango hand. (*For some unseen reason, which I did not understand on first hearing the tape, there was a long break here, when the only sound appeared to be fingers tapping the table.*)

Also, in the yard my mother grew yams and sweet potato. You remember I told you about the potato pone I made for Dwayne and Molly? My mother made that from the sweet potato she grew but we did not have the luxury of custard. Also, in the yard we had a nanny goat. She gave us milk and in return she ate everything she could get her mouth near. She was tethered to the breadfruit tree but still managed to stretch the rope somehow. So, you see, we did not starve.

Water we collected in a tank at the back. It was pure rain water that ran off the corrugated iron roof and I don't remember the tank ever running dry. It only served for drinking and washing though. There was a privy a few yards from the house for all the other business. Fortunately, Mandeville is blessed with a climate that produces a fair amount of rain, unlike the plain down on the south coast, which often suffers from drought. I have heard of people who manage to grow strawberries up in Mandeville, although I never ate one or even saw one before I came to England.

It is hard to know what to tell you about how we lived then. It is a very long time ago and, you know how it is with children, they accept that how it is for them is what is normal. It is only when you see how other people live that maybe you question if things could be better for you. So, when we saw smart cars passing through our village, or looked up in the sky to see an aeroplane overhead or maybe were told stories by your schoolteacher of the greater world outside, that you began to think, or even to wonder if there is a way to escape and experience these things. But, for the first five years of my life there was no escape from the reality of our poverty, and this was never more painful than when the weather turned bad.

In my youth, in Jamaica we suffered two bad hurricanes. Usually when these storms sweep through the Caribbean, they come close to the land and then push back out to sea. Of course, with the smaller islands they go right over and cause a lot of damage. But, when I was about six or seven, a really bad one — in those days they only had girls' names — came right inland and even hit Mandeville. I have never been more frightened in my life. The corrugated iron roof was ripped off and ended up nearly a mile away and the breadfruit tree was knocked out by its roots. Many people drowned nearer the coast when the rivers came up and I heard that a bridge over the Rio Minho in Clarendon was washed away. You probably don't know this, but it is a sad fact that most people who die in a hurricane, are killed by the flying debris. If a piece of corrugated iron hits you at a hundred miles an hour you have no chance. After that hurricane it took my father a week to get the roof back on. Fortunately, the goat did not blow away and we didn't lose much else. Maybe when you don't have much to lose anyway that is not such a bad thing. (*I could almost hear Moule smile at that comment.*) Jamaica was not a rich island then and it took many months before those in poor areas recovered from their losses.

You ask if we went to church. Yes, my mother was deeply religious and unquestioningly and devoutly believed that Jesus Christ was the son of God. She took my sisters and me to the local Anglican Church every Sunday. Of course, we wore what was our Sunday best. My mother and sisters had white dresses and straw bonnets, which they managed to keep clean for this occasion. However poor you were, there were standards to maintain not only in the sight of the Lord but in the sight of your neighbours. I wore the one shirt I had which was not torn and which had all of its buttons and a pair of khaki pants (*shorts*) that my mother had picked up from a charity stall in the market. I think the pants must have been donated by the parents of a boy from the fee-paying preparatory school up the road. I will talk about that school later. It is an important part of my story.

I also had one pair of shoes, which were sandals. I wore them to church only. Most of the time I ran around barefoot and soon the soles of my feet were so hard that it took the sharpest macca (*thorn*) to penetrate them. If I was going to walk a long way, I wore what we called sham-patters on my feet. This is a simple form of sandal made from a cut-out piece of car tyre and held on the foot between the toes by a piece of jack-ass rope. Very effective and probably as comfortable as any flip-flop you can buy in the shoe shop.

The Church service was held by a pastor, who lived in a grace and favour house on the hillside near Mandeville. I can't remember his name but to us children he looked as old as Methuselah himself and he preached fire and brimstone as he thumped the pulpit with his bony fists. The echoes of *Amen* from various parts of the Church helped to emphasise the parishioners' fear of the wrath of God. None of his words meant anything to me and I think I just sat there in silence, playing with the marbles in my pocket.

Marbles? Yes, I was never bought any but just seemed to gather them from ones I found discarded in various places. My friends and I would play games with them in the dirt, and we regarded them as a form of currency. If you had as many as ten you were rich.

But even more important to me than marbles to play with was my go-cart. My father was not a caring kind of man when it came to helping others or having any concern for their needs but the one kind thing I remember him doing for me, was to build that cart. But I now suspect that he did it not just for me but just to show himself that he was capable of doing such a thing. The base of the cart was a plank of splintery wood. At the back there was a nailed-on strut onto which two wheels were fixed. These were taken, with their axle, from a discarded baby's pram. On the front a shorter strut of wood was fixed with a pivot and the other two wheels bolted onto the side of the strut. Steering was with a length of strong string attached to either side of the strut. There was no proper seat, but I nailed on a thick piece of cardboard to make it less hard on the backside. Downhill, I could pick up a lick of speed but as there were no brakes, I had to use my foot to try to stop.

This cart gave me a lot of pleasure for about a year until one day the steering string broke and I hit a tree. The cart was a wreck, and I had a bad cut on my leg. When my father came home and heard what happened, he hauled me out and beat me with a piece of hose pipe. He never fixed the cart.

At this sad point in Moule's tale, the first session with Sonia came to an end. It was tempting to let the tape run on to the next session, but I resisted, put it aside and thought about this man's start in life. Was he richer than most of us from his base beginnings, or had his world view been warped for the remainder of his life? While I pondered that question, I decided that it was important for me to get to know the man better. At that point in time, I had only had a brief introductory meeting with the Grand Moule of Clapham and that only happened as a result of an unfortunate incident.

After a brisk walk and a cup of coffee I sat down at a table in my son's house in Wandsworth and began transcribing the second session from Sonia's tape. The reason I was not in my own home will become clear later in this narrative.

As I mentioned earlier, the transcribing was not easy work. I had to keep stopping and starting the tape and sometimes rewinding. Also, it was necessary to transcribe the text from the Jamaican idiom into some form that was intelligible to an English person of an age similar to Sonia herself. I also had to weave in Sonia's scribbled notes.

So, session two begins:

You ask if I ever saw the sea in those days. Mandeville is up in the hills in Jamaica and is therefore not close to the sea. About thirty miles to the north, there are the tourist hot spots although in the late fifties, the tourist industry was not booming in the way it is today. But there are the beautiful, long beaches with golden sand and even back then some very grand hotels. Where we lived, we were only about fifteen miles from the sea as the John Crow flies but it was on the south coast and very different from the north. I don't know any detail as to how Jamaica's tourist industry has developed since I left but I would be a surprised person if even today, the south coast has been built up in the same way as Discovery Bay, Ocho Rios or Negril to the west.

Fifteen miles does not sound far when you are travelling on straight, well-made roads but from Mandeville to where we went to visit the sea was like a major adventure. We only did it about four times before I was seven years old, and the last time was nearly the end of us. In a while, I will tell you about what happened that time.

The roads were very badly made and winding and you could swim in the potholes after it rained. My father took us in the ice truck — I don't think that was allowed as he was using company gas (*petrol*) - but he was not the kind of man to worry about little things like that. The journey began down the main road from Mandeville to a place called Spur Tree. It was a very steep road with many bends, as I remember. Then we took a much smaller and even worse made road through villages whose names I cannot now recall until we finally reached a place called Alligator Pond.

You know, it's a funny thing but I was a grown man living right here in Clapham, before I discovered that the so-called alligators in Jamaica are not alligators at all. They are in truth and in fact, crocodiles. But that was how it was then and probably still is now. I never actually saw a live *alligator,* but they lived down there amongst the mangrove that grew for many acres, almost to the edge of the beach. And the beach itself? It was not the golden sand you see in the tourist advertisements. It was grey. Fine grey sand. But to me and my sisters and maybe my mother too, it was wonderful. My mother used to bring a picnic of whatever she could find that morning. Pau-pau, mango, some goat's milk and breadfruit that we roasted when my father got the fire going. He cursed and swore when the wood was too wet and when he poured gas onto it, he nearly burnt his face. I have to say that on that occasion I laughed, and he hit me around the head. I don't think he enjoyed the beach trips as much as the rest of us.

Unfortunately, one of the problems with our sea visits was that none of us could swim. The sea level from the beach sloped away quite gradually, so we could easily judge when we were going out of our depth but there was one occasion, when I was too boasy (*bold*) for my own good. I was standing on the tips of my toes when a wave, or maybe the current, pulled me out and I was thrashing around trying to find the bottom. My father saw me, but he was enjoying a puff of ganja and didn't move. My mother looked up and saw the trouble I was in and came wading in to reach me, while she hollered at my father. He still didn't move. She reached me and stretched out a hand. I grabbed it and she pulled me in, just as another wave tried to fight back. My mother hauled me back while I was spluttering sea water and, when she reached the beach, she kept yelling at my father. He just lay back and laughed and said something like *that will teach him not to be a nyamps* (*a stupid person*). After that, my opinion of my father sank even lower.

There were no more trips to Alligator Pond after that

incident, but it was for a reason other than that of my near drowning. It was because of what happened near Spur Tree on the return journey.

On the way back home that afternoon there had been a sharp shower of rain, so the road was slippery. Of course, at my age I knew nothing of tyre traction on wet asphalt but looking back now it seems probable that neither did my father. Also, maybe Mr Bronstoff ran his trucks on bald tyres. Spur Tree hill is notorious and has claimed many lives over the years through careless driving. My father was probably going too fast in the truck for the conditions, but we might not have had the crash if the damned fool man had not been lying in the road.

Even after all these years I can see it still. Father saw the man and immediately swerved to avoid running him over. He succeeded in doing that but then lost control of the steering. The truck hit a bank, swerved across the road — luckily nothing was coming from the other direction — and came to a stop against a tree. If it had not been for that tree, we would have gone down a steep gully and maybe all been killed.

I forgot to mention that because the cab in the truck was cramped for space, my younger sister and me were in the back of the truck, trying to keep steady against a pile of crocus bags, while my mother and older sister were in the cab. With the impact of hitting the tree, everybody was flung forward. I hit my head and blood started to pour down my front, while my sister landed on top of me and cracked her shin against something hard. Inside the cab, my mother hit her head against the windscreen and my other sister broke her wrist against the dashboard. My father was okay as he had the steering wheel to hold on to, but he sat for a few minutes, suffering from the shock of the impact.

Everything went quiet immediately after the crash but gradually, we could hear what sounded like laughing from outside. I still can hear that sound clearly; it was such an unreal thing to reach our ears after such an event. Slowly, my father opened his door and the first thing he saw was the man in the road jumping around on one leg. I was mopping my head with a kerchief, and I saw him too, as he suddenly started shouting, "Compensation! Compensation!" And there on the other side of the road was a group of men, all laughing fit to bust. It was totally unreal and all I could do was sit next to my crying sister, mopping my blood and watch what was happening outside.

Then my father reacted at last. He jumped from the cab, holding his ribs that had been jammed against the steering wheel and began yelling at the man in the road, "What you mean compensation? You nearly kill me an' me family. You wreck de truck. What kine of fool you is?" He carried on shouting and throwing in a lot of bad words, while the group of men, who turned out to be road repair workers, carried on cackling like cane cutters.

This is a long story. I hope I'm not boring you? (*a pause in the tape and then he continued.*) So, what happened next was the arrival of a policeman on a motorcycle. In those days we called policemen *corpie*, probably short for corporal. Anyway, he arrived on the scene and started to try and calm down the situation and at the same time take notes. The man in the road was still calling for compensation for his imagined injury and my father was waving his arms around and calling the man a lot of bad names and saying it was he who wanted compensation for damage to his truck. Of course, it was the ice company's truck, but I'll come to that point later.

Most of this was beyond my understanding but I climbed into the cab with my mother, and she did what she could to stop the bleeding, even though she was not too good herself. The sister with the broken wrist had fainted and the other one was still crying in the back. Soon somebody came by in a Land Rover and took us all to Mandeville hospital, where they dealt with our injuries. Much later, when I asked my mother what happened after we left, she told me that the man had been lying in the road because he had a bad headache.

Can you believe such stupidity? He had been breaking up rocks with his fellow workers for road repairs when he had developed a migraine, which was so bad that he decided anything was better than going on living with pain. So, he lay in the road. And, when the truck didn't kill him, he forgot about the pain and started shouting that he wanted compensation for his injury. Meanwhile, his companions found the whole situation so amusing that they simply stood by the roadside laughing. Jamaicans have a great sense of humour and maybe they favour the ridiculous as a trigger for laughter, but can you understand the mentality in this situation?

Although even at a young age I had little sympathy for the predicaments my father found himself in, I do feel that he was the innocent party in the Spur Tree crash. But, his employer, Bronstoff, was not so understanding. The man in the road continued to demand compensation, although that claim eventually died when the facts were established. I would not be surprised if his reward was to be removed to a mental institution. The ice company, Bronstoff's, was in no hurry to take my father's side though. They claimed that he had no business to be using their truck to take his family to Alligator

Pond, as the truck was insured for company use only and he was also stealing the company's gas by driving there at all. Now there was a crash and a damaged truck. Who would pay?

In the end, after the story hit the *Gleaner* (*Jamaica's national newspaper*) and the insurance company reluctantly paid up, my father was taken back as a driver but not for long. Bronstoff's never forgave him or trusted him again and eventually, found some excuse for making him redundant. So, for a time that year he was unemployed, and we were living off his meagre redundancy pay. This did not help his temper or make life at home any easier. Certainly, my beatings for minor infringements seemed to increase in regularity.

That is a long story about one single incident, but it is important, as it marked a turning point in our lives.

One good thing I will say about my father is that he had some magical way of bouncing back when life — often through his own fault — knocked him down. He must have persuaded Bronstoff's to give him a fair reference as a driver, because one day he came back home, drunk from celebration, to say that he had a job as a truck driver for the Bauxite company, Alcan.

Alcan Jamaica is the subsidiary of a Canadian Aluminium company and one of its operations was at the Kirkvine mine, located not far outside Mandeville. I think bauxite was discovered there in the 1940s and certainly by the early '50s it was in full production. My father was given a job driving trucks for the company when I was about seven years old. I don't know what he carried in the trucks, but they were much bigger than Bronstoff's ice carrying vehicles. I think it must have been some kind of bauxite waste he was taking away. Anyway, he was obviously paid a lot more because we soon moved from the shack by the side of the road and into a much smarter bungalow, with neighbours who also mostly worked for Alcan. Maybe it was a company house, but I don't know and now there is no one to ask.

My father's money might have gone up but that did not improve his behaviour towards his family. In fact, in some ways it was worse, because with more cash in his pocket he could afford to buy more rum and ganja. He still joined up with his friends in the rum shop on a Friday night and played dominoes until the small hours of the morning. He returned home reeling, falling over and cursing. I think at those times my mother was afraid of him and would keep out of his way if she could. When she could not avoid him, then he would have his way with her, shouting that it was his right as a husband. In the next room I could hear all this, and I hid my head under the pillow, wishing I was older so I could go and protect my mother.

Although the house was an improvement on the shack, there were things that I missed. The goat came with us but as the house was quite new there were no mature, fruit-bearing trees. My mother planted some, but it was years before they produced anything worth picking. This meant that I had to exercise my mango hand much more than before.

My sisters and I did get some fresh clothes. I don't say new ones, but they were a better quality than we had grown up with and my shirts had a full set of buttons. But, just because we had more to wear did not mean that I stopped roaming round the countryside looking for trouble. I freely admit it now, I was a wild child. This might have been in defiance of my father and his bullying ways, I don't know. I am no psychologist. But I loved my mother and it really caused me grief when I did anything that made her be disappointed with me. I think even at that age my emotions were a mixture of love and hate, in equal measure.

(*Moule let out a long sigh and, I assumed he was reassessing his last statement, because he continued thus:*)

No, hate is too strong a word. Because I had only one father, I knew no different. At the age of seven, maybe I thought his chastisement was justified. Perhaps it was me who was at fault, and I was in some way a disappointment to him. So, rather than hate, my feelings towards him should be described as a kind of wary bewilderment. (*I have to admit that these were not Moule's actual words. I was taking the liberty of interpreting what he was attempting to express in a less articulate way.*)

You ask what we did to get food on the table. I told you about the fruit and milk we produced when we lived in the shack but to add to this, my mother used to shop about once a week at the market in Mandeville. By the standards of hygiene today these markets were very basic. Vegetables were on open display but that was fine, because you took them home and cooked them. But the fresh meat just hung from hooks in the open, covered with swarms of flies and other insects. I am surprised there was not more sickness on the island, or maybe there was, and I did not know about it. Some of the meat was actually rotten. One day, my mother brought home a cut of pig for the stray dog — a mongrel of the type that were commonly known as *brown musku* — that wandered around our yard, only to find that it was crawling with maggots. She threw it as far into the bush as she could, but I expect the scrawny animal still found it.

I will also say this about my mother; that she was a good

cook, and we never went hungry.

The tape stopped abruptly at that point. Maybe the mention of hunger suggested to Moule that it was time to end the session. When Sonia left him late that afternoon, she would never have guessed that the next time they met it would be under very changed circumstances.

CHAPTER 6

The sun shone weakly through the fine carpet of early morning mist that hovered over the Common as Moule stepped out of his front door and onto the pavement. He had to stock up with a few provisions, which also included diet coke for Sonia. She got through a couple of bottles as she interviewed him, even though he was doing the thirsty work.

To his surprise Moule found that he was enjoying the interview sessions with the young girl. There had only been three so far but if it continued in the same vein it might even turn into a form of therapy. At her prompting on each aspect of his early life a dusty old veil had been lifted and once more the days of his youth had been rediscovered. For him it was a re-varnishing of old paintings, sometimes in colour, sometimes in black and white and for her a revelation. Casting subtle glances at Sonia as the stories poured out effortlessly Moule could see quite clearly that the girl was awestruck. In fact, to admit the truth, after so many years living such a different life in South London, he was equally impressed at the contrast between his own deprived beginnings and subsequent developments. It was a comparison he only rarely considered and certainly never in conversation.

But not forgetting Abe's advice, he had to remember to keep a tight editorial lid on the amount he revealed. What had Abe called it? Yes, redacting the past: especially when he got near to the reason for the family leaving Jamaica.

So, it was with eager anticipation that he prepared for the fourth interview session that Thursday morning. After stopping to chat with a couple of people in the High Street, he went back inside and started cleaning up the flat. Since his wife and his daughter had gone away it did not come naturally to him to be house-proud. Not that he lived in squalor; it was just that he turned a blind eye to some of the more detailed aspects of cleanliness.

He had completed the tidying and had a lunch of leftover chicken with sweet corn and gravy, when the mobile began dancing tunefully on the kitchen table. He picked it up.

"Moule? It's Sonia."

"Yes, Miss Sonia. You comin' today?"

"Yes, that's why I'm calling. You'll be at home?"

"I will be at home, my dear. Look forward to session four."

He rang off, put the phone back on the table and turned to look at himself in the kitchen mirror.

"Moule," he said sternly, "the time has come to write a poem about Sonia Benjamin and what she's doing. But first, we must take a walk in the park."

He returned home an hour later, disappointed that he had not seen Abe anywhere. He had been keen to let him know how it was all going. Now that the interviews were underway Moule regarded his friend as being the catalyst for the whole venture and he had a right to know the state of progress. He was not to know on that fine autumn afternoon that progress was about to be abruptly arrested.

At a few minutes before four o'clock Moule was ready for Sonia's arrival with some prepared notes on the kitchen table, a couple of diet cokes in the fridge and a fresh shirt on his back. This was about the time she usually rang his intercom. But at ten past four he was still waiting.

Half past four came and he was beginning to worry. He picked up his phone, put on his glasses and ran a finger down a sheet of paper pinned to a board on the wall. He picked out a number and then stabbed it into the phone. It rang three times.

"Hello, Mrs Benjamin?"

"Yes?"

"It's Moule here, Mrs Benjamin. Is Sonia wid you at home?"

There was a delay in her reply and, when it came, there was a hint of anxiety in the voice. "No, Mr Moule, she should be with you. She said she was going straight there after school."

"She's not here, Mrs Benjamin. That's why I'm callin'. She rang earlier to say she was comin' but…"

Both parties were silent in their sudden mutual concern. Eventually Moule spoke, trying to be encouraging. "Maybe she stopped off for something. Let's not worry yet. She's only about half an hour later than usual."

"Well, I hope you're right," she said uncertainly. "But give me a call when she turns up, will you?"

"I'll do that for you, ma'am."

He rang off but continued to fret.

Shortly after five, Moule reached for the mobile just as it rang.

"Mrs Benjamin?" he answered eagerly.

"No, Moule, it's Molly. The young girl you were telling us about the other night… is her name Sonia?"

Moule had a foreboding of something not good coming. "Yes. Sonia Benjamin. What about her?"

"Well, I have some bad news I'm afraid. She's had an accident. I found her on the Common and took her to A&E."

Moule sat down and gripped the phone more tightly.

"Tell me wha' happen', Molly."

"I can't believe that this happened in broad daylight on Clapham Common but from what she told me, she was set upon by a couple of youths and beaten up."

"No!" Moule gasped. "Who would do such a thing?"

"I found her crumpled up on one of the benches. She was crying and bleeding, but people were just walking by. I don't understand how uncaring some people can be. It was clear that the girl was in distress. But maybe they just thought she was a druggy or something."

"But you stopped to help. Did she know the people who did this?"

"No, but I don't know if that is because she doesn't know or if she won't say. It's something the police will have to find out."

"The police? You told them yet?"

"The first thing I did was ask her name and where she lives. I had my mobile, so I called 999 and asked for an ambulance as soon as possible and then called the police. Of course, by then a few nosey parkers had stopped to see what was going on." She stopped to take a breath. "The ambulance was there in ten minutes."

"Did she tell you she was on her way to see me?"

"No, I didn't know that."

"And her mother? Does she know?"

"I got her number and called her after the ambulance

95

drove off and she said she would go straight over to the hospital."

"I must go over and see her. This is terrible." Moule began pacing the kitchen. "And have you heard anything from the police? What they doin' about it?"

"Moule, don't rush over there, because she might not be there by the time you arrive. She didn't want to go there at all, but the paramedics said it was necessary to get her injuries seen to. I think after they do that her mother will take her straight home. Maybe you should contact Mrs Benjamin? As for the police, I'm sure they'll talk to her as soon as she's well enough. Moule, I'm very sorry to bring you this bad news."

"Molly, my love, you have done this poor girl a great kindness and I thank you for callin' me about it." She heard him curse quietly and then repeat, "Who would do such a thing?"

Immediately after ending the call with Molly, Moule phoned Sonia's mother. He had no reason to feel any responsibility for what had happened to her daughter but the very fact that she had been on her way to see him, instilled in him a form of vicarious involvement.

When she answered the call, he could tell instantly that she was distressed and equally perplexed as to why anyone should attack her daughter. Nothing had been stolen, although she had been carrying a mobile phone, some money and the tape recorder. She had suffered severe bruising to her face, a cut on the back of her head and a broken finger from her attempt to ward off the attack. Her shirt had also been badly torn and there was a bruise on her leg.

Sonia had insisted on going home after she had been attended to and patched up at A&E but, when asked by her mother and other interested parties, she would not say whether or not she knew her attackers. She hedged their questions by saying they wore hoods and so she was unsure of their identity. All she had noticed was that one youth had a tattoo on his hand.

Moule asked if he could go over to see Sonia that evening, but her mother said she was resting, so maybe tomorrow. He accepted that and said he would call again the next day.

He opened a cupboard door and took out the Appleton.

When Moule arrived at the Benjamin household the next morning, he was self-consciously carrying a bunch of flowers. Earlier, he had phoned Sonia's mother who confirmed that Sonia was out of bed and feeling less sore.

However, he was not Sonia's first visitor that morning. WPC Sanders was sitting opposite Sonia in the front room, taking notes on a pad resting on her lap. Mrs Benjamin quietly relieved him of the flowers as Moule put his head around the doorway. He gave the girl a wan smile and a nod of acknowledgment to the officer.

"Hello, Sonia. How you doin'?"

She smiled back at him, and the policewoman looked up.

"I'm sorry," Sonia said.

"What you sorry about, darlin'?" Moule's eyes opened wide, and he sucked his teeth. "Someone beat you up an' you say to me you're sorry."

"I'm sorry I missed the next session and now…" she looked at her damaged hand. "… and now it's probably the end of the project."

"No, man! No way." He glanced at the WPC whose hand hovered over the note pad. "Look, we'll talk when the officer has finished wid you."

Moule went into the kitchen and watched Sonia's mother arrange the flowers in a glass vase.

"Did she say anything as yet?" he asked.

"No. If she knows who did this thing, she is not telling me." She shrugged. "Maybe she will say something to the police, I don't know."

He shook his head and walked over to the window. The back yard was small but full of interest. Round the compact area of mown grass there were borders of a variety of flowers and in one corner, a circle of maize huddled together bearing healthy-looking cobs. In the middle of the lawn there was an ornate bird bath, into which a sparrow was busily dipping its beak. Moule turned around to face her as she placed the vase on a shelf.

"De corn looks ripe for pickin'."

She looked out at the object of his comment. "When I was a child in Spain, we always grew it in the garden. But then we had a lot more space than I have here."

"Same as when I was boy. I am from Jamaica, you see. The land of wood and water. Corn grew all over and big, sometimes nearly two feet long. My favourite was when my mother roasted it on an open wood fire." For a few seconds his eyes clouded over dreamily. "I can almost smell it now."

"Mostly we boiled them but roast sounds good." She went to rinse her hands in the sink. "But you're right. These need to be picked. Would you like some coffee while we wait?"

"Thank you. That would be good."

She boiled the kettle and invited him to sit at the kitchen table. While she poured boiling water into two mugs, she apologised for the fact that it was instant and then sat opposite him. The Spanish woman and the old black Jamaican fiddled awkwardly with their steaming mugs, with eyes averted, as they sought some common ground for conversation.

To their mutual relief they did not have long to wait.

The door opened wider, and WPC Sanders came in, tucking the notepad into her breast pocket.

"Well, that's all done," she announced. "I've got a statement from Sonia, so I'll go back to the station and log it. Oh, by the way, I asked Sonia, but she says she doesn't want counselling. It's her choice."

Mrs Benjamin stood up. "Okay, if that's what she wants. Did she say any more? I mean, did she tell you if she has any idea who did it? Or why?"

"No, she just said they were white boys wearing hoods. I don't think she's deliberately hiding anything, but I do think she's scared even to suggest who it might have been. This was an assault causing actual bodily harm, so we'll do all we can to apprehend the culprits."

"I know who it was," Moule said from the table, without looking up from his coffee mug.

Mrs Benjamin appeared to be astonished but the officer maintained a professional expression of mild interest and waited for Moule to expand on his statement. He looked up at them and shook his shaggy head gently.

"It must have been fren's of dat dirty little rat who broke into my flat." He lifted his hands and his voice rose by an octave. "It stands to sense, man. This Jason fellow ran off and left Sonia behind, then, when the police catch him, he thinks is Sonia who grassed on him. So, he gets his nasty little fren's to take revenge on de girl."

"An interesting theory, Mr Moule but until there's any kind of proof you shouldn't…"

"It stands to sense," he repeated. "These bad boys did not steal anything. In the middle of the day, they beat up an innocent girl on the Common, who is just goin' about her business." Spittle churned through his molars as he sucked his teeth loudly. "You don't need to be a detective to work this out, officer. I know, because I know the mind of these people. They are no different all over the world. I know dem."

For Moule, this was a long and impassioned speech and the two women simply stood and stared at him for several seconds. Then, feeling he had said too much, he clasped the mug and stared down at his hands.

The officer didn't respond to the tirade but turned and thanked Mrs Benjamin for her time, nodded at Moule and then left the room. Mrs Benjamin saw her out of the front door.

Moule was still sitting at the table, looking morose, when she returned.

"You really think that's what happened? That's why they did it?"

He leaned back in the chair and just nodded.

"Is that how it would have been where you come from?" she asked quietly. "Is that how you know?"

"Jamaica's the land of wood and water, mother and son, father and daughter," he replied enigmatically and stood up abruptly. "Now, is Miss Sonia ready to see me?"

She regarded him quizzically and then replied, "Yes, unless the police officer has tired her."

Moule followed her into the front room, where Sonia had her head resting on a cushion at the back of her chair. Her eyes were closed but she was not asleep. He sat down opposite her, while Mrs Benjamin hovered in the doorway.

"Sonia," Mrs Benjamin said softly, "do you feel well

100

enough to talk to Mr Moule?"

"Yes, Mum. I'm fine." She opened her eyes and switched her attention to Moule.

Mrs Benjamin slipped out of the room and pulled the door closed.

"What are we going to do now?" she asked pleadingly.

"We carry on, Miss Sonia. When first you arks me to do this I was reluctant but now we are under way I want to see it finish."

"But how can we?" She held up her bandaged hand. "I can't write. This is my writing hand."

"You can still use de tape recorder and write later, when your hand is mended."

"That will be too late, Moule. I have to complete it before the end of term and the hand won't be better by then. And I still have all my other schoolwork to do."

Moule rocked gently as he contemplated the situation. Suddenly he snapped his fingers. "You need a scribe. Someone to listen to de tape and write out long hand what is recorded. Dat is exactly what you would have done if dey hadn't bust your hand."

"But it wouldn't be in my handwriting, would it?"

"Chuh, man! In the circumstances who is goin' to mind that. At de school, when dey hear what happen dey must make allowances. It's still your work, just written out by some other hand. I mean, if you was going to type it, no one would know whose fingers was on de keys, eh?"

She laughed at that but suddenly stopped short with a wince and put a hand to the side of her face.

"Okay, so, assuming we can finish the interview, who's going to write it out?"

"Well, what about your mother?"

Sonia rolled her eyes in the manner that teenagers do when confronted by adult ignorance.

"She's Spanish," Sonia explained. "Her written English is just not good enough to write out what we have recorded on the tape. It needs to be written as I would have done it."

She thought it but didn't want to say to Moule's face, that his idiomatic Jamaican patois was probably too undiluted for her mother to interpret.

They had reached an impasse. So, after Moule had talked to her further about the incident on the Common, he stood to leave, promising that he would think of a solution to the problem. Then, turning at the doorway, as if on sudden impulse, he looked back at the reclining figure on the armchair.

"It was Jason's fren's wasn't it? It was dem that beat you."

She didn't reply but looked at him for a few seconds before being unable to hold his stare. Sonia shook her head but in that lowering of the eyes, Moule knew he had been right.

He sought out Mrs Benjamin, said goodbye and then left the house.

A couple of days passed after his visit to the Benjamin's and Moule was sewing on a shirt button, when the mobile began warbling. He cursed as he pricked his finger with the needle and then got up to answer.

"Mr Moule? This is Sergeant Grant. You might remember…?"

"Oh, yes, Sergeant Grant," Mould replied eagerly. "You callin' to tell me you caught the ruffians dat beat up Miss Sonia?"

He heard Grant chuckle. "Er, no but it is about Sonia that

I'm calling. It's a bit unusual and not in my normal line of duty but I have a suggestion to make."

Moule sat down.

"WPC Sanders filed her report about the unfortunate incident on the Common and obviously it now has a crime number. But she also mentioned that Sonia now has a problem regarding… what is it, a project she is carrying out with you?"

"Dat's right. It's a schoolwork project. With her hand broken she can't write it up before de end of term."

"Yes, and that's why I'm calling with a possible solution to the problem."

Moule's mind raced wildly, wondering how the police could possibly help to complete a schoolgirl's work project. Were they going to offer the services of a stenographer, or perhaps someone on probation? Or was it some kind of community service that he was about to offer?

"A solution?"

"Yes, but as I'm busy at the moment could I call in on you this evening on my way back from work? We could discuss it then."

"Okay but my place is not exactly on your way home."

"That doesn't matter. It's only a small detour."

Moule hesitated. This would not look good. The whole neighbourhood had talked for a long time after the visit by the police following the break-in. Now, if a uniformed policeman arrived on his doorstep the tongues would start wagging again.

"You can't tell me on de phone?" Moule pleaded.

"Don't worry Mr Moule," Grant replied, detecting Moule's anxiety. "I'll go home and change into civvies first."

"Okay then, sergeant. That would be good. I'll expect you about… when?"

"About eight. I'll have a bite to eat first."

In fact, Grant arrived a few minutes before eight that evening. Moule had eaten his meal and downed a couple of Red Stripes and was busy tidying the sitting room, when the intercom crackled into action. He pressed the release button and waited by the landing door.

Sergeant Grant came in, wearing the same jacket as when they had met on the Common, but his mauve shirt was open at the neck. Moule produced his sweeping gesture of welcome and then closed the door.

"Take a seat, sergeant." Moule paused to consider what you offer an off-duty copper. This was a new experience for him. "Can I get you something to drink? A coffee maybe, or a Red Stripe beer?"

"A beer would be great, thanks." Grant sat down. "And it's Noel when I'm not in uniform."

Moule nodded in acceptance of this privilege and went to get the beer. As he cleaned out a glass, he thought desperately of some piece of small talk to kick things off. But then, Grant had come to see him, and it was up to him to say why. He went back and placed the glass and beer on a table by his guest.

"Noel is a name of a well-known Jamaican policeman from when I was a boy in the island," Moule volunteered. "Noel Crosswell was Commissioner of Police."

Moule was just sitting down when Grant said something so unexpected that he almost lost his balance.

"I know. He was a school friend of my grandfather's, and I am named after him."

"No... so... so, your father was in Jamaica?"

"My father was born in Jamaica," Noel, said calmly as he poured Red Stripe into his glass. "And that is part of the reason

I'm here tonight."

It did not take a detective to note the sudden change in Moule's expression. From sudden surprise at hearing of my country of birth, to a flash of panic on being told that there was a connection with my son's reason for visiting, was palpably obvious to Noel. It puzzled my son at the time but not knowing Moule as I came to know him later, he thought no more about the reaction.

Moule settled uneasily in the armchair and waited stone-faced, for Noel to continue.

"My father was a solicitor in a country practice for most of his working life but retired nearly ten years ago. He and my mother live in a village near Tunbridge Wells, and he potters around, doing some writing, a bit or carpentry and gets involved in local activities. Apart from that, there's not a lot to keep him active, so when I heard from Wendy Sanders about Sonia's project stalling, I thought of the old man." Noel smiled. "I mean my father."

He paused and sipped from his glass. Moule was now looking slightly more at ease and was regarding Noel with a beatifical expression of total absorption.

"So, with his Jamaican connections, his knowledge of the expressions you often use and the fact that he can type as well as write good English, I suggested to him that he might like to transcribe the tapes for Sonia. What do you think?"

For several seconds Moule appeared to be overwhelmed and when he did reply, it was with a croak in his voice. "Well, dat would certainly be… a solution to de problem. No, it would answer a prayer. This is a most unexpected offer. But what does your father say? Will he do it?"

Noel's face creased in the shy smile I know so well, and

he made an awkward gesture with his hands. "To be honest, Moule, I haven't asked him yet. It's only correct that I clear this with you first as it's your story. And also with Sonia, of course. So, what do you think?"

"Man, if it's okay with Sonia, then it's okay with me." Moule was clearly warming to this policeman, never having previously dealt with one in a private capacity. "I will ask her tomorrow and as soon as I get her answer, I will tell you."

Noel finished the drink, leant forward and then extended his hand to his host. Moule unconsciously wiped his own hand down the side of his trousers before grasping and shaking Noel's. It was like the sealing of a deal. A small matter in the scale of worldly affairs but it was a significant one in terms of social bonding between authority and a representative of a minority group.

Noel stayed on for a while and the two of them discussed community matters before he prepared to leave. He handed Moule a business card.

"It was good to meet you... Noel," Moule said awkwardly at his front door. "An' give my best to your father... a fellow Jamaican."

"I will. And thanks for the beer."

As the door closed behind him, Noel's thought turned automatically to his mantra. If only the public and the Force would keep constantly in mind the fact that police officers are merely civilians in uniform. There is always an ordinary human being under the badge of authority.

Moule duly contacted Sonia and explained the proposal put forward by Noel Grant. At first, she was suspicious of the police involvement, albeit off-duty, but Moule eased her concerns and eventually she agreed. As the alternative seemed to be total failure of the project, she accepted that there seemed to be no choice. As soon as he had her agreement, Moule called Noel and gave him the word to proceed.

So, one quiet autumn evening, while I was inspecting a row of ageing runner beans in the vegetable patch, my wife called me in to take a call from our son. I have to admit that his suggestion that I should transcribe a Jamaican's life story from tape recordings was well off-piste but as he went on, I slowly warmed to the proposal. The idea cemented itself when I heard that I would be helping out a young girl who had been violently attacked in broad daylight in a public park.

It would involve my moving up to London for at least a week, but I checked with June, my wife, and I got the impression that she might actually welcome me off the premises for a short while. That settled, I contacted Noel again and said I would pack and then take the train up the next week. It was reckoned that Sonia's interviews would be coming to an end by then. My base was to be the spare room in their Wandsworth house.

So, that was how I became involved in the Moule saga project.

Sonia resumed her interview sessions with Moule as soon as she was fit enough to do so, and I arrived at my son's house as planned. Noel said that he would take me to Moule's Clapham flat on his way to work the next day and introduce me to the old Rastafarian.

During my working years I spent as little time as I could in London, never having liked city life. However, on occasions when it was necessary to visit clients or attend court up in the capital, I did make the most of it, by going to the theatre or a museum. Latterly, we had been going to visit our granddaughter in Wandsworth but apart from that, I now steered clear of what used to be called The Smoke.

I will admit though that it was very pleasant that first morning, strolling through Clapham Common. In spite of the constant drone of traffic, there was an urban serenity to the two hundred and twenty acres of tree-lined parkland. It was one of London's many lungs. As we passed the largest of the ponds, I noticed ducks and Canada geese floating contentedly on the still water and looking up, I noted the browning edges of fine mature chestnuts. It was all quite agreeable, and I said as much to my son.

"London's not all bad you know." He acknowledged a greeting as someone passed. "But, like anywhere, it looks better when the sun is shining."

"I hope the sun's shining on Lavender Hill station. I read that Mayor Khan is trying to shut you down."

"Yes, you're right. All in the name of cost cutting." He stepped aside to let a mother and child pass. "But there's a strong opposition group working on it, so we might get him to back off. There's a fine balance between cost cutting and effective policing and to close Lavender Hill could tip the balance the wrong way."

"Hmm, I hope you're right."

We crossed over the road and walked briskly up the High Street until we arrived at Moule's door. He was expecting us and to avoid our arrival looking like a police raid, he was standing outside his street door in order to greet us as friends. No doubt he felt that would look better to inquisitive passers-by.

He was exactly as Noel had described. Tall, craggy-faced,

with the shoulder-length dreadlocks and not unlike I imagine Bob Marley would look, had he lived to be seventy-four. He beamed a flash of strong, white teeth, looked me square in the eyes, shook my hand firmly and said, "I also am from the land of wood and water."

"Father and son, mother and daughter," I completed the couplet, and he threw back his head and screeched with laughter.

A man passing by shouted, "I see you, Moule."

He was still laughing when we went up the stairs. Noel had bidden us a hasty farewell and then taken the route to Lavender Hill.

Up in Moule's sitting room, he offered me a seat while he went off to percolate some of *the best coffee in the world*, from the Blue Mountains of Jamaica. While he was out in the kitchen, I let my eyes rove across the many treasures around the room. There was the map of Jamaica on the wall, different shaped conch shells on tables and surfaces, a female figure carved from lignum vitae, a table lamp converted from a bottle of Appleton rum, a tee shirt with a scrawled signature across the front and... I was attempting to decipher the signature when Moule returned, bearing two mugs. He followed my gaze.

"Lord Kitchener," he said, and then added with a smile, "the great calypso singer, not your great English warrior."

Over the next hour we discussed many things, mainly from our past as children in Jamaica. We were from different backgrounds, different class systems and even different parts of the island but somehow, there were no barriers from the start. In short, I found him delightful company and I assured him that I was looking forward to hearing his story. We agreed to go together to the Benjamin's house the following day.

I returned to Clapham High Street the next day and, as arranged, we left Moule's flat together at ten o'clock after he had called Sonia's home. Mrs Benjamin had answered and confirmed it would be okay to visit, so Moule said we would be right over.

Sonia met us at the front door, explaining that her mother had gone out shopping. She was much as I expected, because Moule had given me an accurate description. At that point however, he had not elaborated on their initial unfortunate meeting, and it was sometime later that I heard the details. It was as if he had not wanted me to prejudge the girl through any past misdeed and I found that rather endearing.

Sonia greeted me politely but with a layer of reservation about her demeanour. Maybe she saw me, an ageing white man with what she might call a posh voice, as representing an authority of which she was innately wary. I did my best from the beginning to make her feel at ease, without also appearing patronising. By the time Moule and I left the Benjamin's house, I think that I had achieved a strong degree of thawing.

And so, I settled into my new temporary quarters in my son's guest room and began transcribing Moule's reportage. Although familiar with the still undiluted accent, it was at times difficult to piece together his ramblings, as he tended to switch suddenly from one topic to another. That said though, the challenge made the task even more interesting. I was not only transcribing but editing and writing in a way that an educated sixteen-year-old might. I also found Sonia's pre-injury notes were helpful in creating continuity to the story.

Anyway, I have now reproduced my best effort up to the

time when Sonia was attacked on the Common. The following is Moule's story, continued after Sonia was able to resume the recordings.

"Now, where were we, Miss Sonia?" Moule had enquired after ensuring that she was comfortable. "Ah, yes, my father had started at Alcan."

At about the time my father changed his job, I changed my school. It was the school I would have stayed at in Mandeville until I was about fifteen, if we had remained in Jamaica. By English standards it was quite basic education, sufficient to teach us to read and write. Enough for us to get a better job when we left. There was little in the way of history, because what history there was in Jamaica related to slavery and colonial empowerment and that was not a popular back-story with the teachers. We did learn a bit about the Arawaks but then they were wiped out by more invaders. Jamaica's was not a happy history for descendants of enslaved people. There was some history of the Mother Country but at the time, that was like learning about the craters on the moon.

And when it came to Geography, all we were taught related to our small island. Something must have gone in because even today, I remember that Jamaica is one hundred and forty miles long and forty-four miles wide. Anyway, although I was not a grade A pupil something stuck and for that I am grateful.

You ask about other schools in the area. Yes, there was one up on the hill for people with money. It was a fee-paying school called 'de Carteret'. (*At that point I stopped the tape, sat back and had a vision of that place through the eyes of a twelve-year-old boy.*) The school was quite small, with, I think, only about fifty boys at any time. It is what in England would be called a prep school, with pupils leaving at the age of thirteen and going to elite secondary schools such as Munro. Obviously, we had no connection with these boys, except when we — my friends and me — used to go up to the boundary walls and watch them playing cricket or football.

Like most of the area around Mandeville, the soil was a rich red colour, scattered with small, round, grey pellets. I used to think that it was bauxite coming to the surface and maybe I was not wrong. As I said, Kirkvine was just up the road from there. One of the playing fields at de Carteret had been cut out of the hillside and sometimes after dark, I used to go and look at the roads the boys had cut with their penknives into the bank to play with their toy cars. I had never owned anything like that and, one night, I found one of these cars left on a dirt road cut by the boys and I took it home. I read the name under the car and saw that it was called a Rover and made by a company called Dinky. I kept that car to play with secretly, because I knew my father would beat me if he knew that I had stolen it. I was too young at eight years old to recognise hypocrisy, because my father was a far bigger thief than me. I found that out much later. That car is the only store-bought toy I ever owned — if stealing is owning. If today I would meet the true owner of Rover, I would thank him most sincerely and give it back immediately. Yes, I still have it, somewhere in a box under my bed.

Apart from that stolen car I never had any other toys. Anyway, not ones you can buy in a store. Modern children have so many toys, games and gadgets they don't know which ones to play with. I had my go-cart of course but the only other toy I can remember was a gig. It was made for me by a man who used to carve all kinds of things from wood. He must also have had access to a lathe because this gig was beautifully round and smooth, with a nail sticking out of the base for it to spin on. I spent hours spinning that top, sometimes making it turn for several minutes before it flopped over. I took a lot of care winding it up with the string as tight together as possible in order to give it a chance for the longest spin. I was happy with that gig, so it was a sad day when my father backed the truck over it and mashed it into the ground. I know he didn't do it on purpose, and it was my fault for leaving it in the dirt, but I still think it was unkind of him to beat me because the nail punctured the truck tyre.

But, going back to what I was saying about de Carteret, we boys from the council school had no contact with those from the prep school on the hill. They were the sons of businessmen, traders and planters. It was a boarding school and some of the boys must have come from many miles across the island. I believe a few came from as far as the Frome sugar estate over in Westmorland. In many ways we actually felt sorry for them. It must have been like being in prison, seeing their parents only maybe a couple of times a term, while we went back to our homes every afternoon. Okay, some of the homes, like mine, were not all sweetness and light but at least we were not prisoners. I also heard that the headmaster was a bully and enjoyed beating the boys for the smallest wrongdoing. No, we had no contact with them. None at all and that's the truth.

(*I did pause to wonder why Moule had been so adamant on this point, but he then moved swiftly on to another topic.*)

I did quite well at school, but I soon discovered when starting at secondary school in England, that the standard was very low in Jamaica. In England, history was something from a different world and also no one was interested in how long the island of Jamaica is. Meanwhile, my friends and I continued to get up to high jinks. Nothing really dishonest but just the sort of things we bush kids did. For example? Well, one trick was when it rained heavily, many of the dips in the roads used to fill up with water. This was not a problem for tractors and trucks, but cars had a struggle. Some drivers did not know how to keep the engines going as they went through the deep water and we boys watching could easily see which ones they were. So, when they reached the deepest part, two or three of us would run out into the water and jump up and down on the back bumper. This motion caused water to rise up to the spark plugs, or maybe just make the car stick in a pothole. Either way, the result was the same. The car either got stuck or stalled. Then one of the boys, usually the bravest one, rushes to the driver's window and says he and his friends will push him out if he pays them.

Of course, the driver and other people in the car are vexed as hell and curse at us but what can they do about it? They pay up and we push them clear of the water. Sometimes we got as much as two pounds a time for this mischievous act. Depending on how many cars there were and how long the water remained deep, we could make about ten pounds in a day. Man, those were riches. Of course, it would be a foolish boy who told his parents of this prank, because the money would be taken away and maybe a beating administered.

There were other things we got up to, like stealing mangoes and making mud dams in the culverts but nothing too serious. There always seemed to be a corpie not far away, so we had to be careful.

There was a pause in the tape here. It was a shorter session than the previous ones and I suspected it was because Sonia was tiring. My typing fingers were also tiring, so I gave them a rest and leaned back on the wooden chair to contemplate what I had written. Much of what Moule had recorded was familiar to me but it was also like looking at the same picture from the reverse side, or in a mirror. I was twelve years old when I left Jamaica with my parents and even in the leaving, I guessed there would be fundamental differences in our modes of departure. I was writing of a period of my life that was running along a parallel line to that of my subject, but those lines had not deviated to within touching distance before last week. It was all very weird and also quite mysterious.

I had a drink of water and then went out for a walk to clear my head. Noel's wife, Mary, was out and so I took the dog with me for company. After a pub lunch, with the dog tied up outside, I returned to the tape. I had promised not to be a burden to my daughter-in-law, and this included not having me around for midday meals. She said it was no trouble, but I knew she had her own life to lead.

I sat down, switched on the tape and Moule continued his rambling reminiscence:

I think I was nearly ten years old when my mother began to branch out. Although my father was earning decent money at Alcan, he was also spending it just as fast, so my mother took a job up at de Carteret. She joined the team of washer women. The money was poor, but it was all her own and this independence also helped her to get out of the house more often. She had a cousin who lived in Kingston and about once a month, she took the bus down there to see her and do some shopping as well.

I must tell you about the buses we had in Jamaica at that time. By today's standards they were ramshackle vehicles but always painted in bright colours to make up for their other deficiencies. I can't remember the make, but they must have been constructed in England long before they found their way to the West Indies. The seating capacity was about forty, but baggage and sometimes extra passengers found their way onto the roof. I never heard of anyone falling off, but it was a precarious way to travel, especially up and down hills and on sharp bends. Animals travelled inside too: goats, chickens and anything that could get through the door and not have to sit on the driver's lap. These vehicles were known throughout the island as Romance Buses. What a fine name for such beaten up, fume-belching people carriers.

Anyway, that is how my mother travelled to Kingston. It was a long and bumpy ride that took several hours, so she usually stayed at least one night with her cousin.

At about the same time, my father also began to travel around but having learnt something from the experience of the ice truck, he also used the bus service. Most of the time we didn't know where he went but many of his longer trips were also to Kingston. If we asked him what he was doing in the capital, he either said we should mind our own business or just that he was doing a favour for some unnamed person. Even at my young age, I guessed that he was up to no good on those trips, but I never knew what that mischief was. Maybe now I never will but it was on one of my mother's visits to Kingston that something happened to make me fear for my life at his hand.

Some dates fade with time. Now, I can't tell you what I was doing this time last week, but other dates have a great significance, and you know exactly where you were and what you were doing at that time. For example, most old people like me, remember what they were doing at the moment they heard the shocking news of President Kennedy's assassination. I was dancing in a night club in Soho but that's another story. Anyway, my mother was in Kingston on the second of June 1953 when I left school early, right after lunch. It was the day of Queen Elizabeth's coronation and the headmaster had declared a half day's holiday in honour of the occasion.

When I look back on the coronation, I have to smile at our ignorance. Several months before that event, King George died, and a very solemn headmaster announced to the school assembly that His Majesty had passed away. Jamaica was a colony and so the King of England was also our king but as it was likely that none of us had even seen an image of him, his death meant little to us. In fact, for a short period after the announcement, some boys thought that a pupil of the name King had died. It was not until we saw the boy kicking a football around outside that the mistake was corrected.

Anyway, the moment I arrived back at my home I knew that my father had a visitor because there was a bicycle propped up by the wood shed in the yard. I must have gone in quietly, probably not to cause a disturbance and be rewarded with a clip round the ear, because they obviously had not heard me. As soon as I went into the front room though, I heard them. I thought there was some kind of fight going on, so I went into the bedroom and there they were, wrestling on top of the bed. Only it was not any kind of wrestling that I knew about. I stood there for long enough to recognise the woman, because she assisted her mother at one of the vegetable stalls in the market.

Woops, I thought. Steady on Moule, this is for school kids. But then, I reasoned they are really quite sophisticated at sixteen these days.

The floorboard must have creaked because the action on the bed suddenly stopped and both of them turned and stared at me. It was the first time I had seen my father with no clothes on, even in the sea, but in his rage, his nakedness did not faze him. He leapt off the woman, grabbed the first thing he could reach — it was a shoe — and flung it at my head. I turned and ran as he chased me up to the front door, yelling and screaming. He grabbed me just as I was opening the door and hauled me back into the room. I put my hands up to protect my face and he would have hit me with his fists, if the woman had not shouted at him to stop. She had a gown round her and she threw my father's pants at him and told him to put them on before the neighbours saw.

I was surprised when he obeyed her, because when he was in a rage usually nothing stopped him, but he told me to sit on a chair in the corner, until he was dressed. The woman went back into the bedroom and also dressed. As she slipped past me on her way to leave the house, she smiled and winked at me. I will never forget that small gesture. It was as if to say, one day you also could be in this situation. But it is not part of this story to say if I ever was.

On this occasion, to my surprise, my father did not take the belt to my backside. Instead, he made me stay sitting down while he finished dressing and quite calmly said to me that if I ever told my mother what I had seen he would kill me. He would chop me up with a machete and throw the pieces into the mangrove for the alligators to devour. Yes, man, that shut me up good and proper and I never told anyone, not even my sisters. In fact, it was a good thing the girl's school did not also have half the day off as well, as my father's machete might have become quite busy.

I don't know how often that kind of entertaining went on at my home, because after that he took greater care of secrecy. It probably happened at the woman's home, if it was the same woman he kept up with. I don't know why my mother stayed with him as she must have known he was... what's the word...? a philanderer. I don't have to tell you, after that incident I was even more scared of him and kept out of his way as much as possible.

You are wondering if I had grandparents alive when I was growing up in Jamaica. My father's parents I never knew, and he never talked much about them. All I heard was that they used to live somewhere up on the edge of the cockpit country, quite close to a place called Sherwood Content. That is the village where Usain Bolt came from, and I believe his parents are still there. There was a bad bout of diphtheria at some time between the world wars and it carried both of my grandparents away. Now, I don't even know where they are buried. My mother's parents finished their days on the north coast, at a town called Oracabessa.

It makes me smile now when I hear that name, because that was where the mystery man lived. Let me explain. The main radio station — there was no television in Jamaica in those days — was RJR. It was a commercial station and there were several record-request programmes. For some reason, many of those requests came from 'Guess Who' from Oracabessa. I don't know if it was always the same person writing or phoning in, but the requests were usually for

119

different women.

Again, I was never sure what my mother's father did for a living during his working years, but they had quite a nice house, in the hills behind the town. We went to visit them a few times and they came to stay with us after my father got the Alcan job. I know that grandma never liked my father and now I know the reason why. But my main memory of grandma is that she used to give us sweets called Paradise Plums and she made the best dumplings in St Mary Parish.

My grandfather died not long after we left Jamaica in 1956 and my grandmother went soon after my mother returned to live there in the eighties. When we sailed to England, she thought she would never see either of them again.

From about the middle fifties, things started to change in Jamaica. The island was attracting more tourists, mostly from the USA and they brought with them the mighty dollar. Even simple people in country districts began to detect the smell of the greenback. When an American left a tip that was nearly half a week's wage, then the underprivileged began to wake up. So, there was a lot of unrest, with strikes and demands for increased pay. I remember a calypso at the time with the refrain, *Strike, strike, strike, all about me is strike* but I can't remember who sang it.

I don't think Alcan ever had a walkout at that time but there was a lot of disruption on the sugar estates and also at the docks, especially when perishable goods were being loaded onto ships. If dock workers refused to load green bananas into the refrigerated hold of a ship, then after a few days, the whole load was only fit to be tipped into the sea or be fed to pigs. Politics were also hotting up, with the two main parties, JLP and PNP, both having a rough house element. At election time there was shooting and beatings happening in most big towns but especially in the poorer parts of Kingston. As I said, my father made a lot of trips to Kingston, but I don't think he got involved in that kind of thing. He was not political. He just looked after himself. Number one was all that mattered to him.

I was about eleven years old when I discovered I could sing. The transition between calypso music and the beginnings of rock-steady was just happening at about that time, so it was a small step for me to go from singing a solo in the chapel choir to performing with a group of local musicians. They were probably self-taught but were good enough on drums, guitar and maracas to perform at some of the local hotels. My voice had not broken but they thought it would be a useful gimmick to have a young boy as lead singer. They travelled to the richer hotels on the north coast, places like The Arawak and Shaw Park but my father would not let me go up there. He said I was too young and might be subjected to some bad influences. That was a joke, coming from him. So, I sang at the few local hotels in Manchester Parish and made some helpful pocket money, which I hid away in a Black Magic chocolate tin box. I lied to my father about the money, because if I told him I was sure that he would have helped himself to it.

The singing did not last long, as my voice began to break early, and the band did not want to ruin their reputation by having a screeching adolescent behind the microphone. But I had made some money for the first time in my life and had also built up some confidence for dealing with affairs in my future life.

My mother continued to work up at de Carteret and must have caught the attention of whoever it was who employed the domestic staff, because she was promoted to a job in the school sanatorium. I think the job title is an auxiliary, not a nurse but someone who assists the nursing staff and does a lot of the dirtier jobs. Her pay went up but like me, she kept as much of it as she could away from my father.

The sanatorium was at the highest built-up place on the school's property, about fifty yards behind the main building. From there and also when she went down to collect things from the school's storeroom, she saw a lot of what went on and used to tell me about it when she came home. My father, when he was home, was not interested. He had no time for what the sons of rich people got up to. But one of those things that interested me most was the car racing.

From the top of the slope by the sanatorium down to the yard by the school kitchen was a stone wall, about two feet wide and twenty-five feet long. This wall was capped off with smooth concrete and the boys used to let their cars go at the top and let them run down the slope to the column at the end of the wall. Most of the cars fell off long before reaching the bottom but if one did not and hit the column, then it was declared a champion and the owner earned a lot of respect from the other car owners. My mother said that the cars were called Dinky toys. When she told me that, I went to look again at my Rover, which I kept hidden in the Black Magic box with my money and noticed for the first time that the front axle was slightly bent. From that moment, I saw my Dinky Toy as one of the champions that ran the whole length of the wall.

The other treasure that my mother brought to me from the prep school was wrapped in a piece of cloth and packed around with ice inside a newspaper. By the time she reached home, the newspaper was a sodden mess but inside the cloth, was one of the most delicious things I had ever tasted. Soursop ice cream. She told me it was made in the school kitchen in a wooden churn with a handle and when ice was packed round the inside, the handle was turned until the liquid inside froze. I have yet to find sour sops in the markets here, but I will never forget the beautiful, bitter-sweet taste of that ice cream. Maybe one day…

Another thing my mother managed to bring back for me was clothes that some of the parents had thrown away. Maybe they were torn or even a bit faded, but she used to fix them up and then to me, they were like new clothes. Of course, being a boys' school, my sisters did not get anything like that and, I am pleased to say, they did not like soursop ice cream either.

I took a rest from the tape then and, as was becoming my habit after these sessions, I moved into a more comfortable chair after easing my limbs and threw my mind back to those far away days of my youth. Moule's early life was so different from mine and yet in his narration, he kept hitting memory keys that rang familiar notes through my head. I knew by now that we had both left Jamaica in the same year and I was becoming increasingly intrigued to hear how his life had developed, since arriving in what was a strange and alien land. I knew that was how it was for him, because that was how I found England on first arrival. In fact, as a young black boy it would have been far worse for him, with the prejudice that existed throughout England in those days. However, at that point I never envisaged the twists and turns that would develop from Moule's narrative before we finally arrived at its denouement.

That evening, Mary was later than usual from work. She had a four day a week job as PA to a senior executive in a city-based company and sometimes was required to fill in more than the standard nine-to-five. The neighbour who collected Alice from school on Mary's workdays, brought the little girl over while Noel and I were busy preparing dinner. It was a routine I was happy to follow, and it gave me a chance to talk with my son.

I didn't discuss Moule's tape and the strange feelings of connectivity his words aroused but I did ask if any progress had been made in tracking down Sonia's attackers. The answer was negative. No one was talking and that included Jason. I also got the impression that Noel's concerns were more immediately with the future of his station, than with catching another mugger. I really couldn't blame him for that.

CHAPTER 7

Although I was becoming deeply involved in Moule's story, I was also beginning to sense that it was about to enter a darker phase. There was nothing tangible, just the increasing periods of hesitation, as if he was trying to negotiate his way through that period of life as he approached adolescence. One can pick up those sorts of intonations and subtle alterations in cadence if one has been tracking a verbal report for a decent length of time. He seemed now to be inching his way through the proverbial minefield. I was not to know at that stage that he was simply exercising his redacting skills, as Abe had suggested.

On a more prosaic level I was also concerned about the length of the entire transcription. Other than translating what at times was *raw-chaw* Jamaican, I had not carried out any editing of the narrative, so I wondered how Sonia was going to condense it all into a school essay exercise. At present, the whole thing was heading into novella territory and Sonia was about halfway through her term. But I felt that we still had time to sort that out later.

Meanwhile, she continued to visit Moule, and he seemed just as keen to relive his youth for the girl. However, she was now more cautious in the route she took to visit the High Street in Clapham, avoiding the quieter areas on her way.

Moule continued his story:

By the middle of the fifties there was a lot of talk about independence, although most of it passed over my head. But the two political parties, Jamaica Labour and People's National, were shaping up for who would run the country when that time came. I only knew about this because my father told us of shootings in Kingston when he returned from his visits to the capital. I could be wrong about the timing, because it is something I only read about much later but there was, for a few years before independence, a Federation in the West Indies and the two main islands in this uncomfortable union were Trinidad and Jamaica. Of course, the Federation did not survive independence in 1962 but unfortunately, the political rivalry and the shootings did and maybe still do, to this day.

1955 was an important year in Jamaica's history, because the island's first Prime Minister, Alexander Bustamante, always known as Busta, was defeated in the general election and Norman Manley's PNP won. Manley was a clever and well-educated man, but many employers were fearful of his politics, as he was a man of the Left. Of course, my father thought he was Jamaica's saviour and never seemed to stop talking about what the PNP was going to do for the working man. As you can imagine, at the age of eleven, my knowledge of politics was only what I heard from my father and, as I had little respect for him, I didn't care much anyway.

It is very difficult for youngsters in the UK today to imagine living in a world with no instant communication through mobile phones, internet, TV or even landline telephones. I have told you that in the mid-fifties in Jamaica, there was no television network but of course, neither was there such a thing as internet and where we were in our new

Alcan house there was no telephone. But at last, we had electricity and for the first time in my life I could turn on a switch for light. We still kept the oil in the kerosene lamp though, as the power had a habit of failing quite regularly. One day my father proudly brought home a radio, so we could listen to recordings of the music we loved. Before the radio, we only heard live music from bands on a Saturday night or in the market. I can still see my mother dancing round the kitchen table to Byron Lee's music playing on that radio.

The other form of entertainment we did have was cinema, or as it was better known at the time, the picture house. I went two or three times with my friends to see pictures in Mandeville. I suppose in England this kind of place would be called a *flea pit* and the one we went to probably did have an infestation of those creatures. The films were mostly American imports in black and white and mainly of the 'B' variety. But to us, who had paid the large sum of one shilling and sixpence, it didn't matter what they showed as long as there was plenty of action. Sometimes, the action also took place inside the picture house, when fights broke out in the cheap seats. Maybe the men responsible had visited the rum shop before, or perhaps they were taking rival sides from what was happening on the screen. I don't know but when that happened, we just kept out of the way and watched the fun. Mostly the fights broke out when the film snapped, which happened quite often. Anyway, it helped to give us our money's worth.

Towards the end of 1955, about the time my mother was wondering when the new fruit trees would start to bear, my father began to talk about going to England. As far back as 1948 the immigration authorities in the UK had been encouraging West Indians from their colonies in the Caribbean to come to England to fill the gaps where there was a shortage of workers as a result of the war. I did not know why my father wanted to move away from Jamaica and of course my sisters and I were not allowed to question his reasons. If we did, we would either be bawled out or get a clip round the ear, or both. I expect he discussed it with my mother, but she never said anything to us. But the idea of going to England was as frightening to me as a trip to the moon. Jamaica was my home, where I had friends and where I intended to grow up. It was my world.

But something must have happened in my father's life to make him think that way. I suspected that it was somehow connected with his frequent trips to Kingston, where maybe he was developing big ideas from hearing people talking to other people. You know, it sounds crazy now but there was so much ignorance about the *Mother Country*, that some country people believed that the streets of London were paved with gold. I mean, that kind of thinking is for fairy stories, man. I don't believe my father ever had those kinds of thoughts, but something was drawing him towards leaving the island. He was not a well-educated man, but he was clever; in the way a fox is clever. The trouble is you never knew what was going on in his head.

As his plans developed and his talk of emigrating increased, so my plans grew for running away from home. It seemed to me the only way to escape going to England. Then, about a week before Christmas when my father returned home drunk, swearing and kicking the furniture about, I did just that thing. I packed a few useful things and fled into the night.

My knowledge of Jamaica and its geography was limited to the Parish where we lived, Manchester, and to what I learned at school, so I was setting out into the unknown. I did not count our few visits to Oracabessa as having acquired travel knowledge, because I spent most of the time sleeping at the back of the bus and anyway, Oracabessa was too far to run.

I worked it out that if I went south in a straight line, I would eventually reach the sea by Alligator Pond. Down there I could try to get work by helping one of the fishermen who kept their boats and nets pulled up on the beach. I had seen them there when I was younger, and they always looked like they could do with some help. But I decided to go there on the old road through Cedar Grove and not on the Spur Tree Road. That was too public and also, that route still held bad memories for me.

I think I walked for most of the night. Every time I saw a vehicle light or a mule cart coming, I hid on the side of the road until it passed. It was not until I had left Marlborough behind that I stopped and lay down under a fruit stall. I slept for a few hours until I was woken by a woman putting out some yams. She bawled at me for frightening her and she told me to go back home, or she would call a corpie. I don't know where she expected to see a policeman out there on a bush road, but I moved on anyway, stealing a mango from her stall as I left.

I am sorry to say that I had no thought of how my mother would react to my disappearance. I just knew that I wanted to get far away from my father and maybe by doing so, make him change his mind about going to England. It was foolish but I was eleven and confused and angry.

On that first morning away from home, I walked on and made it to Alligator Pond. Down by the water I climbed up a coconut tree — a skill most of us had as boys — and threw down a ripe one. I had no cutlass, so had to break it open with a rock. This was not easy but eventually I succeeded and saved most of the water inside. I also scraped out the soft, white flesh from the inside and that was my breakfast. That and the mango. Then I went to find a fisherman.

I was down at Alligator Pond for nearly four days before they found me. In that time, I met a fisherman called Moses who said he would give me work in exchange for food and a roof over my head. He never once asked me why I was there or where I had come from. In fact, he said very little, only speaking when it was necessary to do so. He was the first Rastafarian man I had ever met, and I soon held him in high regard for the way he lived and for his natural humility. He had the dreadlocks and a scruffy beard, but he was clean, washing in the stream, morning and evening. I helped him sew up torn nets, clean his boat — which was more like a canoe — and gut the fish. He caught all kinds of fish, such as snapper and bonito but he also pulled in crabs and lobster. Being a true Rastafarian, as I believe he was, he was careful as to what he ate. He didn't drink any alcohol but at the end of the day, as we cooked fish over a wood fire on the beach, he smoked fat ganja spliffs. I think once he was about to offer me a smoke but then shook his head. Maybe he thought I was too young. Instead, I just breathed in his exhaled smoke. Although he spoke little, after he had finished smoking, Moses used to sing quietly. He had a good bass voice and, if I knew the song, I joined in with my cracked and breaking tones.

I never found out where Moses lived, or if he had a family. At the end of the day, after eating and smoking, he just bid me goodnight and then disappeared into the bush. I still was unable to swim but enjoyed a dip in the sea after he left, careful to avoid the poisonous sea eggs underfoot. If I splashed around in the water, the phosphorescence, I think is the word, sparkled under the light of the moon. When I came out, I washed the salt off in the stream and then dried myself with the piece of towelling Moses had given to me. Then, after checking there were no alligators in the area, I lay down under the coconut leaf roof he had made to cover the nets and went to sleep to the sound of the bullfrogs croaking. At that point in my life, I don't think I had ever been happier or felt so much freedom. It's a pity it did not last.

Moses was out in the boat when they came. I was gathering up firewood at the edge of the mangrove when I looked up and saw a corpie striding down the beach, with one of the local fishermen beside him. The fisherman pointed at me and for a moment I thought about running. But, as there was nowhere to run to, I just stood and waited for them to reach me. The policeman asked me if I was Meshach Moule and I said I was. He was a decent fellow, but he said quite firmly that he was there to take me home, as my mother was scared about what might have happened to me. So, after giving the fisherman a scowl for betraying me, I went quietly.

I looked out to sea and shouted for Moses. I don't know if he heard me or just sensed that something was going on back on land, but he looked across the water towards us. He didn't say anything as he was too far out, but he made a strange sign with his arms, which I assumed was a kind of farewell signal. I waved and shouted back at him, just before we went out of sight behind the bushes that grew nearly down to the high-water mark.

I never saw Moses again, but I never forgot him. He taught me that there can be wisdom in silence.

The policeman had arrived on a motorcycle and that was how we returned to my home. Before I got on the pillion seat behind him, I asked how he had found me. He said when I had not returned after the first night my mother had reported me to the Mandeville police as missing. After a local search they began asking people along the roads out of town and when the woman with the yams had said she had chased off a boy of my age, they had guessed where to look. Finally, a fisherman down at Alligator Pond told the policeman he had seen Moses with a young boy. As I mounted the pillion, I said to the corpie I would only go home if he made sure my father would not give me a beating. He said child welfare between father and son was not his business, so I jumped off the pillion again and threatened to run back into the bush.

The corpie looked at me for a long time and then laughed, telling me okay, he would threaten my father with a charge of assault if he took the belt or stick to me. His word was good enough for me, so I got back on, and he kick-started the engine.

When we got back, I was covered in dust and must have looked to my mother as if I had slept on the road for four nights, but she still hugged me and thanked the corpie. He gave me a wink and then drove off. As we walked into the house, the first thing I asked my mother was, *Are we still going to England?* She didn't answer me right away but just said to come and have some pumpkin soup.

The policeman who picked me up must have kept his word and spoken to my father at the Alcan works, because when he came back that evening, he did not even look at me. And, when he didn't talk to me for nearly a week, that suited me just fine. He must have remembered I still held his secret.

I switched off the tape when we reached that point as it seemed to be a natural place to end the session. It was tiring work but as I plunged deeper and deeper into Moule's story, so I became increasingly curious as to its eventual outcome. Somehow, I felt that there was a sinister underlying motive for Moule's father deciding to leave Jamaica, other than the simple desire to make more money in the Mother Country. So far, there was nothing tangible to suggest it was anything other than an opportunity for self-improvement, but the apparent devious and self-centred nature of the man's character gave rise to my suspicions. I had become eager to find out if the son, Meshach Moule, knew the true reason why they had been uprooted from their homeland and if he would reveal that motive later in the narrative.

Sonia had been in the habit of dropping tapes off at my son's home after school, but I didn't often see her. This day I hung around downstairs waiting for her to come, as I knew it was an interview day with Moule. She arrived at about six o'clock and I heard the package plop onto the doormat. I managed to open the front door before she dashed off down the road.

"Sonia,' I called out, 'how's it going?"

She stopped and walked slowly back, pulling her school bag more tightly to her shoulder.

"Okay. How are you getting on?"

"It's a bit hard to follow in parts but I'm getting there. And how's the finger now?"

"It's mending slowly." She held up the strapped digits. "But it'll be a long time before I can write again properly."

"Well, don't push it too soon. Give it time." She nodded. "Would you like a drink of something, or are you in a hurry to get back?"

"No, I'd better go."

"Okay. And Sonia, you realise that when you've finished taping Moule's story we'll have a lot of editing to do. There's enough here for a book already, so we'll have to cut a lot of it out."

"I know but," she added shyly, "it's a good story. I'm enjoying it."

"I hope it gives you time for your other schoolwork."

She laughed, baring pink gums above her even, white teeth.

"And what about Moule?" I asked. "Are you sure he's still prepared to go on?"

"Oh, yes, he says he's happy to go on to the end."

A gust of autumn breeze shuffled some early fallen leaves across the pavement. Sonia hitched her school bag again and made an awkward movement with her feet that indicated it was time to move on. I said goodbye to her and then turned to go back inside.

"Whenever the end might be," I muttered to myself.

As I pushed the door open, I heard my name being called and looked back to see Mary approaching along the pavement. We went in together and I asked her about her day. She declined my offer of help with preparing dinner but asked if I would go the short distance down the road and collect Alice from the neighbour.

Noel was due to be late home that evening as he was attending a group meeting, so the three of us dined at seven. After that, Alice went to do her homework and I stepped out for an evening stroll to ease the limbs that had spent much of the day hunched over a word processor.

I rose early the next morning and went downstairs to find Noel in the middle of eating breakfast.

"Morning, son. Are you managing to keep the Barbarians from the gate?"

"The cost-cutters, you mean?" He pushed a cereal packet across the table for me. "It's an on-going battle but we have some big guns on our side and I'm hopeful."

"Good luck then. I'm so glad to be away from the political side of business. It can wear you down."

"I think we have a strong case to keep Lavender Hill open, but the next few weeks are going to be crucial. We'll see."

Noel pushed his chair back and excused himself. I finished breakfast and then returned to my room. After calling June to check that all was well at home, I slipped the tape back into the machine and prepared for another long session of Moule memoirs, attuning my ear once more to the Jamaican accent.

Meshach Moule continued with his recollections:

My brief escape from the confines of my home and our neighbourhood must have done something to my mind and it was not all good. Looking back, I realise that I had become resentful of the life we were living, restless and rebellious. More and more I drifted off on my own, sometimes just looking for trouble. I suppose I had become a trouble maker, but at the time I didn't see it that way. I was living day by day with the knowledge that my father was planning to take us away from Jamaica, from my friends and the life we knew there.

Sometimes, I tried to talk with my sisters about it, but they did not believe it would happen and anyway, they said, if it did, they were not going. I asked if I could stay with them if my parents did lift up and go but they dismissed that idea immediately. They were both well into their teens and the last thing they wanted for the future would be a young brother tagging along. So, I was on my own, a rambunctious and resentful kid.

One of the pieces of mischief I got up to was sneaking onto the grounds of the prep school on the hill. I knew that behind one of the playing fields, there was a shooting range where some of the more senior boys practiced with .22 rifles. I didn't know anything about guns, and I certainly did not know the bore of the rifles then, but I did know that the bullets they fired became embedded in the thick planking on which they stuck the targets. A friend had shown me one of the spent bullets that he had dug out of the wood, and I wanted some of them too. So, one evening just before it grew dark, I went up to the school, jumped over a wall and ran across to the shooting range. There was no one around, so I got out a nail I had found and began to dig into the wood.

It was not too difficult and soon I had three of the bright, copper-coloured bullets in my pocket. I was about to look for another one when I heard a noise in the bushes and turned to see a dog. In Jamaica at that time, most dogs in the country parts were mongrels, what we called *brown musku* dogs (*I did not know how that word should be spelled*) and you never could tell if they were friendly or not. Many times, I heard someone call out to a dog owner, *Is a bad dog dat?* Or just *Hold dog!* I did not wait to find out the answer to that question but dropped the nail and ran. The dog ran also but he ran faster than I did and when he caught me, his teeth grabbed the back of my leg. I fell but the dog held on, and it was making a noise like he was enjoying a nice, juicy bone.

Then suddenly out of the same bushes, a man appeared while I was screaming. I expected the man to call off the dog but no, he shouted at it to hold me. When I knew that help was not coming, I reached out for a rock lying next to me and hit the dog as hard as I could. It let go with a yelp and I got up just before the man reached me. While I ran for the boundary wall the man, who must have been some kind of caretaker, was shouting at the dog to get me. But luckily the animal had had enough, and I was running faster than the man, so I went over the wall and disappeared into the bush. All I left behind was some blood and a piece of my pants.

When I got home I was bleeding badly and trying hard not to cry. The pain was bad, but I did not want it to show in front of my family. Fortunately, my father was not home, or I might have been dealt another beating on the spot. Instead, my mother bathed the wound in hot water and bandaged it up after applying iodine. I tell you, man, that stuff pained me more than the dog bite, but she said it was necessary to kill off any infection the dog might have been carrying. I don't know if there was rabies on the island then, but it was always a case of 'better safe than sorry'. My mother, God bless her, never asked me where I had been to get mixed up with a bad dog. But the next day, before I limped off to school, my father did. He had a way of finding out everything that went on in the area.

When I did not answer him, he went for his stick, but I was then twelve years old and big enough to face up to the bully. So, when I threatened to punch him if he raised the stick to me, he backed off. I was amazed. I had taken it from him all my life and here he was now, suddenly backing off like a beaten cur. As we stood there in a face-off, I glanced at my mother and saw that she was smiling. I was proud of myself at that moment, because I could see in her face that I had become her hero.

My father never touched me again after that but very soon after the dog incident, he did get his revenge in a way that neither of us had planned. It was a form of revenge that changed the course of my life.

As a boy of twelve, I did not know what was going on in the world of adults and their schemes, so it came as a shock to me two weeks later when my father announced that we were packing up and going to take a ship to England. It was something I had long feared but hoped would never happen. I will skip the period between the dog bite and when he made that announcement, not because I have forgotten any of it but because there was an incident that I do not want to go on record. It is enough to say that my father used me and that incident as an excuse for us leaving as soon as possible.

When I think of it now, he must have planned this weeks ahead, because of course papers had to be obtained, emigration forms, tickets for the ship and landing cards for when we reached England. There are many questions that could have been asked but I was too young and also, too much in a state of shock to ask for answers. It never even occurred to me to ask where he got the money from to buy the tickets or what he was going to do when we reached England. When I asked my mother about these things, she just told me to be quiet and accept what was happening. But I knew she was also reluctant to leave Jamaica and fearful of what might lie ahead.

My sisters, both teenagers, had already made it clear that they would not be going. My mother was sad to know this, but she had arranged for them both to travel to Oracabessa, where they would make their home with our grandparents. They had left school and were able to get jobs, so that would help with the finances at the grandparents' home. If circumstances had been different, I would have stayed as well but I knew that I had no option but to join my parents on the voyage into the unknown.

After my father's announcement, the time passed very quickly. He left his job at Alcan, and we packed up our few possessions but left all furniture behind. We said farewell to my sisters, with my mother in tears. They caught the Romance Bus from Mandeville to make the long and uncomfortable journey to the north east of the island. I never thought about the future then, so it never occurred to me that I would never see them again. I was probably thinking too much of myself and what I would be leaving behind.

Soon after that, we also piled into a bus and went due north to the port of embarkation. I had heard of other departures from Jamaica to England and had seen pictures in the *Gleaner* of friends and relations waving from the dockside as a ship pulled away. As the side of the ship was always lined with hundreds of black people waving back, I assumed these were special ships taking emigrants to their new lives. But somehow my father had done things differently and again, I did wonder how he got the money to buy the tickets. In fact, it was not until we were on board the ship that I realised it was a banana boat on a regular voyage that would be taking us to England.

Most of the loading into the refrigerated holds had been done before we went aboard but after all the necessary clearance procedures had been completed, I managed to look down into one of the holds before the hatches were pulled over. We settled in our cabin, and I discovered that I would have to sleep on a camp bed on the floor, while my parents had the bunks. It should have been the beginning of an adventure, but I was scared, disorientated and feeling that all I ever knew was about to disappear into the ocean we were about to cross.

When we cast off from the dock and moved slowly away from my homeland, I began to experience a sensation I had never felt before. I had only ever been in a small fishing boat but now everything under my feet was beginning to move. For a second, I thought the ship was going to sink and I still did not know how to swim. In panic I held firmly onto my mother's hand and looked into her eyes. To my amazement she looked as scared as me, which did not make me feel any easier.

We were soon out into the Caribbean Sea and gradually Jamaica was disappearing. I stood as near to the rear of the ship as I was allowed and watched my homeland until it sank below the horizon. I am not ashamed to tell you now that I cried. It was the last time I ever saw the Land of Wood and Water.

The ship was the SS Ariguani. When years later I checked on her details I found that she was one of the oldest vessels in the Elders and Fyffes fleet of banana carrying ships, being launched in 1926. The ship also carried a maximum of about one hundred passengers but on this trip, there were only about half that number. I also found that we passengers were on the ship's final journey as she was destined to be broken up later in that year. I also discovered that the Ariguani was the last coal burning Atlantic liner, so, as there were only five children on board, it is possible that I might be the only surviving passenger of that last coal burning ship's final journey. But at the time, I knew none of those things. All I knew was that if I could swim, I would have jumped off the back of that ship and swum back home, disregarding the consequences. I knew why I had to go with my parents, and it was not just because I was twelve years old. My father had explained the reason and I had accepted it without question.

No, maybe explained is too mild a word. He had rammed it down my throat so far, I knew I could never bring it up again.

When we reached the open sea with no land in sight, the old ship really began to roll. The Ariguani had no stabilisers, so she went up and down and sideway with every movement of the sea. It was not even the hurricane season, but the sea was rough enough to test the stomachs of most of the passengers. But for some reason, my stomach rose up and down as if synchronised to the movement of the waves and on that journey, I was never seasick. So, when half the passengers were vomiting or resting in their bunks, I was enjoying every meal. Never in my life had I eaten so well, even if much of the food was new to me.

Before we sailed out into the Atlantic, we made a stop to pick up more bananas. My geography did not stretch much beyond the shores of Jamaica, but I did know where Cuba is. At its nearest point it is only ninety miles from our island's north coast and many years later, when Michael Manley was prime minister, this proximity gave much concern. But in 1956, Cuba was still very much under the influence of the USA and ruled by the corrupt Batista regime. At that time Fidel Castro, Che Guevara and their rebel friends were still planning their revolution up in the thickly wooded hills. We were allowed to go ashore in Cuba and if you look on my wall you will see a couple of Havana pennants and some maracas that my father bought for me from a souvenir shop. We were there a few hours and then when the bananas were safely on board we set sail again and into the Atlantic.

Being a regular passenger liner there were many different types of people on board. The majority seemed to be English people going back home for a spell of leave from sugar estates, engineering plants or government positions. Others were Jamaicans who had made their home in England and were now returning from holiday. To those I wanted to ask, *why you not staying back in beautiful Jamaica*? There were not many black people on board and certainly none from as poor a background as us. But as the ship had only a single class of passenger, we all had to rub shoulders together.

On the calmer days there were games to play on the deck. One of those games was quoits, played with rings made of rope, which were pushed along the deck into marked out squares. I was quite good at that game. Maybe that was thanks to my mango hand judgment. There was no fixed swimming pool on board but what they did was sink a large sheet of canvas into one of the open holds and then fill it with salt water. There was a man amongst the passengers who volunteered to teach the youngsters to swim, and I put myself forward for this challenge. I swallowed a lot of sea water, but after a few days I was getting the idea. He was a good teacher and by the time we were halfway across the Atlantic, I knew that I was not going to drown. The only trouble was that as we got closer to Europe the sea water in the pool got colder.

It was not only the pool water that was cooling. As we went north the temperature started to drop and I began to shiver like I had not done since being in the back of the ice truck. We had taken with us our best clothes, but this did not include such things as pullovers or coats. When the wind blew up on the open deck, I kept to our cabin. You will never see a black man's face turn blue, but I am sure that I heard my father's teeth chattering. My mother had made a friend of a planter's wife and had been lent what I discovered is called a cardigan, so she was okay for most of the time.

The distractions on the ship helped to dull the pain of leaving Jamaica but I was still fearful of what lay ahead. My father said he could get a job as a bus driver in a place called Wolverhampton, where he had a contact from Mandeville, but he did not seem sure where we were going to live when we got there. I heard my mother asking him about this and where the money for living was coming from, but he never gave a straight answer. So, when this happened, my mother just sighed and muttered something about God will provide. Even at the age of twelve, I doubted that her faith would overcome our material shortcomings. So yes, I fretted about a lot of unknown things that lay ahead of us.

I can't remember exactly now but I think the journey took about two weeks. However, I do recall very clearly my first sight of England. As we approached Southampton, I stood in awe at the deck railings looking at the greenest fields I had ever seen. I didn't know about the streets of London being paved with gold but now I knew for certain the fields of England were sprayed with green paint. Even after the heaviest rains in Mandeville, the grass was never more than a pale imitation of what I was now seeing. I think even my father was impressed and kept saying that the cows must produce very rich milk.

We gathered together all of our possessions and stuffed them into our two battered suitcases. My mother went to give back the cardigan, but the owner very kindly said she should keep it. I saw the lady's suitcases and guessed she must have at least a dozen others in there. The man who taught me to swim came up and shook my hand and I realised it was the first time I had ever made physical contact with a white man. I felt very funny about that gesture because where I came from these people mostly represented authority and I was very remote from all that where we lived out in the bush.

Docking took place soon after midday and the passengers began to file off down the gangway, while the bananas were offloaded. I'm not sure but I suppose they were shifted straight into refrigerated trucks to keep them from ripening too soon. But as I shivered in the weak English sun, I wondered how they would ever get ripe in that climate.

When we walked down the gangway, I saw some men with cameras, and they were taking pictures of the passengers as they descended to the quay. I thought at first they were police undercover in plain clothes and tried to hide my face. My father saw this and told me not to be so stupid, because they were press photographers. I never knew we were that famous, but I accepted what he said. Maybe it was because it was the old banana boat's last voyage, or perhaps there was someone famous amongst the passengers? I don't know. All I know is that I was confused and a little scared as we walked into the customs shed.

The richer people had their luggage taken from the ship, but we had all we possessed in the two suitcases. We had dressed up in our finest clothes to walk off the ship, so my father wore a tie, a brown fedora hat and a jacket. He kept the travel documents and boarding papers in one of the jacket pockets and when I looked at him, I was hoping the customs people did not think he was carrying a gun. But nearly worse than carrying a gun was what he had in his suitcase.

As we got nearer to the customs desk, my mother saw one of the officers ask a West Indian man to open his case. It didn't take much rummaging around for the officer to find down the lining of the case a plastic envelope. Mother turned to my father, nudged him in the ribs and pointed to what was going on. After a whispered conversation my father broke away from the queue and carried his case over to the corner of the shed. I saw him open it and take out something, which he held up to a watching customs man. It was a scarf that my grandmother had knitted for him in haste. When the customs man turned away again, he did not see my father drop a packet into the waste bin beside where he was standing.

The man at the counter was being led away by two uniformed officers to a room at the corner of the shed as my father closed up his case and then coolly walked back to join us. His recreational ganja was gone but at least he was not going to spend his first night in England in a prison cell.

We passed through customs without any trouble and then into our new world. For me and almost certainly also for my parents it was a world of confusion, strange sights and a sudden feeling of being one of a small minority. The colour of our skin stood out like a piece of chocolate on top of a sheet of cake icing.

The first thing my father did after leaving customs was to change some US dollar notes into English pounds. He could have done it on the boat, but he claimed he would get a better rate of exchange — something I knew nothing about — at the port. At that time, I never knew how he got the US dollars as the only money I had ever seen was Jamaican pounds and very few of them had ever come my way. But, as I say, I was twelve and did not ask those kinds of questions.

After that, it is all a blur in my mind. We found the railway station and bought tickets to Wolverhampton. It meant changing on the journey, of course but I did not mind. To me, the train was like a luxury liner. The only public transport I had ever used had been Romance Buses, so this beautiful train pulled by a real steam engine was something I had only dreamed about. We had a lot of searching looks from passengers, but I hardly noticed, as I watched the amazing countryside speed past the window. When I looked at my mother's face, it must have mirrored my own in its expression of wonderment. When I looked at my father, he was only counting his money.

We reached Wolverhampton quite late in the day and when we had taken our bags off the train, my father looked around for his friend. Of course, he was not there but we had a telephone number and so he went off to make a call. He found a red telephone box, but he was soon back out, cussing and waving his arms, because he did not know how to use the phone and he didn't want to lose his change. My mother put on her Jamaican charm and asked a passing man how to make the call and what to do with buttons A and B. At last, after my father had calmed down and successfully made the connection, he was able to talk to this friend of his, who said he would come right over to the station.

I don't know how much of a friend this was to my father, because he took us to a poor part of the town, where the buildings mostly looked deserted and in a poor condition. He took us into one of the terraced houses and I could see my mother open up her nostrils at the smell. But it was late in the day, and we had nowhere else to go, so my parents kept quiet about it as we were shown into a flat on the first floor. There was electricity but no curtains and the carpet looked like it needed a good clean. In the small kitchen there was a stove and the room beside that was a bathroom with a rusty stain running down from one of the bath taps. There was only one bedroom, with a double bed and a mattress on the floor. There was one grey blanket and no sheets.

The man said it was not quite the Savoy, but it was the best he could do in the circumstances. I think he found that funny but when I looked around, it did not seem much worse than the shack I had spent my first years living in. So, when the landlord left, we did our best to settle in. My father went out to buy some food and my mother started to clean up the bathroom. She said they would look out for some proper bed clothes the next day.

I discovered much later that round about this time in Wolverhampton there was a lot of new housing development in progress and whole streets like the one we were in were due for demolition. This West Indian man had bought one of the houses cheaply and was using it to let out to immigrants like us, at what he called a reasonable rent. Some might say this was exploitation but when you have nowhere else to lay your head, you will not create a fuss. We soon discovered that we were just three of thousands of newcomers to this part of England. At first, I thought that was the reason the area my father had chosen was called the Black Country.

One day soon after we arrived and my mother had made the flat a bit more comfortable, I went out into the large park not far away and was surprised to see the number of Indian people around the place. Most of the men were wearing turbans and the women were in saris. Not only was there a large Sikh community in Wolverhampton at that time but there were also Irish, Dutch and Poles. We had landed in a melting pot of different races and cultures, and I started to wonder where the real England was and where the English people were hiding.

At my age I should have been in school, but it was the middle of term and therefore there was no way that I could get any formal education before Christmas, so my mother did her best to help me with basic learning. Meanwhile, my father was having no luck with employment. He thought that he could walk straight into a job as a truck or bus driver, but he found that his Jamaican licence was worthless in England. Also, most of the buses in Wolverhampton were in fact trams and he had no experience of how to drive that kind of vehicle. So, he took whatever job he could while he made arrangements to take a driving test.

Although there were a large number of foreigners in Wolverhampton, I soon found that in fact the majority of people in the area were white locals, so that did create some racial discrimination. Mostly this took the form of quiet disapproval, and I certainly did not experience any direct hostility for being different. It mostly took the form of refusal to accept black people in lodgings or difficulty in finding employment when local applicants were looking for the same job. You know, maybe I am different in saying this, but I have an understanding of this type of resentment. How would a Jamaican feel if, in his own country, a white man fresh from England took a job for which he was qualified? But after sixty years here, perhaps I now have a wider perspective of life.

Another thing that I found very difficult to get used to was the ordinariness of the food. Having grown up with all those wonderful spicy Jamaican flavours, with rice an' peas, breadfruit, yams and sweet potato we now had processed meat, cabbage and mashed potato. You've probably never heard of something called spam. Man, you had to be really hungry to want to eat that stuff! In the mid-1950s very little West Indian food was being imported into England, so we had no option but to eat this bland stuff. We also had little choice as it was only a few years since food rationing had been removed. I have always enjoyed my food, so this lack of choice was one of the most depressing things about England for me. That and the weather too.

Thank God we were not in Wolverhampton for too long. My father took his driving test for heavy duty vehicles and passed. He had a number of manual jobs during our time in the Black Country, which did not bring in much money but somehow it seemed enough to keep the wolf from the door. I only discovered later that in fact, he had enough to keep a whole pack of them howling outside but I will come to that in a while.

We spent a cold Christmas in the flat of the condemned building and shortly after that my father announced that we were going to London.

CHAPTER 8

It was just as well that I stopped the tape at that point because the mobile started warbling. It was my wife, to say that the boiler was not coming on and what should she do. We ran through the options, most of which she had already tried and then I suggested that it might be a blown fuse. She said she would try that and if it failed, she said she would call the plumber in the morning. I told her where to find the fuses and we then talked generally about the current state of our lives apart.

It was nearly six o'clock, so I drifted downstairs and out into the narrow garden at the back of the house. I was admiring the late-blooming roses when Noel came out to join me.

"Good day?" I asked.

"More bloody politicking." He handed me a whisky glass. "I'm still hoping we'll come good in the end but it's all a diversion from the regular job."

"Maybe what you need is a good meaty, crime to convince the mayor and his crew that Lavender Hill is essential. Is your Super batting for you, or is he also playing politics?"

"Oh, he's on our side but I don't know if that's because he also has the backing of the Tories. They are the ones who run Wandsworth and he reckons they will have at least as much clout as Mayor Khan."

"Let's hope so."

"Mary's going to be late tonight, so I'm in charge of dinner. If it weren't for Alice and her homework, I'd suggest a drink in the pub."

"Maybe another night." I swallowed the whisky. "Actually, if you don't need my help in the kitchen, I might go for a stroll. Need to clear my head from a surfeit of Moule."

Noel laughed as we turned to go back in. "How's it going?"

"We are just leaving Wolverhampton and about to head for London."

"Wolverhampton?" Noel exclaimed.

"Wolverhampton," I replied, as we stepped inside the house.

The next morning, I resumed listening and transcribing from where I had left off:

I don't know how my father made his contacts but there always seemed to be someone there when he needed some help in getting things done. On this occasion he announced to my mother and me that he knew someone in London who could find us a place to live and also that there was a much better chance of getting a job down in the capital. He had his licence now and there were big red double-decker buses there and no trams. So, we packed our bags again and took the train down to London. I was not sorry to say goodbye to Wolverhampton and I must tell you that I have never been back there.

The acquaintance of my father said he knew of a place to live in the south London District of Clapham, and he arranged to meet us outside Clapham Common tube station. This was another challenge for us. After we got out at the mainline station, we went underground. It was a very confusing experience because, although all the various lines were marked in different colours, we had to change trains and got lost trying to locate the correct platforms. My father had to ask many times how to get to our destination and he got cross when some people did not understand what he was saying. Maybe they did but just could not be bothered to help out a black man with a very unfriendly face.

When finally, we arrived at Clapham Common station my father's contact was waiting but he was not very pleased, as we were an hour past the appointed meeting time. He was a rough-looking fellow with a broad brimmed fedora hat, dark glasses and a blue scarf wrapped twice around his neck. It was not that cold, so it looked to me like he was wearing some kind of disguise. He just nodded to my mother and ignored me before we walked off down the road.

I might have guessed that there would be a problem. The contact man took us to a rundown-looking building and led us up a flight of rickety, uncarpeted stairs. He must have thought we would be accustomed to a rat-infested hovel for a home, because this place was worse than the flat in Wolverhampton. There was the bare amount of furniture, the wallpaper was peeling and there was a smell of drains. My father started berating the fellow, my mother began crying and I kicked an empty bean can across the floor of the front room.

The man said, "*What do you expect for twenty-one shillings a week and when it was so hard to find a place in Clapham for a black family anyway?*" I thought for a moment my father was going to hit him and for once I would not have blamed him. Instead, he shouted the fellow off the premises and started hitting the door with his fist.

We spent one very uncomfortable night in that place.

The next morning, before having anything to eat for breakfast, we packed up and hit the street. For an hour we walked around Clapham looking for accommodation until my mother collapsed on a bench and said she could walk no further. I sat down beside her, and we both looked up at my father as if to say, *what you going to do now?*

My father had few fine qualities but one of them was that he never gave up. Whether what he was trying to achieve was legal or not, he just kept on trying. So, when he came back with sandwiches and a big smile an hour later, I knew he had found something.

He grabbed our cases and told us to follow him quickly. We followed as fast as we could, but my mother was tired and her feet were hurting, so I helped her to keep up. Finally, we stopped outside a house which looked as if it had once been fashionable but now had weeds growing outside and a front door with peeling paint. My father pushed open the front gate, walked up the short path and used the brass knocker.

It was a boarding house, and the landlady must have been more broadminded than many in that part of London, because she was prepared to take us in. She had one room to spare but she was charging thirty shillings a week, payable in advance. In those days that was not cheap, especially as we had to share a bathroom with others and had to put shillings into the meter for heating and light. Meals of course were extra. But as we were desperate my father said we would take it for a week.

In fact, we were there for nearly two weeks, while my father looked around all day for a more permanent place to live and for a job that suited his qualifications as a driver. I said he was persistent, so after the tenth day at the lodgings he had found a flat and he had been taken on as a temporary delivery driver, for Simmonds brewery in the Wandsworth Road. He had the job until the regular driver recovered from sickness. It seemed then that our fortunes were at last on the rise.

The flat was on the first floor above a café in the High Street, run by an Italian family whose name I cannot now remember. They were very kind and generous people, who obviously were sympathetic towards immigrants like themselves. They had left Italy shortly after the end of the war and had taken a long lease on the house in Clapham High Street. The only difference between us was that, as white people, they were able to merge more easily into their surroundings, in spite of the strong Italian accent. I think everyone just loved their food. Pasta was probably more acceptable to the English palate than Jamaican patties. At that time there were very few West Indians in Clapham and not everyone was as tolerant as the Italian family, so we did experience some discrimination as we moved about the area.

The Italian café has long gone, and the ground floor of the house has changed occupation and activities many times but, after sixty years I am still here in the same flat. It is my kingdom and my sanctuary. I will tell you how I came to remain here for so long later in the story.

Another small group of refugees from conflict arrived at about the time we settled in Clapham. In 1956, there was an uprising in Hungary against the Communist regime. This was brutally suppressed, with the help of the Soviet Union but many managed to escape to seek out a freer life in Western Europe. One man who arrived in Clapham with his family was a dentist and he set up a practice in the Wandsworth Road. My mother heard of their arrival and wasted no time in enrolling herself and me in that practice. My father had no time for dentists, so did not join us. I went to have my teeth checked about twice a year and it always made me smile when the dentist told me to *'open your mouse'*.

My mother amazed me by adapting remarkably well to her new life. I think that, in spite of her humble beginnings and poor education, she had a natural way with people and was not in any way judgmental. She also had a wicked sense of humour and all those qualities helped her to be accepted when others might have been shunned. I learned a lot from her example, and this helped me when I went to my first English school.

Once she had sorted out the flat and we had bought a few basic items for everyday living my mother, Mavis, needed occupation. So, she went along to the Sunlight Laundry in Acre Lane, and they gave her employment. She worked at Sunlight for many years and made some good friends through her job there.

Meanwhile, my father managed to get the job he was really looking for: driving a red double-decker bus. So, when the contract with Simmonds came to an end, he signed up with London Transport, or whatever it was called at that time and was given the route to Camberwell. But, like many things in his lifetime, he nearly blew it after only a month. It takes a lot of effort to turn over a Routemaster bus, but he nearly succeeded one day, when he went round Elephant and Castle as if he was a Port Royal driver in a Cadillac. Many of the passengers screamed as the bus tipped and the conductor swore that the wheels left the ground for a second. My father was severely reprimanded and told he would be fired if it happened again. Naturally, he never told us about the incident, but the rumour soon reached Clapham and my mother gave him a hard time about it.

Another thing Mavis managed to do in our early days in Clapham was to get me into the local secondary school, even though term had already started by then. If I had been a year younger, I might have gone to a primary and taken the eleven plus exam but as I was so backward by English standards, I would have failed anyway. So, as a poor, ill-educated, black boy I went into the lowest class and, at the beginning, I was given a tough ride.

I got into a few fights, but I was big for my age so mostly the bullies came off worse. This earned me some respect for a short time, but I had no wish to be feared as well as hated, so I learned to win my classmates over in another way. I have heard Lenny Henry talk about how he succeeded in being liked and respected from an early age but of course I didn't know such a person existed when I was only twelve. Instead, I took my lesson from my mother and employed humour as my weapon.

When somebody tried to start a fight with me, or ridiculed me for the colour of my skin, I just played up to them and clowned around, as if I was part of their joke, rather than the butt of it. I found that in no time this was working and after a while, I could see that I was becoming popular *because* of my difference and that personality I developed has seen me through my life ever since those early days. Yes, even now I am a clown as I stride down the High Street in my *uniform* and swinging an umbrella. You know the saying: *all the world loves a clown*? But you know, it's also true that behind the face of every clown there are also tears.

I stopped the tape there.

I could hardly believe my reaction as I transcribed those last few words. I leaned back in my chair as I gazed at the world outside through misty eyes. I don't really know if I was thinking of Meshach Moule or Lenny Henry, but I do know I was thinking of the power of personality, that is required to overcome what those boys had to and then to succeed in life. Okay, as far as I was aware Moule had not conquered any mountains or risen to fame and fortune in any field of activity, but he was his own man and obviously had the power of character to become respected for the individual he was. It appeared from what he had said that almost single-handed he had managed to overcome the vicissitudes of his early life.

So, the family had finally arrived in Clapham, South London. Moule had landed at the age of twelve in the place that would certainly be his home for the rest of his days. The family from the bush back in Manchester Parish in Jamaica had put down roots and were beginning to establish themselves in a new land and in a new parish.

And for me it was also time for a much-needed leg-stretch.

In fact, as I left the house, I acknowledged that I had had enough transcribing for the day, so I strolled down the road to the pub. As I sat at a small round table with my pint and a ploughman's lunch, I tried to turn my mind to everyday matters that I had left behind at home but Moule's past kept lunging back into the foreground. I also worried on behalf of the schoolgirl who had vicariously commissioned me to carry out this project. I had already filled many pages of A4 paper with the story and her subject was only twelve years of age. I felt like a man who is swimming further and further out of his depth in unknown waters, not knowing quite how to turn back to dry land.

I accepted now that I couldn't just walk away from it all,

even when the typing was complete. Sonia and I would have to condense the narrative drastically and also perhaps rewrite it in such a way that resembled a teenager's account. None of these thoughts filled me with joy as I sipped at a pint of London Pride.

I finished my lunch and left the pub having decided that the whole process needed to be speeded up, even if it meant Moule terminating his story before adulthood. It was delightful being with my son and his family, but they had their own lives to lead. I had been going back to Kent at weekends but now I felt it was time to make a complete break, perhaps returning once Sonia needed assistance with the editing.

That is what I should have done but unexpected events put my departure on hold.

That afternoon I had collected Alice from school, and we had a long chat as I walked my granddaughter home. Later, I had packed my bag after discussing the matter with Noel and Mary and told them that I would be getting ready to leave early the next morning. We were preparing dinner when the front door bell rang. Noel went to see who it was and from the kitchen I instantly recognised Sonia's voice.

I went through to greet her and to tell her my plan, but I could see instantly that she was troubled. Noel disappeared back into the kitchen, and I invited the girl into the sitting room.

"Mr Grant," she began, "I've brought the next tape but there's something here that… I mean, I never expected… It's such a shock."

"Sit down, Sonia, and tell me, what's such a shock?"

"No, I won't tell you now, because I think you should hear

it from Moule in his own words. Then when you hear it, please tell me what we should do."

"Very mysterious but I'll do it your way. I was actually planning to go back home tomorrow but I'll listen to the tape first."

"You're going home?" She sounded quite alarmed, as if I was leaving her to some unknown fate. "Aren't you going to finish writing it out for me? I can't write. My finger's still strapped-up."

"Yes, of course I'm going to help you finish but there's so much of it that I was wondering if we shouldn't call it a day at the point where Moule and his family set up home in Clapham. It's going to take a long time just to condense it from the material we have up to that stage."

"I know but I think you should listen to this tape first, before you decide if you want to go on or not."

"Okay, I'll do that for you." Then I had a thought. "Your half-term break is coming up soon, isn't it?"

"Yes, next week."

"Well, maybe at that time we should review the situation."

"Okay but you will still listen to the tape?"

"Of course. I'll do it tomorrow. And when I've done that, I'll contact you after school and we can discuss where we go from there. Okay?"

"Okay."

She stood up and I led her to the front door. She glanced back at me as she went down the three steps to the pavement and her expression still held a look of perplexed anxiety. As I closed the door, I felt a strong impulse to listen to the tape immediately, but Mary called out that dinner was ready. After a relaxed meal and a couple of glasses of Claret I pushed the

159

urge to listen to the back of my mind. However, without explaining the reason why, I told my hosts that I would be taking a later train the next day.

Alice had gone to school, Noel to work and Mary out shopping when I went up to my room the following morning and slotted the tape into the machine. The now familiar Jamaican patois continued the saga of Meshach Moule:

After a couple of terms at my school, when I had sorted out the social business, I found that I was not as stupid as my father often called me. I discovered that there was geography beyond the confines of the Caribbean and that England had a history, that went back a bit further than the first slave riots in Jamaica. My English vocabulary also broadened expansively, in spite of the fact that sometimes I found the cockney of the local children difficult to follow. Anyway, I was catching up quickly and getting a proper education for the first time.

Outside the classroom, I also played a lot of football. I had played in Jamaica but on rough pitches, where often you could not tell where the boundaries were and where the goal posts had no net. But I was fast and knew how to dribble a ball, so I was soon one of the stars of the school junior team.

I think my mother could see how I was managing to sort out my new life, because of the small things she said. Comments that expressed approval and the fact that she went out of her way to find good Jamaican ingredients to cook my favourite meals. In his own way, I think even my father was impressed, because one day he brought back a new radio for my thirteenth birthday. I started to listen to the pop records of the day on a scratchy station called Radio Luxembourg. I never forgot my calypso roots to this day, but I also enjoyed the pop music of the late 1950s.

My father managed to keep his job as a bus driver but in his spare time, or days off work, he often disappeared to places he did not even tell my mother about. It used to be like this when he went off to Kingston, but now I was older, I began to suspect that he was getting up to no good. One clue to this suspicion was when I smelled the distinctive aroma of ganja drifting through to my bedroom. My mother and I said nothing, because that was how he had always been, but I was aware of the much tighter rules about marijuana use in England and did not want him to be caught. Worse than that, if he was caught, it might also implicate me and my mother. I can say, hand on my heart, that as a young boy I never smoked the weed but up 'til then, I had breathed in a lot of my father's second-hand fumes. Later, in my Rastafari days, is a different story.

So, for nearly two years after we moved to Clapham our lives went along quite well. I soon found my way around the shops, the Common, the cinema, where there were no fights in the cheap seats and the pubs. I was too young of course but I loved to stand around The Windmill pub on the Common and further up the road, The Sun, just to listen to the music from the juke box. There was also a hot dog stall near the Common tube station, and I spent a lot of my pocket money there. I also liked to talk to the fellow who sold the hot dogs. He did most of the talking and I didn't understand most of what he was saying but it was a form of education in the ways of London for me.

Another thing that was around in those days and you never see or hear today is the rag and bone man. Today, if something breaks you take it to be recycled, or throw it in the dustbin.

Back in the fifties there was this old fellow who regularly pulled or pushed his cart along the High Street and back roads of Clapham, shouting out something I never understood. Maybe even the locals did not know either, but they knew to take out their broken junk for him to take away. One day he didn't come any more and that was the end of the rag and bone trade, which made me sad. I suppose he died and went to the great scrapyard in the sky.

There was a pause in the tape for a few seconds here and then it clicked off. On reflection, I think Moule was gathering himself for what was to come next, or maybe just chuckling at his joke about the rag and bone man.

He continued:

I think I told you earlier that we always remember incidents when they are connected to world events, such as the assassination of John Kennedy. Well, if it had not been for something that happened over three thousand miles away in the very early hours of the third of February 1959, an incident that happened in London might have been given more publicity. It's a long time before you were born but on that freezing night, a small plane came down in a North American state, killing everyone on board. As the time zone was about six hours behind us, it was not reported in our newspapers until the fifth and then it filled many pages of all the nationals. In the same newspapers, tucked away in the middle pages was the report of a stabbing near a night club in the West End of London that occurred a few hours after that plane crash.

Yes, Buddy Holly's death shocked America and also everyone who loved his music, so there was much news coverage. He went down with The Big Bopper and Richie Valens, so as Don Maclean sang, that was the day the music died. But it was not for a couple of days that we were aware of the stabbing incident, because my father was not as famous as Buddy Holly.

When he had not returned after one of his mysterious trips up town my mother was not worried. He sometimes did not return overnight, and she assumed he had drunk too much and was sleeping over somewhere. But when he was away for a second night and his foreman from the depot was calling the café downstairs asking where he was, she became a bit worried. I was at school when later that day the police called and told my mother that her husband had been found dead in a doorway somewhere in Soho. He had a knife wound to his chest and was already dead when a street cleaner found his body. He did not appear to have been robbed of any money, so the police were able to trace where he lived from papers he was carrying in his wallet.

I stabbed the stop button, stood up and went to the window overlooking the street. No wonder Sonia had been shocked on hearing that from Moule. His father had been murdered and his body dumped in a doorway but on tape, he had stated it quite calmly and without any sign of emotion. Okay, it was nearly sixty years ago but how often had he told anybody about this tragedy? It was possible that this private man had never told anyone at all, and it must have been a blow for Sonia to hear Moule state it so dispassionately. I fully understood why she was in a quandary as to what should be done now. It must also have been extremely embarrassing for her to sit in front of the man, as he calmly talked about his father's murder.

As light autumn rain spattered the pavement below, I realised it would not be possible to come to a decision and advise on a course of action until I had listened to the remainder of the recording. I went back to the desk and replaced the headphones, almost fearful of what was to follow.

Moule continued:

When I came home from school, I found my mother in a state of shock. In those days there was no such thing as counselling for the bereaved and I had never seen Mavis in this state before, so it took a while before she told me what had happened. I almost surprise myself to say this now, but my first reaction was not one of disbelief that the deed had been done. Yes, there was shock that my father had gone but there was no grief in my heart.

My father had always lived life on the edge. Whether it was in picking unnecessary fights, dealing in ganja or just being reckless in his relationships with people; he had many ways of making enemies. With him it was a natural hazard. But to die in this manner just raised a multitude of questions in my mind. If he was killed by someone who was an enemy, in what way had my father provoked this kind of vengeance? But if he was simply in the wrong place at the wrong time, was it a case of mistaken identity? Or again, was it something to do with the mysterious trips up town? I was very confused, but I have to admit, not heartbroken. How could I be, when there had never been any love between us? My mother and his three children had tolerated his bullying and inconsiderate behaviour for many years but still Mavis grieved for his loss, so I did my best to console her.

A police car took us to the mortuary where we had to identify his body. I think up to that point my mother still had a faint hope that it was somebody else but no, it was he. When she saw that for a fact, she broke down again. I asked if I could see my father for the last time and it was not until I saw him laid out peacefully that I felt any sense of loss. But I could not bring myself to reach out and touch him. I told myself that he would not like me to do that, because in life I had never touched him in a loving way. It was not something he had encouraged. To touch him in death seemed to me to be like a hypocritical act.

There was some police procedure after that, with questions about when we had last seen him and if we knew who he was with that night. Of course, we could offer very little help, except to say that he often went off without saying where he was going. My mother was then handed the few possessions they found on him, except for the spliff of ganja in his jacket pocket. They kept that. He had owned a quite expensive wristwatch, which he claimed he won in a game of dominos but that was all that was missing. Everything else seemed to be there, including his wallet and driving license. From that, I expect the police came to the conclusion that it was not merely a robbery that had gone wrong. It just looked like a murder that had gone right.

Naturally, there was to be an autopsy as well as a full police investigation into the killing, so it was going to be a few weeks before we could bury him. When the formalities were done, I took my mother home with the sudden realisation that I was now at the age of nearly fifteen, the man of the family.

We had not been in contact with my sisters for many months but assuming they were still with my grandparents in Oracabessa, Mavis sent a telegram to that address. All she said was that their father had had an accident and died. You don't want to write in a telegram that someone has been murdered, when that someone was your father.

Back home Mavis decided that she did not want to deal with my father's possessions right away, so I agreed that we would leave that for a few more days. We thought maybe after the autopsy would be a good time. Meanwhile, I was expecting another visit from the police. I think I was hoping for some kind of discovery, like them finding the murder weapon or further enquiries about my father's contacts but then this was not like a crime story in a book by Franklin Dixon. My expectations had obviously been coloured by the Hardy Boy adventures I had started reading.

Mavis did not take long to recover from the initial shock of losing her husband but then she soon began to worry about how we were going to live. Her income was very small, and she was sure my father had not taken out a life assurance policy. He was not the sort of man to look that far ahead. There might be some kind of compensation from London Transport but that was not likely to go far. So, she fretted about food, my clothes for school, the gas bill and ground rent payments. I said to her that I should leave school and get some work to bring in some more money, but she said no to that suggestion. I was not yet fifteen and she said my education was important. I accepted that but I did have an idea.

I went along to The Sun pub and read the notice about entertainment events to take place inside. Some evenings they had folk singing, others there was bingo and then jazz or skiffle. It was a long shot, but I went along on the skiffle evening and stood outside, as I had often done before. The group playing inside had a washboard, a bass, a banjo and drums but no lead singer. It was what I was looking for. When your needs are great you become bold, so in the break I walked in and went right up to the banjo player and asked if they would like a front man to sing. I was nearly fifteen, but I looked eighteen and no one threw me out of the pub or laughed in my face. There were some looks and quiet comments from the drinkers, because there were still only a few West Indians living in Clapham at that time and I was the only one in the pub. But the frontal attack must have worked, because the banjo player called his mates over and they asked me if I had any experience of singing in a group. I said yes but singing calypso in Jamaica. That did make them laugh and I laughed along with them. Then, one of the fellows said they should give it a try as it would be something different. If I was useless, then that would be the end of the experiment but if it worked, then I could earn a pound an evening.

We shook hands on that, they gave me some sheet music to learn lyrics and we arranged for me to meet at the shed where they practiced on a Tuesday evening. So, that's how I became lead singer with the Sun Skifflers, sometimes belting out their music and sometimes them backing my calypsos as I shook the Cuban maracas. I did this for a couple of years, until eventually skiffle died and the novelty of calypsos in Clapham wore off.

But I am getting ahead in the story too fast. Mavis attended the inquest while I was at school, and she told me about it when I got home. There were no witnesses but the cleaner who found father's body and the policemen who logged the crime were there. The coroner recorded death by homicide and, although the weapon was never found, the instrument causing death was said to be a six-inch blade that had penetrated the heart. Mavis was offered a lift home but turned it down and came home by bus.

I don't know how hard the police looked into the crime. Other than a brief and probably routine visit to our home, I did not get the impression that the investigation was given any priority. Maybe they just saw a dead, middle-aged, black man who had fallen foul of drug dealers and been dealt the ultimate punishment. I hope I am not doing the Met an injustice but the mind-set in the fifties was very different from today and certainly political correctness as an accepted form of response had not been invented. Also, there was no formal counselling, although Mavis did receive support from the vicar at her church and sympathy from some of the congregation.

But no one offered me comfort and I was very anxious that no one at my school should hear of what had happened, as I did not want to be tainted by association. In fact, my fear was that whoever had jooked (*a Jamaican expression for stabbing*) my father might not leave it there and I spent a lot of time looking over my shoulder as I walked down the street. And maybe I was right to be concerned, because when eventually we did look into my father's belongings and affairs we came across a big and quite worrying surprise.

It was a few days after the inquest that Mavis said to me it was time to bring out all of father's things and then chuck away what was of no use or interest to us. So, we settled down to do that, beginning with the junk he kept in his private cupboard above the food store in the kitchen. He obviously did not trust us, because there was a padlock on the cupboard door and when we could not find the key, I prized it off with a hammer.

A lot of stuff fell on the floor, and we began to sort it into two piles: one that should be thrown away and one that needed further investigation. As most of it fell into the first category it began to look like it was there just as camouflage, because right at the back of the cupboard, was one of the suitcases he had carried from Jamaica nearly three years earlier. When I pulled that out, I found that too was locked but Mavis had the bunch of keys for our cases, so we didn't have to break that lock.

To our surprise all that there was inside were a pair of swimming trunks, two Tower Isle shirts, a copy of the *Gleaner* and a mouth organ he used to play when he was drunk. When I looked carefully at the mouth organ, I think it was actually once mine. Anyway, I cleaned it up and used it later at our gigs.

Mavis and I looked at each other, both thinking why trouble to lock a case with almost nothing inside? Then I looked more closely and saw a tear along the lining at the bottom of the case. I found that the tear went most of the way around the bottom, but he had made an attempt at disguising it with some tape. I ripped off the tape and pulled back the padding that covered the inside skin of the case.

For several seconds Mavis and I stared in silence at what was under the padding. I glanced at my mother and the eyes in her head were nearly popping out.

Spread out evenly across the bottom of the bag were layers of cash. US Dollar notes, in denominations of ten and twenty. They were all neatly laid out, so that it looked like a green and white patterned rug. But it was like no rug you could buy in a furniture shop. It was like a small sea of greenbacks.

I stared up at Mavis with my mouth hanging open and saw that she was swaying. I thought she was going to faint, so I jumped over and held her. *Where did all this come from?* she asked and then kept repeating the same question. I had never seen so much money all in one place at one time before in my lifetime, so I had no answer for her.

We were still staring at the greenbacks when eventually she whispered that he must have smuggled it out of Jamaica back in 1956, so when he ditched the ganja, he must have done that willingly in order to protect the money in the case. I agreed this was most likely, but it still did not explain where it came from and to this day, I do not have an answer. I have my guesses and those guesses might be right, but I think the truth will never be known. All I knew for sure was that my father would not have acquired so much money by legal means.

We sat down at the kitchen table to discuss what to do next. Mavis made up some of her favourite herbal tea and she allowed me, on this occasion, to have one of my late father's Red Stripe lager beers. We talked around the subject for some long time until at last we decided the first thing to do was to count it. I think what was going through both our minds was that if there was not too much there, we could keep it. After all, we were not the thieves and, for all we knew, my father might have won it in a lottery. Who was to say he didn't? But if there was a very large sum then maybe we should let the police know about it. So, the first thing to do was to find out how much was there.

Down on our knees on the living room floor we spread all the dollar notes and began counting. Some were new notes, but many were old and some torn; it was dirty work and our hands smelled bad after we had finished. At the end we had eight separate piles of two hundred dollars each: a total of one thousand six hundred dollars. I did not know what the exchange rate to the pound was, but we reckoned that total amount could be worth as much as one thousand three hundred pounds. My head was reeling, because this was to us a fortune.

It might sound hard to believe now but back then you could buy two houses with that much money. But was it large enough for us to declare it to the police? That was the moral question.

We then sat down again and began to apply logical reasoning. To us it was a lot of money but to a bank or other large organisation it would be peanuts. And if we offered it up to the police, what would they do with it? It was not money stolen in England, because it was foreign money brought into the country. What could they do if we gave it to them? They could contact the Jamaican police but after such a long time, how would they know who had lost this sum of money? Also, if it was dirty money, there would be no record of the loss anyway. With all these considerations, we were gradually convincing ourselves that we would only be causing unnecessary confusion and wasting of police time by reporting it to the authorities.

So, that evening we persuaded ourselves that this was my father's legacy to us but even after that decision, I continued to look around me when I went out. And I think my mother was also nervous because she had the lock on our front door changed. But little did we know that evening that there was an even bigger surprise to come.

Mavis knew nothing about the procedure when someone dies in England, so she went to the citizen's advice bureau just after my father's body was released for burial. The advice was to employ a lawyer to obtain probate for my father's Estate. We found it funny to talk about his Estate, because to us Jamaicans that meant a large sugar cane plantation and my father had never owned even a small patch of land. Anyway, with the money we found in the case, she reckoned we could afford a lawyer to sort it out, but we never had any intention of telling them about the hoard of dollars in the case.

As my father officially owned so little, as we thought, the lawyer said it should not take him long to prepare papers for the Probate Office. But he had to have details of any bank or deposit accounts he owned and also a list of any valuable chattels. So, we went through all his papers and to our surprise we found that he had made a Will, leaving everything to my mother. And then soon after that, we came across another even more amazing surprise. We found, tucked away in a tin box under his passport and landing papers, a Building Society deposit book.

And when we opened up the deposit book, we saw that there was a balance of £2,510 in there.

I will never forget that amount, because it was like a bombshell that hit us. This was nearly twice the amount we had found in the suitcase and all in pounds sterling. But unlike the greenbacks in the suitcase, this sum of money could not be hidden away because in order for Mavis to claim it, the lawyer had to declare it for probate purposes.

As we sat down to supper that evening, Mavis and I discussed the possibilities of where all this money had come from and how he had managed to keep it from us until after he died. We both agreed that he cannot have come by that much legally, so it had to have been stolen from somewhere in Jamaica. Even that much money in large denomination notes does not make a big bulge in a case full of clothes, so he had managed to smuggle it past the UK Customs. But he had been very lucky as I had noticed how many cases the Customs were opening. My mother said maybe it helped that he had with him a wife and small boy and looked like a proper family man.

Then, in the UK he would have opened the Building

Society account and must have deposited the cash bit by bit as he converted the US dollars to sterling. The passbook showed that this was how he had done it. In those days there was hardly any check on money laundering as there is today, so there would only have been very few detailed questions asked when he deposited the money. As for the balance in the bottom of the suitcase, he was probably continuing to change it in smallish amounts and then either depositing it or spending it on his vices. We knew he was buying weed and my mother always suspected that he was with other women on his trips away from home.

You must by now be wondering what we did with the money, and I hope you don't think we did wrong to keep it. It might seem strange to you but for a long time we tried to pretend it did not exist. This way our consciences were clear. Probate went through with no problem and there was no Estate duty to pay as he had left too little to trouble the tax people. Also, the lawyer cleverly established that father remained domiciled in Jamaica for death duty purposes. So, Mavis carried on over the next year exchanging US dollars to pounds sterling and then depositing the cash into the Building Society account. I went ahead with my plan to earn some money singing but now I could keep the money I earned for myself. The deposit account was earning some good interest, so she did draw that down to live on, but Mavis carried on with her job at the laundry. That was where her friends were. She never touched the capital until a couple of years after father died, when she made the biggest purchase of her life.

Mavis made enquiries about the lease of the property where we lived and discussed the matter with the Italian café owner. When he told her that there was nearly one hundred years still to run on the long lease, she said she would like to buy a share of it outright instead of just paying him rent as a tenant. I don't know anything of the legal side of it, but a lawyer drew up the papers which I think split the lease between the two parties. So, my mother was suddenly a property owner and she reckoned that not only would the lease see out her lifetime but would last for me as well.

She was right. She died in 1992 at the age of about seventy-three but I am still here and hope to be here until I die, which should be before the lease expires. As for the cash my father left, the deposit account is still open and the amount in it has grown, although the interest rate is now quite low.

Just before Sonia stopped the tape, I could hear Moule say that he was feeling tired and asked to call it a day. It was my guess, but I think the tiredness was not just physical but emotional as well. He had disclosed intimacies of his past, to a teenaged girl, that he had possibly kept under cover for all of his life since the age of fourteen. Not for the first time I found myself wondering why he would choose to do that. It was unusual for a girl of Sonia's age to take such an interest in an adult's past but now I knew why she had become gripped by the old Jamaican's story. It had started as an innocent but inspired extra-curricular project, which had quite unexpectedly turned into a riveting drama.

I finished typing and then printed off the pages of the day's work. If I hurried, I knew there would be time to catch a train before the rush hour began, so I packed a few things, left a note for Noel and then hurried out to find a taxi. I had promised to contact Sonia but as she was possibly still on her way back from school, I decided to give her a call when I got home that evening.

As I sat back in the train I felt as if the papers in my overnight bag were smouldering with a desire to burst forth into the world. I then smiled to myself at the absurd allusion. I was becoming too involved in this exceptional man's life. However, after the day's surprises I was now prepared for almost any explosive revelation.

It felt good to be home again, this time knowing that it would be for longer than a weekend. There was much to catch up with. June had only been to Jamaica once, when we had taken Noel as a teenager to see where I had spent my formative years, so she knew little of the island or its people. However, I felt sure that she would be fascinated to hear my account of Moule's back-story.

First though I decided to contact Sonia, before she got stuck into whatever sixteen-year-old girls get up to in the evening these days. On the train down to Tunbridge Wells, I had formulated a plan as to how we should proceed with the material we had and hoped that she would agree. After all, it was still her project.

Mrs Benjamin took the call and said that Sonia had not gone out. I heard her call Sonia's name and waited.

"Mr Grant?" She sounded out of breath.

"Hello, Sonia, I'm back home now but I've typed out the last tape."

"What did you think of it?"

"Well, I was as surprised as you must have been. Quite a shock really. I certainly wasn't expecting anything like that."

"I know. He just sat there, with his eyes closed and it all... well, poured out. It was as if he was making a confession or something. I felt…"

"…embarrassed?" I ventured.

"Yes, that and also, a bit like I shouldn't be hearing such personal things. It was weird. I still haven't got over the fact that his father was murdered."

"Well, you heard what he said. He's never confided in anyone before. I think he was so traumatised as a young teenage boy that part of him never got over it. Now, talking to you, he's just offloading the burden. I can't think of any other explanation."

"Could be that. But what do I do with the story now? It's too intense for my project." She gave a nervous laugh. "I never expected it to turn out like this, Mr Grant, what with the murder and the money and all."

"I agree, so I have a suggestion." I glanced at my jottings. "I'll help you condense the whole thing, after we decide how long the story should be. Presumably you were told to keep it to a maximum number of words? We'll take it from Moule's beginnings in Jamaica right through to when he arrives in England but cut out any bits about his father's… what shall we say…? misdeeds. It's certainly not necessary to mention the ganja smoking or anything like that. There's plenty of meaty material without that."

"So, you think, write nothing about what he did in England?"

"I think that would be best, for his sake. Maybe a bit about how they settled in, but I wouldn't want anything to come from this that would cause him problems later. I don't want him to have regrets about anything he's told you."

"Yes, but people at school might want to hear how he got on with discrimination and stuff when he got here. I think that's important. Anyway, he's got to approve of what I've written before I hand it in."

"True. And that's why I want you get it right first go. If he has second thoughts about anything he's told you, he could pull the whole project. I don't think we should water his story down or anything like that but it's important to keep anything out that might reflect badly on his character."

"Or his mother's," she added.

"Absolutely right. She's long dead but she was still his mother, and it was her decision, rightly or wrongly, to keep that money. He was only fourteen, so legally not complicit but I think it would be best not to mention the money at all."

We seemed to have come to an agreement on the structure of her composition, so we arranged to meet up some time during her half-term break.

When I put the phone down, I didn't expect to hear from her again for at least a week, but I was mistaken in that assumption, as I had been with much else over those few strange weeks.

CHAPTER 9

"George," June called from the back door, and I stuck my head out of the garden shed. "Phone call for you."

I took off the gardening gloves and went, not too hurriedly, to take the call. It was nearing the end of the day and I needed to get some things ready for the recycling centre the next day.

"Who is it?" I asked before she handed over the mobile.

"It's that girl, Sonia. She sounds in a bit of a state."

"Thanks." I took the phone from her. "Sonia, what's up?"

"Mr Grant, he's gone."

"Who's gone?" but I already knew who she was talking about.

"Moule. He's left home and gone off somewhere."

"Wait a minute, Sonia. What do you mean, gone off somewhere? The weekend is coming up and he's entitled to go off visiting."

"Maybe but he left a note."

"Oh? Saying what?"

"He lent me keys to get in while I was doing my visits, so when he didn't answer the bell, I let myself in. I told him I was going for a last session before half term, so he must have been expecting me. But then I saw the note on the floor inside his door. It just said, *Sonia, I'm sorry.*"

"Okay, don't let's jump to any conclusions about this yet.

Perhaps he's gone away for a period of reflection after all he's told you. Just don't worry about it yet. You enjoy whatever you have planned for the half-term break and then, if he's still not back home by the end of the week, we'll think about what to do next."

"But, Mr Grant, Moule never goes far from Clapham," she persisted. "He told me. And why should he just say *sorry* to me?"

"All right, if you're that worried then I'll keep calling his mobile during the coming week and if I get a reply, I'll call you. I presume you also have his number?"

"Yes, I've called his number many times, but it's permanently switched off. It's as if he doesn't want to be contacted."

"Well, maybe he doesn't for some reason. Look, we'll stick to the original plan, and I'll call you to fix a date to go through the material you've recorded so far. If Moule is back home by then, all will be fine. If not, then I'll follow it up."

"How will you follow it up?" She sounded sceptical.

"Report him as a missing person I suppose. It's not something I've had to do before."

She fell silent and for a moment I thought she had rung off. Then her voice came back, almost as a whisper.

"Okay, Mr Grant. So, I'll hear from you when? Towards the end of next week?"

"Yes, probably Thursday. And I promise I'll keep calling Moule's number."

We ended the call then and I went straight to my Moule file to dig out his mobile number. She was right. The person I was trying to call had turned off his phone. I looked out of the window and as it was still light, I went back to the shed. At this time in a few days from now, I reminded myself, the clocks will have gone back, and it will be dark.

At odd occasions during the following five days, I called Moule's number, but the message was always the same. By Thursday morning, I was beginning to feel the same anxiety as Sonia, but possibly for different reasons. Had we pushed the man too far? But then, he had not been pushed; he had given up his secrets voluntarily. There had been no coercion. He had perhaps been beguiled by a young girl's disarming and innocent request. And maybe there had also been a certain pride in the story of his past, that for sixty years had remained untold. Just like telling a story to a child. Or, in this case, to an adolescent. I really didn't know the man well enough to put a rational explanation as to the psychology behind his decision to absent himself from home but one thing I was sure about, was that Moule's sudden disappearance was an uncharacteristic departure from his normal pattern of behaviour.

That Thursday evening, immediately after calling Moule's number one last time, I stabbed in the Benjamin number. Sonia's mother answered and then went off to find her.

"Hello, Sonia, any luck with Moule?"

"No, he's still away from home and stuff is piling up inside his door."

"So, he's obviously not been home at any time. Look, will you be free to meet me if I come up to London tomorrow?"

"Yeah, I'm not doing anything special."

"Good, I'll take an early train and I suggest we meet at Moule's place. I'll give you a call as soon as I arrive at Charing

Cross, and you can then set off to meet me in Clapham."

"Okay."

"I'll have all the papers. You just need to bring the keys. Oh, by the way, how's the hand?"

"It's healing slowly. I can move the fingers better now but still can't write."

"And I presume the police haven't found who did it yet?"

"No." It was clear that she had nothing to add on that subject, so we ended the call, and I went to check on the train times.

The train was a few minutes late arriving at Charing Cross, owing to a cow thoughtlessly straying onto the line, so it was nearly noon when I called her.

She was standing outside Moule's front door as I hopped off the bus and hurried across the road. After a rather curt greeting she turned the key and pushed back against a heap of post. After a cursory glance it looked like all junk and bills, so I kicked it aside and left it where it lay. A musty and airless odour hung around the stairwell and the automatic light didn't come on, so I guessed the bulb had blown. At the top of the stairs Sonia fumbled around in the semi-dark until the key slotted in.

I don't know why I ventured into every room in the flat but somehow, I felt it necessary. I knew Sonia had been there since Moule had disappeared, but he might have returned and then had an accident or an illness. Anyway, the rooms were all empty and he had even made up his bed before leaving. All food and eating utensils had been neatly stored, so it did not look like a sudden departure. All that there was to indicate that he had not just popped out to the shops or for a walk onto the Common was the note to Sonia.

While I was going from room to room, she just stood quietly, looking out of the window and seemingly lost in thought.

"Have you had any lunch?" I asked her.

She shook her head.

"Neither have I." I undid a window catch and pushed it up to let in some fresh air. "There's a café just up the street. Shall we have a bite to eat down there?"

She hesitated, so I added with a smile, "Treat's on me."

"Okay. Thanks."

We went out and locked up. As we walked along the road, I noticed Sonia hanging back slightly and glancing furtively at passers-by and I guessed she did not want to be seen by anyone she knew, walking with a strange, older man. It was understandable. She was just short of sixteen and for years had been fed paedophile propaganda.

The café made perfectly decent pizzas, so we had one each and a couple of soft drinks. Conversation was a bit stilted, but I managed to get her to talk about what she was studying at school, what her ambitions were after leaving and how her mother was coping on her own. I was not so tactless as to ask what Mr Benjamin had done to so sour relations with her mother. After a while she seemed more at ease with me and no longer lagged behind as we walked back to the flat.

We set up our stall on Moule's kitchen table and I pulled out my many sheets of typed A4. She sat down beside me, and we began the task of churning through Moule's narrative. I think she was impressed by my interpretation of the Jamaican patois and occasionally she let out an exclamation of surprise. I don't know if she had listened to her recordings before passing them on to me, but it was clear that he had frequently used words, expressions or phrases that she had not fully understood. Moule, for all his years in England, still spoke in the way he had learned up to the age of twelve; except, of course, when he adopted the *Trevor McDonald* voice.

For an hour and a half, we made good and constructive progress, but we were still only a third of the way through the script. She stopped once to help herself to a bottle of diet coke from the fridge, while I flexed the fingers of my writing hand. It was not a one-way edit by any measure, as her input was as important as mine. It had to be seen to be written in intelligible English but also in a way that she would have written it. She had told me that the limit was two thousand words, so that was another constraining factor but by late afternoon we were both satisfied with our progress.

I had contacted Mary and Noel and they appeared happy to put me up again, so I asked Sonia if she was free the next day for another session. She agreed and we arranged to meet outside the flat at two-thirty. It surprised me that she was quite willing to sacrifice a Saturday afternoon but did not question her decision. I gathered up the papers and had a quick look around the room.

We were just about to leave, when I had a sudden idea and asked Sonia to hold on. I went into the bathroom and scanned the basin and bath for the usual toiletries. There was no toothbrush, toothpaste, shampoo or hair conditioner. To me, that was another clear indication that it had been a planned departure and perhaps a lengthy one. I closed the window in the sitting room, re-joined Sonia and then left the empty flat.

We had finished dinner and Alice had gone to bed when I turned to Noel as we stacked the dishwasher.

"What's the procedure for tracking a missing person?" I asked.

"Well, it depends on whether the person is actually missing," was his measured reply. "I mean, just because someone leaves their home for a while and doesn't tell anyone where they are going, doesn't mean they are missing."

"Yes, I get that but after a time, if a friend or relative is anxious and reports it to the police, what would you do?"

"I'd log the enquiry for a start and then carry out an assessment. Ask basic questions about that person's normal movements, their welfare and that sort of thing. From that I would know if the situation were high or low risk. Then I would want to know if the person reporting had any specific reason to suspect that there might have been criminal activity behind the missing person's absence. You know the sort of thing - clues that might arouse suspicion."

"So, initially you would do nothing?"

"Look, Dad." He closed the machine and pressed the start button, "If the person disappeared unexpectedly in a quiet country parish, where the most dramatic thing to happen might be a mower stolen from a garden shed, then maybe the local Fuzz would have the time to follow up the report. Here, in the Met, we have rather more serious crimes to deal with, so yes, we would apply the tests I just mentioned before sending out a search party."

We drifted into the sitting room and Mary looked up from her iPad. "I heard you talking about missing persons. Is this your man Moule?"

"Not exactly my man, Mary," I laughed. "But, yes, his sudden disappearance has puzzled me."

"You do seem to be getting rather deeply into this girl's

project, Dad," Noel said, as he stretched his legs out from the sofa.

"Well, it's your fault old chap. You introduced me to Sonia and asked me to help her. I had no idea that Moule's story would turn out to be a minefield of mishaps. Some of what he's said has even shaken the poor girl a bit."

"And are you thinking his revelations are connected with him buggering off?"

"I can't think of any other reason. He's lived a perfectly quiet and undisturbed life in that flat for so many years, that this abrupt disappearance just seems out of character."

"You hardly know the man, so how can you judge his character?"

"You're right of course," I sighed. "I've only met him once but Sonia, young as she is, has worked him out and I've heard the tapes. So, my judgment evolves from that."

We sat silently for a few seconds with our own thoughts until Noel said, "Okay, if you really want to pursue the missing person angle, there is something else you can do."

"I didn't say I was going to pursue it, Noel."

He smiled knowingly at me. "But you are, aren't you?"

"Possibly, but my reason goes beyond what I've agreed to do for Sonia. I'm genuinely curious because of loose ends in Moule's story and his disappearance just seems to compound my suspicions." I frowned at my wonky logic. "So, what is the something else I can do?"

"Well, there is a charity called Missing People and they have a massive data base. They carry out their tracking through computer profiling. So, if you are really keen to dig deeper into Moule's supposed disappearance, then you could contact them. But my advice would be to leave it for a while before you go down that route. He's only been gone a week."

"But do be careful, George," Mary cut in. "As Noel says, you know very little about Moule. Remember what happened to his father. He might have been mixed up with people who deal in drugs."

"You mean the Yardies might have kidnapped him?" I asked with a smile.

"It's possible, Dad. You just don't know enough about his lifestyle," Noel added. "You could easily be stepping out of your comfort zone."

"Okay, warnings noted. But before I start any sleuthing I have to finish Sonia's project." I saw a knowing glance between the two of them. "Can I stay a couple more days to do that?"

"Stay as long as you need to," Noel replied. "I presume Mum can manage without you?"

"I expect she welcomes having the house to herself for a while." I stood up and looked at my watch. "Anyway, thanks for the advice. I'll go out for a stroll before bed."

There was something else I needed to ask Noel but decided to leave it until the next day. There was a small matter involving Moule's father that was bugging me. I saw it as one of the missing pieces of the increasingly complex jigsaw.

The following day Sonia and I met up as planned and we spent another couple of hours on the digest version of Moule's story. This was long enough but it was a mere precis of what was on the tapes. We had already agreed that the finished article of just less than two thousand words should stop at the point when the family arrived and settled in England, so I was pleased that she did not again raise the subject of Moule senior's demise.

However, I did ask Sonia if she knew the man's first name, but it seemed that Moule had never mentioned it during their many hours together. It had always been *my father*.

When we parted at about four thirty, I decided to start my enquiries by talking to people up and down the High Street. He was after all the Grand Moule, who had lived there for over six decades, so he would be known to most local people.

It was not a fruitful venture. Although many shopkeepers, local residents and even a street sweeper knew him, very few could give me a clue as to where he might have gone. It was as if over the years he had taken deliberate steps to be widely noticed as a somewhat eccentric, local personality, without ever revealing what lay behind the façade. The nearest I got to finding out anything about his movements was from a restaurant waiter who had worked there for fifteen years. He said Moule had talked about visiting friends on the other side of the city and that he also travelled somewhere regularly on a number thirty-five bus. Not really very helpful, as it only seemed to enhance Moule's enigmatic persona.

Or, I paused to wonder, was he now merely a rather boring, old man who did nothing with his life? Maybe I was totally wrong in characterising him. Perhaps his only pleasures were passing words with acquaintances, drinking Appleton rum, eating Jamaican food and living with his memories. I realised I knew very little of what he had done with his life from the age of fourteen up to whatever age he was now. If those years had been mundane and uneventful but disguised by his carefully embroidered image, then suddenly ripping the past open might well have spooked him into running for cover.

But I didn't buy that theory. Instinctively, I knew there was something Moule had not given up in his life story to

Sonia. One could sense it through vocal expressions, long pauses and subtle vocal inflections. It was as if he were editing his autobiography as he went along.

At that point in my tortuous mental analysis, I had no inkling as to how close I actually was to the truth.

That evening, back at my son's house I had an opportunity to ask him my second question.

"Noel, you know I told you about Moule senior's sticky end?" I began.

"Yes," he replied warily.

"I know absolutely nothing about police records or how long they are kept before being destroyed, other than the fact that there are cold, unsolved cases that can at some stage be reopened if there is subsequent evidence."

"Or, if new forensic methods are discovered."

"Quite. But how long are these records kept?"

"If unsolved they could be kept for a generation. It depends on the seriousness of the crime, or under which police jurisdiction that crime has been committed. Where is this leading?"

"Possibly deeper than is your knowledge," I laughed and then drew a deep breath. "What chance is there that Moule's father's murder in 1959 might still be on an unsolved case file somewhere?"

Noel puffed out his cheeks and blew. "Highly unlikely, especially if the Met didn't make much of an effort to follow it up at the time."

"Not even on a microfiche in an archive somewhere?"

"I could ask our archive people, but it would surprise me if that sort of record is kept. What would be the point anyway,

Dad, when the perpetrators will all be long dead?" He shrugged. "Anyway, why do you want to know about this man's murder?"

"I'm guessing it's part of the missing link, somehow connected with Moule senior skipping from Jamaica in 1956. If I'm right, then the story he fed his family about looking for a better life for himself and his family is all cock-and-bull."

"Blimey, you really have been drawn into the Moule saga."

"Well, it beats dead-heading the roses."

We both had a good chuckle at that, but I was actually in earnest about tracking the facts of the 1959 murder. It could have long-tail repercussions.

The next day Sonia and I wrapped up the Moule Saga, as we were now calling it. I asked her if I could keep the tapes for a while and she agreed without hesitation. I had already copied my transcription, but it was always possible that I might like to rehear some passages. We read her version through, and she filed it in a bright blue cover. It was still in my handwriting, but we agreed that the final version should be typed. The school would surely accept that in view of her inability to write.

I was not sure when I would be in Moule's flat again, so before we left I checked the rooms one last time. I didn't expect to see anything that I had not noticed before, but it was an instinctive thing to do. When we locked up, I told Sonia to hang on to the keys until she heard from me. I didn't say, until I find him but that was what I meant to imply. She thanked me very sweetly and we rather formally shook hands before she skipped across the road to catch a bus.

I walked back to Wandsworth slowly. Leaves were falling from most of the deciduous trees on the Common now and I reflected that we were only a couple of days off the end of British Summer time. There was already a slight chill in the air from an easterly breeze. A young woman passed me, and I noted that the baby she was carrying was snuggled in a woollen shawl.

The band stand on the Common looked as if it had closed for the season and youngsters were larking about under its domed roof. A man shouted at his dog, which was cocking its leg against one of the plane trees. A few people lounged on benches, some chatting in twos, others listening to music through ear pieces and some dozing singly or just watching life pass by.

A quiet voice in my head was saying that I should be going home now. I had finished the job I had come up to London to do and it seemed to have been completed satisfactorily but a louder voice kept shouting that down. The simple job had exploded unexpectedly, and I knew that I would feel as if I had walked away from something unfinished, if I did not attempt to see it through to a conclusion.

I had my head down in contemplation as I neared the Grant's Wandsworth house, when I nearly bumped into my son.

"Hello, Noel, you're home early."

"Hi, Dad. I've got a report to write up, so I've decided to do it at home. Just hope that I'm not called out tonight."

"You still do nights, do you?" We went up the steps to his front door.

"A few nights every other month. It's hit and miss. Sometimes there's very little action, other times you'd think south London had blown up."

"Mary must worry about you on those nights."

"She worries most of the time, but I do my best to keep my work and play completely separate. You just hope that the villains don't know where you live."

We entered the house, and I was about to go upstairs to freshen up when he said, "I have some information about cold case records."

"Encouraging information?"

"Could be. For instance, about fifteen years ago new data produced evidence that convicted someone for a 1957 murder."

"Good grief, the murderer must have been in shorts when he did it. But it's good to know that records can go back that far."

"So, what do you want to know?"

"Could we discuss it further when I come down? I'm sure you want to get on with your report and I need to call your mother."

"Right, see you for a drink before dinner then."

I twirled the glass gently and heard ice slop around the generous malt whisky Noel had poured. He held a beer bottle by the neck as he leant against the back of a chair and waited for me to speak. Mary was in the kitchen talking softly to Alice.

"What I'm actually hoping to find goes beyond any cold case data on Moule's murder that you might come up with," I began. "I really would like to know what went on in Jamaica before the family left in 1956. For instance, did the man have a criminal record, or was he mixed up in the marijuana trade?

I know that it was rife in the late fifties, round about the time the Rastafari cult was beginning to spread widely around the island. Your grandfather was good friends with Commissioner Crosswell, so I heard some of the stories of the troubles the police were having at the time in containing the drugs trade. So, if you know anyone in the Met who has a contact in the Jamaican police, if it doesn't compromise any confidentiality restrictions, it really would be helpful to know if Moule's father's name was on a wanted list."

Noel did not answer for a while, and I feared that I was asking for too much of him. He was well respected at Lavender Hill but was not a high-ranking officer and maybe this request was pitched above his pay grade. But he was merely thinking in his measured way before replying.

"As it happens, there has been dialogue between the Met and Kingston recently, but" he held up a cautionary hand, "obviously I can't divulge the content or subject matter. However, I do know someone who has been involved, so I could ask him to throw out some feelers. Nothing guaranteed though."

"That would be great but only if it doesn't put you in a difficult position."

"There are ways of being discreet, Dad. If necessary, I could always link the request for information with Moule's disappearance. Slightly left field, but you never know..."

"So, if your contact does put in a request with Kingston, we'll just have to hope that the Jamaican police records still exist."

"The island was still a colony back in fifty-six, so maybe records were of a high standard back then. But what's happened since, who knows?"

"Yes, would they have archived them this long? That's the key question."

"One can but ask." Noel finished the bottle and went to draw the curtains. It was not yet dark outside, but the temperature had dropped and some of the old sash windows were not draught proof.

"If you follow this up, say, tomorrow, how long do you think before you'll get a response?"

"You're in a hurry, are you?" he asked with a smile.

"If possible, I would like to have an answer before Moule turns up." I frowned as a dark thought crossed my mind. "That is, if he ever turns up alive."

Alice came through from the kitchen, having completed her homework. She bent down and gave me a kiss. "Good night, Grandpa."

"Good night, Alice. Sleep tight."

She trotted off upstairs and, as I watched her go, I could not help thinking how much she would enjoy having a brother or sister. However, it was not a subject June, or I would ever raise with our son or daughter-in-law.

"Come on through, Dad," Noel said and from his half smile, I feared that he had read my thoughts.

The next morning, I had an errand to deal with, so left the house soon after breakfast and sought out the nearest boutique-type shop. Having made my purchase, I went back to the Wandsworth house and wrapped it in fancy paper I found in a drawer.

I then called Mrs Benjamin on the mobile and asked if I could visit that afternoon. I told her I was about to return home to Kent and needed to give something to Sonia before I left

London. She didn't make any comment about that but confirmed that Sonia would be home between three-thirty and four, so I said I'd arrive at about that time.

I spent the rest of the morning and some of the afternoon in the public library looking up, or in many cases, revising, facts about Jamaica and its history in the middle of the twentieth century. Being an English urban library there was not a great deal on minor foreign countries, but I did find one book that covered the turbulent politics of that period. I had not realised how close the island had come to embracing communism under the Michael Manley regime, but Cuba was only a short distance away and Castro seemed to have cast a hypnotic spell over Jamaica's prime minister. I recalled that my parents had once met Manley at a party when he was a young man and from that meeting my mother had formed a deep distrust of the man. Fortunately, Jamaica's strong constitutional attachment to a democratic political system eventually saved the day.

I also found some information on the battle that the governments of the late fifties had with the drugs cartels. On the whole it seemed to have been a losing battle.

I'd paused for a beer and sandwich at about one o'clock but then had to drag myself away from some fascinating text in order to keep my appointment with Sonia.

Mrs Benjamin must have been hovering around near the front door, anticipating my arrival, because the door opened seconds after my knock.

"Come in, Mr Grant. Sonia's upstairs. I'll give her a call."

She shouted up the stairs and I waited in the hall until Sonia appeared on the landing.

"Hi," she said, as she came down in bare feet.

"Hello, Sonia. I wanted to give you this before I go back tonight." I held out the small package.

"Oh, what's this?" She took the parcel, felt it and then turned it over.

"Birthday present. It's a bit early but I'll be gone by the thirtieth. That is your birthdate, isn't it?"

"Yes, it is. How did you know?" She was grinning broadly up at me.

"Your mother told me when she was checking me out and for once I remembered a date."

"Thank you."

"I hope I haven't blundered in my choice. Not having a sixteen-year-old daughter I had to ask around." I prepared to leave. "Anyway, I hope you enjoy the day."

I opened the door to leave, and Mrs Benjamin came from somewhere to say goodbye, when Sonia suddenly said, "Wait, I nearly forgot to tell you."

I turned and waited, as instructed.

"I had a thought about Moule. It might be a long shot, but I remembered he told me about a friend he used to meet on the Common."

"He seems to have a lot of friends and acquaintances in the area but none of them I asked was able to help," I said.

"I think this is a special friend. He told me they talk a lot about all kinds of things when they meet on the Common. His name is Abe."

"Abe? As in short for Abraham?

"I suppose so. But I don't have a second name, I'm sorry." She pulled a face of pained regret. "So, maybe it's not much to go on."

"If I look for this Abe, do you have any kind of description for me to go on?"

"Not really, just that he's about five years younger than Moule and looks like a tramp. I think he spends nights at a hostel somewhere near Clapham Common."

I smiled at her description. All I had to do now was to walk around Clapham Common until I saw a scruffy individual, perhaps Jewish-looking and ask him if he answers to the name of Abe. Easy.

"Well, that's better than nothing to go on I suppose. I'll look out for him, Sonia."

"Does that mean, when you come back to London?" There was a trace of disappointment in the question.

"No, it looks now as if I'll have to postpone my return home." It was a snap decision but if I left it another week and Moule was still missing, then there might be cause for regret that I hadn't acted sooner. "Yes, I'll give it a couple more days and if I can't find this fellow Abe I'll go home. The police have been alerted, so there's nothing else we can do at this stage."

On my way back to Wandsworth I stopped to buy a bottle of whisky. I'd made a big dent in Noel's supply, so the least I could do was to replenish it.

I didn't place much hope in finding the tramp in the vastness of Clapham Common. The chance of he and I being there at the same time on a cool autumn day seemed remote. Nevertheless, I resolved to give it a try the next day.

CHAPTER 10

"Look, Mary, I really ought to be paying you rent I've been here so long. At least let me contribute to housekeeping costs," I protested.

"George, it's a pleasure to have you stay. It's just a pity that June can't be here as well."

"I know, it's all rather strange. Never thought when I started this, I'd end up carrying out a manhunt in South London."

Mary laughed at that, and I readily joined in, because it was all rather bizarre. A few minutes later she left with Alice, and I then pulled on my coat to go and hunt for a Jewish tramp on Clapham Common.

There was a stiff breeze blowing across the Common and not many people were taking it slowly along the exposed pathways. I could have started with the hostel, wherever that was but decided to begin with the open spaces. Sonia had told me that Abe spent a lot of time just sitting on a bench but surely not in all weathers. At least it was not raining that morning.

Over a period of twenty minutes, I stopped three individuals who looked as if they were regulars to the Common. The woman with the baby slung across her front hardly spoke English and the man with a pair of Salukis said he was just passing through. Anyway, he did not look like the sort of person who would pay any attention to the presence of a tramp.

I struck some luck with the third person, a council worker with a bin on wheels. Yes, he knew who I was talking about scruffy fellow with unkempt hair and a beard. Usually wore a long coat in all seasons. But he had not seen him today. Was I from the Public Health Department? I assured him I was not, thanked him and moved on.

I had done a couple of circuits of the Common's two hundred-odd acres, admiring the fine architecture of what had been built as a fashionable suburb of London. The whole area had gone into decline after the war but as so often happens with London districts, it had risen once again to prominence as a desirable place for the upwardly mobile to live.

As the feet were beginning to ache, I sat at the next available bench after clearing off some damp pigeon crap. I was watching the ground-grubbing techniques of a pair of Canada geese, when he slowly came into view. As the shuffling figure came alongside me, he paused to peer into the waste bin, and I seized the opportunity to address him.

"Good morning." He looked up sharply as if he needed to defend himself. "Do you by any chance go by the name of Abe?"

"Abe? Me? God no," he said, in a tone that implied I had made an indecent suggestion.

"Oh, sorry. I'm looking for him. Do you know where I can find Abe?"

The old fellow straightened himself and pushed a bottle deeper into a pocket of his duffle jacket. He moved his mouth around in a circular sort of way, as if trying to straighten his dentures and then replied.

"He says it's going to rain today." He nodded at the

sagacity of his statement.

"Who says?"

"Abe, of course." The dishevelled down-and-out observed me through rheumy eyes, clearly believing he was addressing a fool.

"Oh, I see. And is it going to rain?" I realised that playing along was essential if I was going to get any kind of answer.

"Of course not. It's Thursday and it never rains on Thursday."

"Never?"

"No, not even when the clock strikes thirteen. Old Jessie taught me that and she should know, being at sea all those years."

"But today's not Thursday."

The moment I said that I regretted it. Although I knew from the newspaper I had read that morning, it was not Thursday, I should not have contradicted such a man on his own turf.

"Well," he returned indignantly, "if you want to take that tone with me, I'll not tell you where to find Abe."

"I'm very sorry. It's my mistake. Of course, it's Thursday. Does Abe always come to the Common on Thursdays?"

"Ha!" he said in a *gotcha* tone of voice, "now you're trying to patro... patroni... trying to catch me out."

"No, I'm not. But if you don't want to tell me where to find Abe, then that's your choice."

His eyes narrowed slyly, and a line of spittle eased its way down the side of his mouth, as the purple lips creased into a smile. He rocked gently on the heels of his old brogues while he considered a suitable rejoinder.

"All right, you win today but I'll get you tomorrow." He

turned and pointed a gnarled and dirty finger. "Abe's over there on the bandstand. He's sheltering from the rain that he says is coming."

Before I could thank him, the fellow loped off, cackling contentedly to himself.

I almost leapt off the bench and a scavenging pigeon took off in fright. Rain or no rain, Thursday or not, I was determined to catch the fellow called Abe before he moved on. As I walked briskly in the direction of the Victorian bandstand, I was praying that he would make more sense than the vagrant who had just given me directions.

I am quite fit for my age, but I was breathing heavily when I reached the elegantly domed structure of the bandstand. At first, I could not see him but on circling the building, I spied a figure reclining against the wall. I couldn't resist it, so in the manner of Henry Morton Stanley on finding Doctor Livingstone, I said to the recumbent figure, "Mr Abe, I presume?"

He looked up sharply and assessed me before replying.

"That I am, indeed, sir. To whom do I have the pleasure of addressing?"

For a moment I was stunned. I had expected to find a semi-literate tramp, not someone who spoke as if on the stage of a Drury Lane production. Certainly, the appearance and apparel belied the voice that came from an unshaven and world-weary face.

"Do you mind if I join you?" I moved across and sat beside him. "My name is George Grant and I'm a friend of Meshach Moule."

He didn't reply but simply raised enquiring eyebrows.

"Well, perhaps *friend* is a bit presumptuous, but I've been helping a young friend of his, Sonia Benjamin."

"Ah, young Sonia. So, you are the scribe?"

"Yes, since her injury I've been transcribing Moule's taped memoirs. The project's practically finished now but I'm trying to find Moule."

"I presume you know where he lives. Is he not there?" Abe shifted his position and began scratching his cheek.

"No, this is the problem. He's not been there for over a week, and he's left no clue as to where he might have gone."

"And you think I might know more than you do?"

"Sonia says that you and he see a lot of one another, so she thought you might have a clue."

"Come to think of it, he's not been on the Common for about a week." Abe looked down at his dirty mac and his features turned contemplative. "Maybe more than a week. I've missed our chats. Much more constructive than listening to the ramblings of uneducated winos."

I wondered what ill-fortune had reduced the man to this low life, but it was not the time or place to pry into his affairs. It was always possible that it was a chosen lifestyle. It happens that some people gain a warped kind of satisfaction by dropping out of society. I'm told that they get their kicks from being kicked but that was one for the psychologists.

"Any ideas?"

"Hush, I'm thinking. Cranking the memory bank into action." Gazing into the distance and moving a surprisingly well-manicured finger about, as if conducting an orchestra, Abe cranked away for about two minutes. At last, he spoke.

"Moule is not a man who discloses much but he has mentioned a couple of friends during our talks. I think one of them was in the transport business with him and the other somehow connected with his family."

"Transport business?"

"He was a bus driver, amongst other things."

"Like his father then. And do you know where either of these people live now?"

"The relation, if that was what she was, resides in Holy Trinity Clapham graveyard I believe, so unless you can obtain the services of a reputable medium, I fear a dead-end looms there." He smiled conspiratorially at his pun. "In that case, dead end would seem to be an appropriate phrase."

"And the other?"

"As far as I am aware he lives somewhere in the East End." He closed his eyes for a few seconds and then snapped his fingers. "I remember now. He's amongst his own in Brick Lane, near Commercial Road in the East End."

"Yes, I know where Brick Lane is. I don't suppose you have a name?"

"Now you are asking too much, Mr Grant. We don't usually deal in names here on the Common's benches and even if he had told me, I would never be able to remember let alone pronounce a Bengali name."

He gave me a searching look and obviously my expression gave away my thoughts.

"I'm sorry, old boy, it's the best I can do. But I will say this - if Moule has decided to go to ground then I think this Bangladeshi chap is the most likely one to give our Rasta friend a bolt hole."

I couldn't help smiling at that cock-eyed piece of advice. He made it sound as if I were looking for a mole, not a Moule.

"So, what do I do? I can't see myself running up and down Brick Lane, shouting Moule's name. I'd probably be arrested for racial abuse."

"No, of course you can't do that, but you could ask around. After all, in an area full of little brown men and women, a six-foot West Indian with dreadlocks is going to be rather conspicuous, isn't he?"

"You're right. I suppose that's what I'll have to do."

"I hope you don't mind me asking but why do you think Moule has skipped off into hiding? He's not done something naughty has he?"

"No, no, nothing like that. I just think he's sort of scared himself off after opening up as much of his past as he did to Sonia. To be honest, Abe, I really don't know but I would very much like to find out."

"Because the story has not yet to reach its denouement?" he enquired gently.

"Precisely that. It's a fascinating tale that is crying out for an ending. Also, it's important for Sonia to complete her project. She can't do anything with it until Moule's given his approval."

"Mr Grant, a word of warning. Moule is a very private man. He might not want to be found and, even if you do find him, don't expect him to be cooperative."

"I know there's that possibility, but he can't expect to stay hidden for ever. He'll have to come back to Clapham some time."

"So, why rush him now? Why not wait for him to sort out his demons and come back in his own time?"

I was not sure whether to confide in Abe my own private fears. Irrational as it might seem, I did have a concern that Moule might not have gone into hiding of his own volition. What I knew of the man was vicarious, through the words on a tape machine, so what did I really know of his recent past, his current connections, or his private life? Somehow, the spectre of his own father's untimely death hung over everything connected with Meshach Moule.

It was a conundrum. The police would do nothing if there were no suspicious circumstances, and no one would know if there were suspicious circumstances if no one investigated. So, for what it was worth, I was investigating.

"Maybe you're right," I said, "but I'd like to give it one more shot before I go back home."

"Well, good luck to you, Mr Grant." Abe eased himself back into a comfortable position and it was clear that our discussion was at an end.

"Thank you, Abe. That's been helpful." I made to leave and then stopped to ask, "I don't know your surname."

"I think it's better that you don't." He winked. "Just Abe will do."

I gave him a sort of salute and then turned and walked away.

I had my head down, tapping in June's number on the mobile as I approached the exit from the Common, so I didn't notice them as they passed by. Neither did I see them when they turned and attacked from behind.

There were two of them. Rangy, white youths, with hoods over their heads and they knew what they were doing. One barged into me and the other grabbed my mobile. Although I was off balance, reflex made me grab at anything, just to stave off a physical blow. What I seized on to was the loose flap of a fleece jacket and for a second, this helped me stay upright.

Then a second instinct kicked in, in the form of my right foot. The scream of pain told me that I had made firm genital contact and it was satisfying to see my assailant double up on the ground in a writhing foetal position. But I was now also on the ground, and I looked up to see the other one splay-footed above me. He seemed for a few seconds undecided as to whether to lash out at me or to help his friend but those few seconds spared me from the first option, as two male joggers suddenly appeared on the scene.

The hoody took off, with one of the joggers in pursuit, while his companion bent down and enquired earnestly if I was okay. I was a bit shaken but confirmed I was unhurt. I was actually more concerned that the fellow on the ground might stop nursing his balls and scarper as well. I stood up gingerly and brushed off my clothes.

The first jogger soon returned, breathing heavily. He said the assailant had got away and I was silently not surprised. Kind as he was to give chase, he clearly was just a jogger while the pursued was obviously a sprinter.

Two off us kept the mugger on the ground, while the other Good Samaritan dialled 999 and reported the incident. They kindly agreed to stay until the law arrived. My mobile had gone with the runner, but I was not too concerned about that. It was a much-mocked pay-as-you-go specimen that I only used for irregular contact purposes. If they had been hoping to grab a smartphone, they were in for a big disappointment. It was the equivalent of stealing a Mickey Mouse watch, when you were expecting a Rolex.

We had a chuckle about this analogy and then talked for a few minutes generally about the safety in public places these days, before a couple of officers arrived. One of the officers was WPC Sanders.

They were in the act of cuffing the man when I noticed a

blue bird tattoo on the villain's left wrist. His hood had been pulled back and when our eyes met, there was pure hatred in his. It was as if it had been I who had attacked him and not the other way around. But maybe he thought I had done permanent damage to his reproductive organs. I smiled at him sadistically as they lead him away.

I thanked my rescuers and they jogged happily away; something to tell the lads in the pub after a shower. I had confirmed to the police officers that no damage had been done to me but said I would call in to the station the next day to make a statement, if one was needed. I got the impression that this particular mugger and his mate had been in the local force's sights for a while.

I will admit that I was shaking involuntarily by the time I reached the Grants' house and helped myself to a stiff whisky once inside. No one was at home, so I changed my clothes and then called June on the landline. To my surprise, she said she was coming up to London the following morning, having made arrangements with Mary. Clearly, she felt it was time to check up on me.

"What about the chickens and the dog?" I asked.

"Bruno's been farmed out to the Johnsons and next door has agreed to put the chickens away at night."

"Good. In exchange for eggs, I presume?"

"Of course. Will you meet me at Charing Cross, or shall I take a taxi?"

I had planned to go straight over to Brick Lane the next morning but rapidly scrapped that idea. "I'll meet you there. What train will you be on?"

She told me and I made a note. I reminded her to bring her mobile phone but did not tell her why it was needed. There seemed no point in concerning her at this stage.

However, I did tell Noel and Mary that evening when they were both together in the house. Mary was shocked that such a thing had happened yet again, in daylight in such a public place as Clapham Common. But to Noel, this was just another petty crime and I happened to be the unfortunate victim. I knew he was playing it down, because his job was a constant worry to his wife.

To lighten the mood, I told them about my meeting with Abe and my plan to seek Moule out in Brick Lane. Noel shook his head and commented that it was a very long shot and Mary said I really should admire some of the art work while I was there. I agreed with both of them and then the subject strayed onto the continuing struggle to keep Lavender Hill station open.

The train was on time. I met her at the barrier and took her suitcase.

"Packed for a long stay?" I enquired with a hint of sarcasm.

"No, just the essentials, plus gifts for Mary and Alice." She prodded me in the side. "You've been up here long enough. I bet you've not thought of a gift."

"Certainly have. I bought a bottle of whisky for Noel."

"Typical, all you could think of was booze."

There was no answer to that, so we hurried along to the taxi rank. Luckily, we didn't have to wait long and were soon doing the stop-start and weave out to Wandsworth. On the way there I filled in the gaps about what my plans were in tracking down Moule. Obviously, there was also a great deal of explanation as to why I was doing it at all. It made sense to me, but June seemed to find it all quite odd. However, she was generous enough not to question my judgment or even my sanity.

I stopped the taxi shortly before we reached the house, just by a coffee shop I had noticed on my way to and from Clapham. We went in and for half an hour, chatted over a cup of cappuccino. Home seemed a long time ago and there was much to catch up with.

That evening we all enjoyed a leisurely family dinner. It was something we had not managed to do for several months. I tried to avoid what June was beginning to call my *obsession*, although I did spend some time secretly plotting my Brick Lane manoeuvres.

CHAPTER 11

It was more than twenty years since I had visited Brick Lane and then it was just a pass-through, on my way to a meeting at the former Truman brewery at the far end. In those days it was a relatively quiet enclave, occupied predominantly by the Bangladeshi community, still with many first-floor clothing sweatshops. Even the name of the street was written in their language underneath the Anglo Saxon one. Prior to that, I believe it had been known as Whitechapel Lane. I will always remember that within yards of entering the lane, one's nostrils were assailed by the smell of curry and spices. It was like suddenly being transported into the exotic East, rather than to the less exotic East End of London.

I got out of the tube at Aldgate East station and turned left past Commercial Road. A short distance on, followed by another left and I was in Brick Lane. Almost from the moment I entered the lane, I became aware of the enormous change in the area. I had heard that it is now affectionately known as Banglatown, and one could instantly see why. In the nineteenth and early twentieth centuries, there had been a large Jewish settlement in the area but now it was overwhelmingly Bangladeshi but with a big difference from twenty years ago. Brick Lane had clearly become fashionable and chic.

I had decided to walk the length of the lane, just to take in as much of the sights, sounds and outlets as I could. The day was dry but overcast and cool, so I turned up my coat collar as I weaved my way along the busy pavement.

The sounds, aroma and variety were astonishing. I passed the art exhibitions Mary had mentioned and marvelled at the unofficial wall art, applied by a skilled spray-gun artist. There were several curry houses, a few coffee bars, restaurants and at least one book shop. I stopped to browse in one of the latter for a few minutes. One of the main features of the lane today, which I did not remember from my previous visit, was the market. There was an astonishing array of clothing, foods and arty items for sale. Bearing in mind June's comment about gifts, I bought Mary a very brightly patterned, silk scarf. As I paid the vendor, I reflected that it was the second such item I had bought in a week but for very different people.

It was shortly after midday when I decided to have a bite to eat before beginning my probably fruitless search. The stomach told me it was too early for a curry, so I went into a takeaway and bought a soft drink and a tuna sandwich. I found a seat near the market and ate, as I watched the citizens go about their business. As Abe had said, there were an awful lot of small, brown men and women in the lane but not a glimpse of a Rasta.

If Moule was hiding away in the area he had to eat somewhere, therefore I decided to begin with the restaurants. So, systematically I began going into each eatery beginning from the top of the lane. Of course, being the lunch hour, they were busy but at that time they were also alert to potential customers. Consequently, there was usually a manager or front-of-house individual greeting me near the door. In each one, I said I was looking for a West Indian friend who might be staying with a former Bangladeshi bus driver in Brick Lane.

The responses were usually polite, sometimes a little wary but all negative after my enquiry. After the fourth restaurant I stopped to assess my approach. Why were they suspicious? Did they think I was a cop or from the Inland Revenue? Surely not - I was too old to be on active duty. Maybe it was my line of questioning that was wrong.

I decided that a more direct approach was required, so began naming Moule and giving a description. I had an important message for him from his daughter and had been told he was staying here in Brick Lane with a friend. That brought a more positive response, in that those being quizzed were less evasive and seemed to make an attempt at recollection.

However, it was late in the afternoon, when staff were clearing lunch and preparing for the evening, when a spark flashed out of the darkness. It was provided by a very small waiter with delicate hands.

His English vocabulary was perfectly sound, but the delivery was so heavily accented, that I struggled to follow what he was trying to tell me. However, when eventually I tuned in, it was clear that he knew the man who had a West Indian friend staying with him. With arms waving, he accurately described Moule, down to the dreadlocks. I could hardly contain my excitement.

He told me the man I should be talking to was called Rohan Iqbal and he was the proprietor of a restaurant further down the lane, unsurprisingly trading under the name of Rohan's Curry House. I thanked my informant, who grinned at me and waggled his head in that idiosyncratic Indian way.

It was not difficult to find the place and I would eventually have arrived at it, as I made my way along Brick Lane. A very thin boy was sweeping the pavement outside the entrance to the restaurant, trying at the same time not to trip up passers-by with his broom. I skipped around him and went in through the open door. A waiter in an oversized white apron looked up from laying a table, paused, and then came hurriedly over to me clutching a handful of cutlery.

"Not open yet," he said urgently in a high-pitched voice. "Lunch finished. Dinner later."

"It's all right, I'm not here for a meal. I'm here to see Mr Iqbal. Is he in?"

"Mr Iqbal?" He made it sound as if he had never heard of the man. "You want to see Mr Iqbal?"

"Yes, is Mr Iqbal here?" In the traditional English manner when speaking to a foreigner, I said it very slowly and perhaps a little too loudly.

The waiter looked at me through narrowing eyes but did not reply. He'd probably been trained by his boss not to admit anything to a strange man asking for him. It could be the VAT man or someone from the Health Standards department. But just as I was wondering how to break this impasse, there was a voice from the darkness at the back of the room.

"Yes, who wants to see me?" A surprisingly tall, grey-haired Bengali stepped out of the gloom.

"Mr Iqbal?" I gave the waiter a cursory tap on the shoulder and slid past him.

"Yes, I'm Rohan Iqbal. What can I do for you?"

"I'm very pleased to have found you. My name is George Grant. I'm a friend of Meshach Moule." I studied his face closely for reaction as I spoke.

There was a discernible twitch of the eyelids but otherwise the lean face showed no response. He extended his hand slowly and I shook it. The bony fingers were cool and dry.

"Pleased to meet you, Mr Grant," he said but seemingly out of innate politeness rather than genuine pleasure. "Meshach Moule, you say?"

"Yes. Let me explain. He and I were working together to help a schoolgirl complete a school writing project. She was recording details of Moule's early life, with his full cooperation of course and I am typing it out for her. We had nearly finished, when Moule suddenly disappeared, and we are both — Sonia and me — worried about what might have happened to him."

"Who sent you here, Mr Grant?" His English accent was almost perfect and his manner urbane. The ideal restaurant proprietorial demeanour.

"Well, actually no one sent me but a good friend of Moule's said that if anyone other than himself knew where Moule is now, it would be you."

For the first time during our tight conversation, he appeared slightly puzzled.

"This friend of Mr Moule's, gave you my name?"

"No, he simply said that Moule had a Bangladeshi friend who he knew from his days as a bus driver and who now lives in Brick Lane. The rest was detective work on my part."

Iqbal suddenly laughed and I saw flashes of gold teeth. I noticed the waiter stop laying table and glance sharply in our direction. Iqbal said something abruptly to the man in his own tongue and then turned back to me.

"Come into my office." He turned and I followed.

He pushed open a glass-panelled door and we went through into a small room lighted with a stark florescent strip.

He moved behind a desk and sat down.

"Please sit down," he said with an elegant gesture. "So, you believe that Mr Moule is here with me?"

"I am hoping so, Mr Iqbal. I don't know what scared him so much as to make him leave home but that's his choice. I just need to talk to him to find out if there's anything I can do to help. But, if he's not here with you, then I'll have run out of ideas."

"If Mr Moule is here and I am not saying he is, why do you think you can help him?" He folded his fingers together carefully. "And anyway, why do you think he needs help at all?"

"Look, I admit I hardly know Moule, but I am sure his sudden disappearance from the home he has lived in for sixty years, has something to do with what he has been disclosing from his past to the girl, Sonia. If that is the case, she and I feel partly responsible and I for one want to help resolve the problem. I can only do that by talking to him. There is no other motive, I assure you."

He leaned back in his chair and turned his gaze to the ceiling. An elegantly manicured forefinger tapped the top of the desk. I pretended to study the garish painting hanging from the wall behind him, while he deliberated. He suddenly stopped tapping and his leather chair groaned as he leaned forward.

"Mr Moule *is* here as my guest. He has not explained what is troubling him, but he says he needs to be away from Clapham until something — he won't say what — is sorted out." He raised both hands. "I don't even know if he has done something illegal, so while he, a friend, is under my roof, I have to be very careful in what I say to strangers."

214

"I understand perfectly, and I appreciate your loyalty to a friend, but Moule has not done anything illegal, as far as I know. The situation is simply as I have told you; so, is it possible for me to talk to him?"

Iqbal pursed his lips and then stood up. He was surprisingly tall for a Bengali and I pictured him as a cricketing opening batsman in his youth. He glanced around his spartan office, as if checking that there was nothing vulnerable in sight.

"Wait here, Mr Grant." He went to the door. "I will ask Moule if he wants to talk to you."

"Thank you. Oh, and please add that Sonia is also anxious to know how he is."

He went out and closed the door behind him.

Iqbal was out of the room for several minutes, giving me ample time to study the décor in his study. I suddenly felt naked without my mobile phone. It would have been an ideal time to contact June and ask how her day had been so far, instead of sitting in a curry-impregnated den. But then, just as I was becoming twitchy, Iqbal reappeared.

"Moule was not greatly happy that someone has found him here, but he says for Sonia's sake he will talk to you. I have accommodation above the restaurant, and he is using my spare room, so please follow me."

We left the room and then went down a passageway to where the stairs were located. The steps creaked under the puce-coloured carpet as we went up and here, the smell of curry was even stronger. At the top we turned right and stopped at a white painted door. Iqbal gave a gentle tap on the door and then pushed it open.

It was a sparsely furnished room, about four metres

square, with a bed, a small table, two chairs and a wash basin in the corner. The floor covering was a thin, chocolate brown carpet and there was a rough-woven rug alongside the table. Moule was standing by the window, looking down at the lane below. He was wearing his usual Caribbean shirt; a pair of blue slacks and his feet were bare. He looked more haggard than when we had last met, and his locks looked unkempt. I have been told that the Rastafari use a dread comb to back-comb their hair until they build up the strands from the roots before twisting it. They also use a great deal of shampoo and conditioner to keep it clean. At a glance, it appeared to me that Moule had forgotten to bring the comb in his haste to leave Clapham.

He turned from his street gazing.

"Hello, Mr Grant," he said without enthusiasm.

"Moule, how are you?" I extended my hand, which he accepted. His was damp.

"I'm okay, while I'm here."

He moved slowly and stiffly across to the table, which was scattered with sheets of newsprint and magazines. I imagined that he had not got out much since leaving home.

"Do you manage to get any exercise while you're here?" I asked.

"A bit. After dark usually." He pointed to one of the chairs and he sat in the other. Iqbal had silently slipped out of the room and closed the door. "Now why are you here?"

I began my rambling explanation and also how I had managed to find his hiding place. When I mentioned Abe's name as the key to discovery, he sucked his teeth loudly in disapproval but made no verbal comment. Then I came to the all-important question.

"Why, Moule? Why the sudden departure, with just a short note to Sonia? She's been really worried about you."

"It's nice to know somebody is worried about old Moule." He managed a half smile. "But I can't tell you. Not yet anyway."

"Can't tell me, or won't?"

"I won't tell you, Mr Grant, because to do so might put my position in jeopardy." He had raised his voice for emphasis. "That is all I can say just now."

I had not come this far to be put off that easily, but I knew I had to play this game with kid gloves. He was clearly not going to give me a positive answer, so I decided to let him have the opportunity to give me some negative ones.

"Okay, I have to accept that, although I cannot imagine what kind of jeopardy you are worried about. But, if it's something relating to what you have disclosed to Sonia during your discussions with her, it might be helpful to know what it is. It could be connected with something I'm following up."

He drew in a sharp breath and stared at me, as if fearing what I was about to say.

"I know you left Jamaica reluctantly at the age of twelve and from what you hinted, your father somehow blamed you or used you as an excuse for the fact that you had to leave. I can't imagine how that can be when you were so young, but I think he was using you as a cover for his own ends. Is that how it really was?"

"Come on, man, how you know these things?" he interjected. "You can't know any of what went on then. And anyway, what has this got to do with anything today?"

"Of course, I don't know anything, other than what you have told Sonia. But what I suspect and am trying to find out, is if your father left the island because he was scared for himself and that the *better life* excuse was just a sham for his real motive. Have you really never thought that was the case? And if you have, is it connected in any way with why you are now in hiding?"

"I told you, Mr Grant, I know why we left Jamaica and it's nothing to do with my father being scared of anything. That stuff is all history." He glared at me. "I don't know why you came here jus' to spin out Nancy stories. This conversation is going nowhere."

"Listen," I leaned towards the truculent figure. "If your father had got on the wrong side of a drugs gang and they were gunning for him, literally, what better thing for him to do than leave Jamaica? Many Jamaicans were going to England at that time but as it might have been easier to get a passage as a married man with a child, he had to con you and your mother into going with him. But as you know in the end it didn't do him any good, because they got him in London anyway. So, if I'm right then you certainly have nothing to worry about now, after all these years. That's all I'm trying to tell you."

"This is fantasy, Mr Grant," he almost spat out. "And I repeat, it is history and has nothing to do with why I am here right now. Please don't take me for fool."

"Is it fantasy? That money you and your mother found after he died. Where do you think that came from, eh? He didn't win on the lottery, Moule. That was dirty money. Drug money, stolen from the gang he was mixed up with. Tell me that's not true."

A little bit of the bravado left him then, like a slowly deflating tyre. He took in a few deep slow breaths before replying to my challenge.

"Mr Grant, I know I was a young boy when we left but don't think I have not considered these things over the years since I became a man. I am not that simple. And don't think my mother didn't also have the same thoughts. I admitted this much to Sonia when I told her about the money we found and what we decided to do about it. I am not proud of that decision, but I was not proud of my father either. He owed us something and what we found, we regarded as our legacy. It helped my mother as she got older and it helped me become better educated and set myself up for the future in this country but," he stopped and jabbed a finger in my direction before stating emphatically, "all of that, assuming it is true, has nothing to do with why we left Jamaica or why I am seeking refuge here in Brick Lane now. I am sorry if that answer does not suit you but that is how things stand. I thank you for your concern, but I think you should now go back home."

With that, Moule stood up abruptly and took a step forward. In doing so, he stumbled as his toe caught the edge of the rug. He put out a hand to steady himself against the table, which lurched with the sudden jolt. A few of the papers slid sideways and I jumped up to stop them falling onto the floor.

"You, okay?" I asked but even as I spoke, my eye caught a single word on one of the newspaper headlines and in that instant, I knew why Moule was in hiding. I had been completely wrong in my line of thinking. I had been fishing entirely in the wrong waters.

"Yes, I'm okay. Come." He had my elbow and was leading me away from the table, but it was too late. I had seen what he had attempted to cover up. I stopped in the middle of the room and faced him.

"Moule, it's *Windrush*, isn't it?"

He stopped suddenly as if he had run into a wall and his face collapsed like a crumpled brown paper bag. He closed his eyes and his whole frame shuddered.

"Sit down," I said quietly, "and let's discuss this properly, because if I'm right, I think you might be running from shadows."

He did as I asked and sat on the chair I had just vacated. I rested my backside against the edge of the table.

"You surely don't think you're in danger of being deported?" I breathed in disbelief.

He didn't reply, so I probed further.

"I don't know when you heard or read about the *Windrush* scandal but it's all over now. I promise you there's no need to hide. The whole issue has been exposed and the Home Secretary resigned back in April. There will be no more deportations of innocent people."

Moule inclined his head towards me, and his face tightened with the anxiety that was obviously overwhelming him. It was clear now what had caused the terror that had driven him into hiding.

"Listen, man," he began in a strained voice, "I might have picked up on this late, because I don't follow the news much, but the fact is that over eighty West Indians have been deported back to where they came from, and some have lived here since they were children. People like me. So, I am not going back home until I can be sure the law is changed so that there is no chance of them catching up with me."

I was aware that nearly half a million people like Moule who had arrived before 1973 had potentially been denied their legal rights, wrongly detained and threatened with deportation, since the amendment to the immigration legislation. These people were now widely known as the *Windrush* generation, after HMT Empire Windrush that sailed from the Caribbean in 1948. The many thousands who took advantage of the opportunity to come to the UK up to 1973 were initially granted an automatic right permanently to remain, unless they left the UK for more than two years. But clumsily revised immigration law in 2014 had effectively removed that protection. That lacuna in the legislation and the resulting iniquities had initially been exposed by the *Guardian* newspaper and then later followed up in the UK parliament.

Clearly all of this had passed Moule by until very late in the day and, without knowing the details, I could see that he was now petrified of being targeted for deportation. I couldn't help but wonder how the scandal, prominent in the news for so long, had evaded his attention until a few days ago. But I now felt it my duty somehow to persuade him that he was safe. That wasn't going to be easy.

"The whole matter has been exposed to public scrutiny and debated in parliament," I stressed. "There will be no more deportations of people who arrived before 1973. You have nothing to fear now."

But, as I feared, he was not to be easily convinced.

"Like I said, man, over eighty people have been sent back already and some have lost their jobs and other rights in the UK," Moule said, jabbing a finger at me. "And you know why? Because we came here with no papers or other entry documents and even those that did exist were destroyed in 2009. The people who came here then were told these papers were not required and now the British government has gone back on that. It was fine when they needed cheap labour after the war but now, we wut nothing, so they deporting us." He was becoming agitated and lapsing into his *raw chaw* accent. "Man, I don't even have a passport. I came here with my name on my father's passport. And now you are telling me he was a fugitive from justice? If dat is so, what chance do I have of them not catching up with me?"

"Moule, I've told you. The law is being amended to reinstate your entitlements. You will not be deported. Anyway, many of the eighty-odd you mentioned had committed crimes in the UK, so it could be said they had forfeited their right to remain."

"And you think that makes me feel better about de situation? You tink I should now feel safe?"

"Frankly, yes. I'm not trying to fool you. Why would I do that? If we were talking about this a year ago then maybe you might have been at risk but now that the whole scandal has been exposed and the injustice seen for what it was, there is no need for you to go into hiding. Anyway, what good is hiding? If the authorities had wanted to question your right to remain here it would have happened a long time ago. You would have had written notification of some kind from the Home Office."

"You tink so?"

"Of course. Whatever administrative blunder has occurred, this is not Nazi Germany, where someone knocks your door down and drags you away without any right of appeal."

I really was unsure as to whether or not I was getting through to him, but I was determined to try my hardest to get him to accept what I was saying. To me, this misunderstanding was farcical but then I was not an ageing Jamaican with no documentary rights entitling him to be in his adoptive country. In many ways Moule appeared to be an intelligent and resourceful man but in this instance his reasoning seemed to be completely awry.

I pushed back from the table and felt the lump in my coat pocket. Maybe a small diversion would help bring about clarity of thought. If that failed then I knew I might as well just walk away. There were no more persuasive tropes in my locker.

"I nearly forgot," I said, pulling a bottle from my pocket. "I'm afraid it's only a half-bottle and it's not Appleton but in case you're out of rum…"

He stared at the offered bottle for a few seconds and then his face slowly creased into a hazy grin. He reached out and took my gift, reading the label.

"Not a bad choice, man." His smile broadened. "So, what is dis? A bribe for me to come back wid you?"

"Of course. But maybe not immediately. I'll go now but think hard about what I've told you."

He laughed at that, but I knew he was still not fully convinced of his safety, if he emerged from his bolt hole. He only had my word to rely on, but I decided to give it one last shot before I left.

"Moule, tell me one thing. Do you or do you not believe what I have told you about it being safe, or do you think I'm giving you a load of flannel?"

"I believe you, Mr Grant, because you seem to me to be a straight and honourable man, but the question is, do I believe or trust the British government?"

"I suppose you have every right not to, on past record but I'll tell you one thing you can trust and that is the judgment of the British people, especially when they have the backing of our free press. Together they will hold the government to account on this matter."

"That is a fair comment." He pursed his lips and began nodding, as if having a silent debate with himself.

"And there is another thing," I pressed on. "Sonia's project. We've finished editing and writing it out, but we need you to review and approve it before she submits it for assessment. She needs you back for that, Moule, or the whole thing will be wasted, and she will have failed to deliver."

I could tell instantly that I had hit a soft spot. He lowered his head and stared at his bare feet. He then spoke so softly that I only just heard the words.

"You're right, I can't let Sonia down."

I held my breath. It was his decision to make and there was nothing more I could do about it. In the silence, once again, I became aware of the scents of the Orient in the atmosphere. Curry is all-invasive as I once discovered after letting a flat to an Indian couple for several months. We had to wash the curtains three times after they left in order to clear the pungent aroma from the material.

"You are very persuasive, Mr Grant," Moule said sagely. "So, for Sonia's sake, I will take the risk and return home."

"Thank you, Moule. I believe that there will be no risk to you at all but I'm grateful to you for coming to that decision. And I'm sure Sonia will be too."

I watched him lift his lanky frame from the chair. He placed the bottle carefully on the table and moved towards the door.

"I will pack up my few possessions here, thank my host and come back to Clapham tomorrow." He suddenly seemed much older than when we had first met, and I had to remind myself that we were the same age.

"Clapham High Street has missed the Grand Moule," I quipped.

"In truth and in fact, Mr Grant, so have I missed Clapham."

"George, Moule. My name is George." He put his hand on the doorknob and turned to me.

"Jarge, man!" He gave a burst of his raucous laughter. "In Jamaica dem would call you Jarge."

"I know, they always did."

"Oh, yes, I forget. You also are a refugee." He held his hand out for me to pass through. "You know, up to a few years ago, upstairs in this house was a sweatshop."

"Moule, I think up to a few minutes ago it still was one." He made no comment to that but dipped his mouth in acceptance of the metaphor.

He followed me downstairs where they were still laying tables and there was a general atmosphere of preparation. Iqbal was not around, so I said goodbye to Moule at the restaurant entrance and he reaffirmed his promise to return the following day.

It was after five o'clock when I reached Aldgate East station and the homeward rush was in full flow. It was many years since I had experienced the crush of a crowded underground train and my return journey was made worse by the fact that I had to change trains on the way back to Wandsworth. It was like a release from Hades to step out into the relatively fresh air of a south London street.

I was back at the house before any of the others, so turned around and went to collect Alice from the neighbour. She was in high spirits and keen to show me what she had achieved that day. We went into the house and for longer than I could remember she and I talked about a range of topics. It was rather refreshing after my intense confrontation with Moule that afternoon.

June was the first to arrive at the house and, before she even removed her coat, she was berating me for not answering her telephone call.

"I tried several times, but it kept going on to *leave a message* mode," she said indignantly.

"Just as well it was not answered. You might not have recognised your husband's voice."

"What do you mean?"

"I didn't want to worry you, but my mobile was stolen a couple of days ago."

"Oh, no. How did you lose it?"

"My dear girl, I didn't lose it. As I said, it was stolen. A couple of thugs attacked me on Clapham Common."

"George, why didn't you tell me?" She looked me over, as if expecting to see signs of damage. "Were you hurt?"

"No, not hurt. And one of them got more than he expected from an old geezer."

She dropped her coat on the hall chair and gave me a hug. "But I wish you had told me before."

"I told Noel and they have one of the muggers in custody at Lavender Hill. I didn't want to worry you unnecessarily."

"Dangerous place, London." She released me and smiled. "Now, how did you get on today? Did you find your man?"

"Yes, I did. The educated tramp, Abe, was right. Moule had gone to ground with an old buddy in Brick Lane, but I'll tell all at dinner. I need a shower right now. I expect I reek of curry."

We sat down to dinner soon after eight and, when prompted, I rolled out my day's adventure, ending with Moule's promise to return to Clapham.

"How extraordinary that he should be terrified of deportation, when he was only a child when he came to England," Mary said. "He must have some sort of documentation to establish residence here."

"Not necessarily," I said. "As Moule confirmed, he arrived on his late father's passport. All landing documents have now either been revoked or destroyed and he has never taken out a UK passport of his own. And don't forget, there is a precedent for child arrivals to have been deported under the current legislation. In those circumstances he probably had every right to feel vulnerable and not to trust the UK government. Especially as he had no one in authority to turn to for advice or reassurance."

"Well, lucky for him that you have championed his cause," Mary added. "How long would he have stayed in hiding if you hadn't found him?"

"He said, until the law was changed." I shrugged. "But if he had stayed away from his flat for much longer, he wouldn't have been able to push the door open for junk mail."

"I'd forgotten you were in there the other day, Dad," Noel chipped in. "Did you happen to look at any of that mail? I mean, I don't suppose there could have been anything from the Home Office that might have scared him off?"

"I only glanced at the mail, but I saw nothing on the floor or in the flat that looked official. No, having talked to him I now realise it was just a case of him hearing a rumour of deportations, or reading a report and not fully understanding the current situation. Believe me, he was genuinely rattled. But it's extraordinary how it turned out. I went looking for him thinking he was hiding from something quite different."

"Well, you've done a good day's work, darling," June said, as she stood to clear dishes from the table. "Pity about your mobile though."

"Oh, I forgot to tell you, Dad," Noel said. "The bloke you tried to emasculate has shopped his accomplice. He was so pissed off at being abandoned that he gave us the fellow's name. We also have every reason to believe that they were the two who attacked Sonia, thanks to your observation and Sonia's statement."

"My observation?"

"In your statement you said you noticed a bird tattoo on his wrist. Well, the arresting officer saw it too and it matches the description that Sonia gave us."

"I thought she wasn't much help in her statement."

"She wasn't, except for her comment about a blue bird tattoo."

"Well, that's some more good news then."

"Do you want to change your mind about pressing charges?"

"No, I was going to change my mobile anyway but surely Sonia will. She suffered actual bodily harm; I think the phrase is."

"Wendy Sanders will be talking to her about that."

We rounded off the meal with coffee and shortly after that I excused myself. It had been a tiring day and bed was calling. I was asleep when June came up an hour later.

CHAPTER 12

Early next morning, I called Mrs Benjamin but was too late to catch Sonia. She was already on her way to school. All I could do was ask her mother to pass on the message that I needed to talk with her.

As I was therefore at a loose end I agreed, reluctantly, to go with June to the West End for a shopping visit. We spent a couple of hours in and around Oxford Street and wound up in a pizza house for lunch. She was talking about domestic and other matters, which would in normal circumstances be important, but my mind kept drifting off to Moule and his self-imposed isolation. I still could not shake off the instinctive suspicion that even now, there was another dimension to his motivational fear.

We took a bus back to Wandsworth, with June giving me earache about not listening to a word she had been saying and me agreeing with her. It was after all a husband's prerogative to be audio selective, but I would only have admitted that to her under fear of death.

My afternoon's plan was to go back to the Common and seek out Abe, so that is exactly what I did after helping June unload her spoils.

By now, I knew it was hit or miss when it came to finding Abe but as it was a fine, late October afternoon my hopes were high as I set off for Clapham Common.

The Common is actually shared with the Borough of Wandsworth, so crossing it at some point one is passing across the boundary between the two. I was speculating where that crossing point might be and whether, like a county boundary, it was marked, when I saw Abe. He was lolling on a bench, wearing his usual long all-weather coat but he was not alone. A stout, middle-aged woman, wearing a medical uniform, was talking to him in an earnest manner.

Obviously, I could not disturb them without being rude, so I decided to walk past very slowly and hope that the educated tramp, as I had begun to think of him, might recognise me. A pigeon helped with this ruse as its sudden flight out of my way made Abe look up.

"Ah, Mr Grant," he called out when I was a few yards past. Was I imagining it, or was there relief in his voice at the diversion my appearance had created?

I turned, as if surprised. "Oh, good afternoon, Abe. Nice to see you again."

The woman scowled at me and when I didn't walk on by, she shrugged her broad shoulders and turned to Abe.

"Now, don't forget what I told you. Winter is round the corner and you remember what happened last year."

She rose from the bench and after giving me a forced smile, waddled off in the direction of the clock tower.

"Sorry about that, Abe. I hope I didn't interrupt anything important."

"Not at all, old boy. Join me in the stalls. The show is about to begin." He chuckled at his witticism. "Old fusspot. She means well but…"

I sat beside him and decided not to enquire as to what

happened last winter. The pigeon returned to peck warily at morsels around our feet.

"I have news," I began. "Your guess was spot on. Moule had sought refuge in Brick Lane. Brilliant of you to remember that detail."

"It was a guess. So, you did find him?"

"I did indeed. It wasn't easy, because most of those I asked seemed either not to know or were not prepared to give him away. Some barely spoke English, which didn't help matters."

"So, where exactly was he hiding?"

"He was holed up above a curry house, owned by his friend the former bus driver. The fellow now owns the restaurant. He seems to be quite well but scared to return home until he knows it's safe."

"Safe? Safe from what? Is someone after him?" Abe stared at me intently.

"Basically, he thinks the Home Office might be after him, as you put it. He went into hiding because he's afraid he could be served with a deportation order. It seems the *Windrush* business got to him in a big way."

"No!" Abe slapped his forehead and his mouth fell open in disbelief. The aperture revealed several gaps where teeth used to reside. "You disabused him, I hope. Doesn't he realise that shameful *Windrush* scandal has now blown over?"

"Except for the recriminations, of course. But yes, I think I've now convinced him that there's no longer any danger of him being sent back to Jamaica."

"But what on earth triggered that irrational thought?"

"I take it the subject never came up while you talked?"

"No, not once. I knew the bare facts of the case of course but never talked to him about it. Thought it tactless to do so."

231

"Perhaps you should have because to him his action wasn't in any way irrational. He was obviously short on detail about the current situation, but he did have some grounds to think he might be at risk. As I say, he took some convincing, but in the end, he decided to put his trust in what I told him."

"Does that mean he'll be returning to his flat soon?"

"He promised that he would be coming home today but I don't want to rush him. I'll see if I can visit him tomorrow. We have some important business to complete."

"Ah yes, the young lady's school project." Abe thrust his hands deep into his coat pocket. "Very important that."

"Well, it is to her," I replied, not knowing if he was being sarcastic.

"I'm no psychologist," Abe added, "but I think Moule sees her as a daughter substitute." He raised his eyebrows and said wistfully, "His own daughter ran out on him many years ago."

"I didn't know that. Poor chap."

A period of contemplative silence between us followed, until I looked at my watch.

"I'm glad to have found you today. I thought you'd want to know."

"Very considerate. Thank you, Mr Grant."

I stood up.

"Shall I say you'll be expecting to see him on the Common soon?"

"Yes, you do that. He'll know where to find me." A mischievous twinkle entered his eyes. "I hear you were set upon by ruffians when you left here the other day. Must keep your eyes open, old boy."

"So, word has got out," I laughed. "But I'll take your

advice for the future."

Abe was still chuckling as I strode off.

When I got back there was a message flashing on the house phone. I pressed the play button and heard Sonia's voice.

"I got no reply from your mobile, so I rang your son's land line. I'm home now if you want to call again."

So, I did that. She answered right away, and I told her about the mobile and then the good news about tracing Moule. She was not the kind of girl who gave much away through her expressions but for a moment, there was a spark of joy in her response. Tomorrow was Saturday, so I asked her if she would be prepared to go to Clapham in the morning. She agreed, so I said I would phone Moule immediately and see if that was convenient for him. If it was then I promised to call her back to arrange a mutually acceptable time to meet.

It was with an uneasy feeling of uncertainty that I keyed in Moule's mobile number. What if he had changed his mind? Suppose my warm words had cooled as soon as I had left and he was still hiding away in the sweatshop, swigging away at the rum?

He answered the call after three rings.

"Moule, it's George." I mentally crossed my fingers. "Are you at home?"

"Yes, mister Jarge," followed by a cackle, "I am back in my home and busy cookin' some proper Jamaican food. Iqbal's was okay but the wrong kind of savoury for me."

I gave a sigh of relief and laughed along with him.

"So, is it okay with you if Sonia and I visit you tomorrow with the finished manuscript?"

"Yes, man. That will be fine by me. Make it about ten

o'clock. I'm going out to buy some provisions and also to let Clapham know that Moule is back."

I agreed and then replaced the receiver.

Yes, Moule was truly back and what's more he sounded in fine spirit. But I stood there in thought for a while, conscious that something was not quite the same as before. Then it came to me. It was the voice. Either consciously or not, Moule had smoothed the edges from his raw Jamaican delivery. It was as if after his fright he deemed it prudent to sound less as if he had just landed on our shores. It was not quite the forced *Trevor McDonald* but something in between. I found this rather intriguing. Was the strong Jamaican accent sustained after more than sixty years merely a front, or was the now smoothed version the chameleon's new colour?

I went up to my room and was surprised to see June sleeping, fully dressed, on top of the bed covers. She woke as I crossed the room.

"Oh, George, this is awful. I never do this at home," she exclaimed.

"It's the putrid London air. Knocks you out. Have you been outside since I left?"

"Yes, I went for a stroll around Wandsworth. There are some lovely houses in the area."

"Very rich ones too. I don't know what Noel's mortgage is, but I expect he and Mary have stretched their budget to the limit."

"Don't forget she put a large lump sum in as a deposit when they bought the place." She swung her legs off the bed and straightened her dress.

"Ah yes, the legacy. That certainly helped."

"If only it helped in other ways," she said wistfully, and I knew instantly what she was alluding to.

"Now look, that is their business. If they choose not to have another child it's not for us to interfere. I'm sure that they will talk about it and ask your advice if they are trying and not succeeding. We must just be careful not to create any friction."

"I know all that, George but Alice is now eight, so the gap is widening all the time. Also, Mary is nearly forty. Also," she added in a whisper, "It might not be a matter of choice."

"Thirty-six is not nearly forty. You'll be saying next that I'm nearly eighty." I took my jacket off and hung it from the back of the door. "Anyway, do you want to hear about my afternoon?"

Whether she did or not I told her what I had been doing, if for no other reason than to change the subject that raised its head from time to time. Our one child had produced one grandchild and that simply was as it was.

We were reading in the sitting room when Mary arrived home with Alice. I put the newspaper down and stood up to give Alice a hug.

"June and I will be going back soon, so that you can reclaim your home," I said

"You're no trouble, George. It's been lovely having you both up here."

"Kind of you to say so but the oldies know when the time has come to move back."

"You're not old, Grandpa," Alice chirped up, "you're ancient!"

She giggled and ran out of the room as I feigned a monster, threatening to chase after her.

Noel returned an hour later, and I explained what we had

planned for tomorrow, adding that after all that had been settled there was nothing further to hold us in London. We had livestock to attend to and I had other essential paperwork to deal with.

But once again, fate had another plan in store for me.

Just before dinner I phoned Sonia and told her that Moule would see us at about ten. She agreed to be there at that time, and I reminded her to bring the finished document. As if she would forget! I said I would bring the bulky full draft version of the tape recordings. With those assurances, I went in to join the others.

It seemed like a last supper as we had planned to leave on an afternoon train the next day. Being a Saturday, there would be no commuters but not having booked ahead I knew the tickets would be expensive. Nevertheless, both June and I were conscious of overstaying our welcome. The five of us had a jolly dinner and afterwards I played a card game with Alice before she went up to bed.

I was at Moule's door before Sonia the next morning. There was a keen easterly wind blowing and heavy rain-bearing clouds overhead, so the walk to Clapham High Street was not as pleasant as usual. There was very little shelter over Moule's street entrance, so I stood in the doorway of the adjacent property and waited.

I didn't have long to wait. A bus pulled up a few yards down the road and the slim figure of Sonia jumped to the pavement. She was wearing a pale blue raincoat and had a school bag over her back. My own papers were in a Tesco's shopping bag that I had borrowed from Mary.

Sonia greeted me with a grin and apologised for keeping

me waiting. As she still held the key to Moule's flat she let us in. The broken stairway bulb had been replaced so the automatic light came on as we stepped inside.

At the top of the stairs, I knocked, and Sonia slipped the keys into a pocket. We heard his feet padding across the floor and then the door was flung open. Moule was in a freshly ironed Tower Isle shirt which hung loosely outside his green corduroys. As I had grown to expect, his feet were bare.

"Come in, people." He waved a welcoming hand and stepped back.

"Good morning, Moule," I said, and Sonia just said, "Hi."

Then, to my surprise and I expect also to Sonia's as well, he seized her in an embrace with his long, spidery arms.

"And a big welcome for young Sonia, my biographer," he said through his infectious laughter. I smiled at Sonia as she was released and saw that she was blushing.

"Well, Moule, it's all here." I pointed at the school bag. "Sonia's and your hard work, now just needs your seal of approval."

"I'm sure it will be fine, my friends. Just take your coats off, sit down and I'll get you some beautiful Blue Mountain coffee."

"Moule, do you mind if…?" Sonia began.

"Of course, my dear, you want a diet coke. You know where it is, so help yourself. I bought some more this morning."

He disappeared into the kitchen. I sat down and Sonia went to the fridge.

"How long will it take you to read two thousand words, Moule?" I shouted through to him.

"Without my spectacles, probably a week but with them on, I should manage it while you have your drink."

Five minutes later he brought through a wooden tray with two mugs of coffee. Sonia was already slurping from her bottle of diet coke. She had taken her manuscript from the school bag and now handed it to Moule. He made a fuss of finding his glasses, which he eventually located on top of the fridge.

"I've taken a copy," Sonia said, as Moule sat down near the window and pulled the A4 sheets from a brown envelope.

"You mean, in case I spill coffee on this one?" Moule chuckled.

I didn't know what Sonia was going to do while Moule read but I had brought a newspaper, which I pulled out of the shopping bag. Sonia seemed content just to sit, sip her drink and watch Moule as he surveyed her work.

I glanced up from the newspaper. "Moule, if there's anything that you think we've got wrong, or anything you don't like, just call out and we'll make an alteration."

"Okay, man." He carried on reading, with his glasses perched on the end of his nose and his lips moving. After forty minutes, when I was halfway through the paper, Sonia got up and went to the lavatory. Up to that point, Moule had not said a word. All we heard was the odd grunt, but I couldn't tell if it was a grunt of disapproval or one of agreement.

Another twenty minutes had passed, and I got up to take the coffee cup to the kitchen. I was beginning to wish we had left Moule to read through at his own pace and then come back later. Sonia joined me and we looked at each other, probably thinking the same thing, when there was sudden shout from the sitting room.

"You can come out now. I've reached the end."

I expect Sonia was more nervous than me about Moule's assessment of what was, essentially, her work. I felt a bit more phlegmatic. If he wanted her to make changes, so be it. My only problem was one of timing as I had agreed to take a train back home in the early evening.

"What do you think?" Sonia asked, trying very hard to look cool and dispassionate.

"You wrote all this?" Moule's long fingers flicked the pages.

"No, I just did the recording and made some notes. Mr Grant gave me a lot of advice on phrasing and things like that and he did the typing." She held up her damaged finger by way of explanation.

"Well Miss Sonia, I think it is brilliant." He removed his glasses. "I don't know who this reprobate is you are writing about, but he sounds like a rambunctious sort of a fellow."

Sonia's face was a mobile picture of fluctuating expressions. There was surprise, joy, disbelief and finally satisfaction, in a matter of seconds.

"You think it's okay then?"

"I think you have made a fine job of my life story and I wish you luck when you hand it in."

Moule knocked the loose pages into a block and reached out to give them back to her.

"So, no alterations or corrections?" I asked.

"None, but I am glad you cut out the bit about... you know?"

"We did tailor it for a young and impressionable audience." I winked at Sonia, and she tried to suppress a giggle. We both know that most of today's sixteen-year-olds are at least as worldly-wise as their adult mentors.

"You obviously noticed that we stopped at when you sailed from Jamaica," I said. "Sonia and I thought that was the best thing to do."

"I agree with you. My early life in England was not something I would want to share with the world. It was not always a happy time."

Sonia pushed the manuscript back into its envelope and then into her school bag, while I gathered my own papers.

"That's it then, Sonia. Good work," I said.

She was doing her best to look dispassionate about the whole situation.

Moule had stood up and was rubbing his eyes. "I expect you'll be going straight home now, Miss Sonia?"

"Yes. I'm meeting friends this afternoon, but I'll put this safely away first." She seemed unsure how to end this meeting and was obviously thinking it over, as she was pulling on her coat.

"Sonia, you have my wife's mobile number, if you need to contact me about anything?" I said.

"Yes, you gave it to me." She looked at Moule and said awkwardly, "Well, thanks for everything. It's been really cool."

Moule bounded forward and gave her another hug, followed by a loud kiss on the forehead. "My pleasure, darlin'. Now, you keep in touch, you hear?"

"I will." She grinned and then turned to me. "Goodbye, Mr Grant. And thank you."

I smiled at her as she turned to leave.

"Walk good, Miss Sonia," Moule called after her.

As the door closed behind her, I turned to Moule who was wiping his eyes with a large, red handkerchief.

"An interesting experience... for both of us," I commented.

"For *all* of us, man. I never thought I would be telling my back-story to a girl like that."

"It can't have been easy... at least, not to begin with. Then we might not have finished it if you had decided not to come back."

"For you I have that to thank," he said generously. "But I must admit, as soon as I returned to Clapham, I contacted my District councillor to hear what he had to say about how safe my position is."

"And presumably he confirmed what I said?"

"Yes, the Home Office will not be sending me back." He smiled broadly.

The moment had come. I couldn't put it off any longer. Before arriving at his flat that morning I had decided what I was going to ask him, and I knew it was not going to be straightforward. He was about to fetch my coat when I said, "Can you spare me a few more minutes?"

He stopped and gave me quizzical look. "Sure, man."

"My wife and I are going back home later today but before I go, I would very much like to hear the rest of your story. If you don't think it's too impertinent to ask, would you mind telling me what you did with your life after your father died? You see, we both left Jamaica at the same age and I know we took completely different paths, but my early years are still very much alive with me. So, if I leave here now and we never meet again, I will always wonder about how you coped after..."

His face betrayed no emotion as I spoke, and I guessed that I might have taken a step too far. What he had poured out to Sonia over the past few weeks must have been hard for him at the beginning but as he went on, it probably became a form of mental healing: a kind of closure. Maybe it was a purging of past demons at the same time as simply helping a schoolgirl with a classwork project. Now, here was I, a relative stranger prying further into his past, with only the flimsy mutual connection of having grown up in the same Caribbean island: he with nothing, from an impoverished beginning and me from a privileged, white background. He was the black son of a no-good truck driver and I the son of someone who once would have been referred to as a backra massa: a white boss's son. No wonder my sentence tailed off.

We stood facing each other for a few seconds, until he shrugged his shoulders and said, "Would you like a beer, Jarge?"

I can't describe what my face revealed at that moment, but I expect it was something akin to a welling up of relief, with maybe a smidgeon of joy. This fine upstanding ex-Rasta was not offended by my request. It was an acceptance of who I am and not of what I might have been perceived as representing.

"I would like that very much, Moule. Thank you."

He fetched a couple of Red Stripes from the fridge and prised off the caps.

"Sit down," he instructed as he handed me the bottle and, with a tentative grin, added, "maybe I should be asking you to give me your story. Mine is not so special, after my father died."

"Oh, compared with mine it is. My story is far too conventional. It follows a regular, middle-class pattern of boarding school, university, professional qualification and then working in different firms for the next thirty-five years.

Yours has probably never lost the flavour of the Caribbean, with a rich variety in the mix."

"I don't know about that, but I will tell you how it has been for me." He took a swig from the bottle and then wiped his mouth with the back of his hand. "But no notes this time."

"No notes."

He stared at the ceiling for a while as he arranged his thoughts.

"I have told Sonia about finding the money after my father's murder and what we decided to do about it. Mavis did what was necessary to get probate settled but the cash in the bag was never declared. As I said, regardless of how it was obtained, my father owed it to us. The money invested in the building society was transferred into my mother's name and later she bought the lease on this flat.

"I was getting on quite well at school by then, but I continued to sing with the small group, mostly in The Sun pub up the road but sometimes we played at other gigs. I enjoyed doing that and as our range of music changed with the times, so my interest in different styles grew. We started with skiffle but when that died in the early sixties, we went on to rock and roll and blues ballads. I also played the mouth organ so that came into the mix when I introduced some rock steady and ska."

"Did you ever think of going professional?" I interrupted.

"No, man, we were not that good, and I certainly wasn't such a great singer. We just had fun and people liked what we did. I told you I was a bit of a comedian. Well, I threw in some jokes as well. Yes, it was fun, and I kept up with those guys for many years."

"You were at the local secondary school for part of that

time. When did you leave?"

"I left when I was sixteen, so that was when my formal education ended. What knowledge I have acquired through the rest of my life has been through reading, observing and self-teaching."

"You've lived here for over sixty years. What was Clapham like in the early days?"

"Very different from today, like everything else. You will have noticed the very smart houses around the Common and that will tell you that this was once a much-favoured borough. It went through a bad spell, but it is back again with a new generation of people with money.

"When we arrived here it was only eleven years since the end of the war and a lot of the damage had still not been repaired. I believe as many as ten German bombs dropped on the Common alone and back in 1956, you could still see the craters. The air raid shelter near Grafton Square used to be a favourite place for kids to play and so was the bombed-out church near The Sun pub. There were a lot of shops and I remember one called Parson's Corner. Not knowing anything about corner shops I thought that it was somewhere the vicar lived." He cackled at that memory. "Yes, much has changed since then and much of my memory of it has as well."

"Were there many other West Indians living in Clapham in the early days?"

"Very few and in truth and in fact there are not that many here today."

"So, when you left school, what did you do?"

"Man, I've done all kinds of things. I was too young to take a driving test, even though I had learnt to drive a truck in Jamaica, so I did odd jobs around the place. I was a strong boy, so I helped at the pub, you know, moving barrels, getting coal in for the fire... you could have coal fires in those days... and washing dishes. I also did some deliveries for the butcher and for a few weeks I did street sweeping for the council. There was quite a lot of unemployment at that time and not everyone wanted to employ a black boy, so it wasn't always easy. It helped though that I was quite well-known in the district and people knew they could trust me."

"I suppose your inherited money helped at times when you were not in work?"

"This is true. Also, my mother didn't need to work but she chose to do so. She carried on at the laundry for a few years and then did shop assistant work in the High Street. She was also a volunteer at the church helping to keep it clean, preparing flowers and that sort of thing."

"You were never a church goer?"

"No, my mother was always disappointed about that, but I had seen too much hypocrisy in the Church of England to want to be part of it."

"Is that why you adopted the Rastafarian beliefs?"

"No, that was some years later, after my mother moved away. I don't think she would have approved." He smiled at some distant recollection. "For a long time, I held no faith, except in my own desire to make something of my life. You know, some way of cleansing my body and soul of the wrongdoings of my father. They never caught the people who killed him, but you are probably right that it was some kind of revenge killing. It took two years for them to catch up with him, but you can be sure that the drug gangs would have Yardie connections in London. But I have to tell you that for many months after they killed him my mother and I were scared they would come after us too. You know… for the money. But that is all long in the past and I am no longer bothered by those unanswered questions.

"As soon as I reached seventeen, I took driving lessons and then passed my test. You might think that there was not much purpose in doing that as we had no car and I was too young to think of a public transport job but at that time, I was always in a hurry. For two years I did odd jobs, working mostly for Wandsworth Council, getting to know my neighbourhood and its people better. Then when the time came, I took and passed my test to drive heavy vehicles. I suppose this is one good thing I inherited from my father — a love of driving big vehicles. When at last I got a job as a bus driver I was not only one of the few black people driving red double-deckers but also the youngest. My mother was very proud of that fact.

"It was while I was stationed at the Hammersmith bus depot that I met Marie. Up to then I had not had many long-time girlfriends but when I saw her, I knew she was the one for me. It was difficult at first because she was going out with a fellow in the accounts office and as he was a white guy and she was a white girl, I thought I didn't have much chance. But as she worked in the canteen, I saw her every day and began chattin' her up." Moule began to chuckle, presumably at the audacity of his younger self.

"How did she respond?" I prompted.

"At first she did not seem to be interested. She was a pretty, white girl and she was accustomed to all kind of comments from people that ate in the canteen. But one day, I was brave enough to ask her to come to the pub near where she lived and where I knew there was going to be some live music. I don't know if her boyfriend knew about it at the time, but she accepted, because she knew someone in the group that was playing.

"We met up at the pub and we sat and listened to the music for a while as she drank Bacardi and rum, and I had a beer. We didn't talk much, and I noticed some looks from people in the place, because at that time there was some strong disapproval of white girls going with black boys.

"It was the middle sixties by then and every amateur pop group was trying to sound like the Beatles but to my surprise, this lot was trying to copy reggae, but they had no front man. You remember how it is when you are trying to impress a girl? You will do something that you would not normally go out of your way to do, just to make her think more highly of you as a person. So, what did I do? I put my beer down, pushed my way through the crowd and after the end of a number I went up and spoke to the lead guitarist. I knew the words of several of the popular reggae songs of the day, including a couple of Bob Marley numbers, so suddenly I was fronting the group and belting out the songs that they had rehearsed. I even had my mouth organ in my pocket, so threw in some of that as backing when the words dried up. You know, man, after a few minutes of this we really had the place rocking."

"And was Marie impressed?"

"I tell you, after that performance she was smitten. I had taken a gamble and it had paid off. She dropped the poor fellow she was going out with and started to go steady with me. He took it bad though and we had a bit of a punch-up at the back of the depot. I didn't want to hurt him, but I was a big, strong boy at that time, and he really should not have laid down the challenge. After I had landed a few blows, we called it quits and even shook hands. He knew he had been beaten but he was a decent fellow and went on to achieve managerial status at another bus depot in London."

He stopped talking suddenly and looked down at the empty bottle in front of him.

"I don't know about you, man but this is thirsty work. You like another Red Stripe?"

I accepted and he rose stiffly to get two more from the fridge. I took the opportunity to glance at my watch. At this rate I would be missing lunch and, unless June had Moule's mobile number, she would not be able to contact me. He came back and plonked the bottles on the table.

"Presumably you took Marie home to meet Mavis?" I asked.

"I most certainly did, and I could see she was impressed." He took a long gulp of beer.

"Your mother approved then?"

Moule looked blankly at me for a second and then roared with laughter.

"No, I mean Marie was impressed. She was impressed at where we lived. A black boy and his mother living in a flat on the High Street in Clapham! She probably thought we lived in a mud hut on the Common. Yes, Jarge, she was impressed."

"But your mother…?"

"Oh, she was polite as she always was, but I could tell she had reservations. I don't know why but she was never very warm towards Marie, even after we married the next year and had a child. I think it was the old throwback of black and white mixing. She was old-fashioned in that way."

"So, you married Marie. You must have been very young."

"I was twenty-two when we married in the registry office,

and she was a year older than me. She moved into the flat with us and slowly my mother accepted the fact that she was no longer number one in my affections."

I couldn't help glancing around the room and speculating as to how this threesome, plus baby, would have rubbed along together.

"But she must have welcomed the fact that she had a grandchild to dote on?"

"Yes, there is no doubt my daughter's birth gave her great joy but at the same time, there was friction as well. Some grandmothers can't help making suggestions about how to bring up a grandchild. They always think they know best."

"And your wife resented this?"

"It is true to say that she did. My wife, Marie, was still working up to when the baby was born, and in those days, there were no long periods of maternity leave. So, as soon as she could she went back to work, while my mother, who by then had left the laundry, looked after the baby. Of course, when Marie returned home, she took over and my mother found it difficult to disappear into the background."

"How long did this situation continue for?"

"I guess it came to boiling point when my daughter, Selma, was about three years old." Moule paused for a period of reflection before continuing. "I can freely admit that it was partly my fault. I was still playing in bands and more and more into reggae music and copying the style of Bob Marley. Some people even said I favoured Marley in looks and maybe that went to my head, because that was when I looked into the cult of the Rastafari. I began smoking ganja, selecting my food with care and attending chanting and discussion meetings. It was both a religious and a political movement and for nearly ten years I embraced it and all its beliefs. Well, not quite all, because I had no desire to go back to Africa." He glanced at me and smiled ruefully.

"And this had a disruptive effect on your family life?"

"It did indeed. Marie never would have anything to do with the Rastafari cult and my mother thought I was a devil worshiper. When I think about it now, I don't know how we all stuck together for so long. But then, in the early eighties the movement almost came to an end with the death of the Emperor Haile Selassie and then Bob Marley. I can't remember which came first but it was like the puncturing of a balloon and for a while I went into a kind of mourning. This proved to be the final straw for my mother, and she announced to me one day that she had obtained a passport and was returning to Jamaica. She was about sixty then and she said she wanted to spend her final days in her own country and with her true family. I found this hurtful but what she meant was, with her daughters and five other grandchildren she had never seen."

"Were both your sisters married?"

"One of them was but the other lived with a man many years older. He had money, so she was okay. My mother arranged to go and live with my married sister who was still in Oracabessa. My grandfather had died by then and my grandmother was not too well, so that was another reason for Mavis to go.

"I was very sad when she packed up and left, because we had been through so much together over the years and I think when the time came, she also was sad to leave me, but I know there was little love between her and Marie, so I suppose the parting was inevitable. One kind thing she did though before she left; she made the flat over in my name and I still have the legal documents in my drawer over there. She also left me some of the money in the building society account, which was a great help to me in hard times."

"Was she happy to be back in Jamaica?"

"Yes, she was. She loved the grandchildren, and she nursed my grandmother until she died a few months after her return to the island. They sold her parents' house in Oracabessa and invested the money in a laundry." Moule chuckled. "My mother had a lot of experience in that line of business."

"I presume that you never saw your mother again after she returned to Jamaica?"

"That is so and that was a cause of great unhappiness for me. I never had a passport to travel, and she had no desire to return to England. She was happy enough with my sister and her grandchildren." Moule sighed. "Yes, it was sad in a way, but it was a natural parting and we carried on writing until she died in 1992. About once a year we spoke on the phone, so we had some contact up to the end."

"How did she die? She can't have been very old."

"You know, I never did discover my mother's year of birth, but I think she was about twenty-five when I was born. That would make her about seventy-three when she died. It was a fever that took her in the end."

"Is she buried in Oracabessa?"

"No, she wanted to be buried near where her own parents lie, so they took her over to Stewart Town for the service and burial. It's quite a long journey across the North coast but that was where the old people originated from."

"Meanwhile, you and your wife and child stayed on here. Did your mother's absence ease the tension in the house?"

"It should have but I was still going through a bad spell. I think the smoking of weed upset my judgment and Marie was finding that difficult to live with. She put up with my goings on for many years, but all the time Selma was suffering from her parents' rows. I was still driving the buses, but I was also doing things like modelling and writing poetry in my spare time. It can't have been easy for them."

"Modelling?"

"I was an artists' model," he smiled shyly, "in the nude. There are probably pictures of a younger and more handsome Moule hanging on walls in homes and galleries around the country today."

"Well, at least the owners wouldn't recognise you now… with your clothes on."

"Not just that, man. Many parts of me now sag where once there was a good strong body." He laughed loudly and I gained the impression that he was rather enjoying talking about this dissipated period of his life. It was almost as if he were distancing himself from it all and expounding on someone else's past.

"You wrote poetry too?"

"Yes, but it was mostly while my mind was under the influence of ganja. Some of it was good enough to be published but I think now that it was nonsense and somehow publishers were fooled into thinking that it had deep meaning, coming as it did from a member of the Rastafari sect."

"Have you kept any of your poems?"

"Not many, because I now find that period of my life painful." He studied his nails. "Those poems and all the other things going on at the time cost me my marriage. When Selma was about twelve, Marie took up with a man who worked in the construction industry. He wasn't the first one but this one was serious, and I knew it was over for me when she announced she and this fellow were going to emigrate to Canada. So, she left me and took Selma with her. She wrote once from Toronto, and she enclosed a few words from Selma but apart from a card at Christmas that was the last I heard of them."

"You mean, you don't even know where your daughter is now?"

"No but she would be over fifty now and if she wanted to contact her old father, she knows where I live."

"Did your mother know about the break-up of your marriage?"

"Yes, she knew but she also knew the reasons why. Even from Jamaica she scolded me, like I was a small boy again. But what was done, was done. But I believe she kept up with Selma up to the year she died."

It was growing late into the afternoon, and I was aware that June and I had a train to catch soon after five, but Moule's story had so gripped my imagination that I found it difficult to draw it to a close. I had never expected such poignancy in this man's past and now, I just wanted to hear of something that would lift the gloom. He appeared now to be such an open, generous and genial soul that something must have gone right in the end.

"Knowing something about you now, you must have straightened your life out somehow," I said. "Was there a cathartic moment?"

"Jarge, I tell you, many things in my miserable life will never be straight but I did change the way I lived. It was too late to get my wife and daughter back, but I stopped going to

Rastafari meetings and I cut out the smoking. All I didn't cut was my hair. By the time I cleaned up my living I was already well-known in the borough, if not for the right reasons but I then I changed something else." He leaned towards me and said in a conspiratorial stage whisper, "I became a *character*. I made myself into the Grand Moule. The Grand Moule of Clapham!"

He slapped his thigh, threw back his head and shrieked with laughter. I smiled back at this extraordinary man and knew instinctively that with that comment he had drawn a line under his story. It was surely time for me to go.

"But maybe someone who is also stuck in the time warp of old Jamaica?" I said, as I stood and slowly straightened my back.

"Exactly right, my man. You can take the boy away from Jamaica, but you can never take Jamaica away from the man." He winked. "But you must never tell anybody about Moule's secrets."

"I understand."

He followed me to the door, and I thanked him for confiding so much. It was the closing of a chapter, although I had not really questioned myself as to why it was so important to achieve such a closure. Maybe it was just my tidy mind, not liking to live with loose ends. Maybe. But still I just could not get rid of a small worm of doubt that a scintilla of the story was still missing. Could there have been yet another reason for Moule to create for himself a new personality?

Moule opened the door, and the stair light came on. I thanked him for the beer and prepared to step onto the landing.

"I have told you everything, Jarge but I know nothing of your life." He stood back to let me pass. "I don't even know where you went to school in Jamaica. I suppose it was somewhere near where you lived in Clarendon?"

"No, when the local primary school closed there was nowhere local for my parents to send me, so I started boarding at de Carteret. I was only aged seven when I went. I have a photograph of me standing with my father on the day…"

I turned to face him and then stopped abruptly and stared. Rarely have I seen a man's face change so dramatically. One moment he was beaming, his wide-mouthed, tooth-flashing smile and in an instant, it had changed, almost to a look of horror as he took a step back. It was as if I had slapped him hard on his woolly cheek.

"You never told me you was at de Carteret," he said accusingly.

"I'm sorry. It didn't seem important." I frowned at him, puzzled. "I didn't think it necessary to stop the flow of your story. Why does it…?"

"I'm sorry but you mus' go now." Breathing heavily, he almost pushed me through the door and as it closed, I distinctly heard him mutter, "Grant."

I stood on the landing for nearly a minute, until the light timer clicked off. As I moved slowly forward it came on again and I proceeded to descend the stairs, my mind in turmoil of speculation. All the way back to Wandsworth I tried to analyse what it was that I had said or done that had resulted in such a sour parting. But all I could think of was the mention of where I was at school until 1956. Perhaps he still held a feeling of resentment towards all that DC represented, after the wrong that had been done to him. Or perhaps I was somehow the embodiment of the privilege bestowed on those who were taught on the other side of the dividing wall. No, it was all too sudden. Also, from what I had learnt of his personality over the past weeks, Moule was not the kind of person to bear such a chip on his shoulder. It was too long ago for such resentment still to fester and I truly believed that his was a generous and forgiving nature. He had proved this through his declared feelings towards his departed family.

It was that scintilla thing again and it was continuing to bug me.

I was still turning these matters over in my mind when I arrived at the house to find June in a state of controlled agitation.

"George, the train is due to leave in an hour. Where have you been?"

"There's plenty of time."

I prepared to run upstairs to pack my few possessions, when she shouted after me, "I've packed everything. Just bring the cases down."

Noel and Mary appeared as I brought our two cases down to the hallway. We said farewell to each other, and I think I made some comment about growing roots in their house. Sadly, Alice was not there, having gone to play with a friend, so we left hurriedly to find a taxi.

We arrived at Charing Cross Station in plenty of time for the train, but the rush had all been in vain. We came to a sudden halt as we entered the station concourse, and I dropped the cases by my feet. Even though it was the weekend, there was a swarm of agitated people static between the platform gates and the entrance. There was an announcement over the public address system, but we only picked up a few words.

I turned to the woman beside me and asked, "What's happening?"

"There's a fire on the line just outside the station and it looks like nothing's moving in or out." She was trying to placate a fractious small child, so I thanked her and turned to June.

"If you could just stay with the cases, I'll try to find out what chance there is of a train out of here tonight."

"George! You can't leave me here in this throng with the cases," she wailed.

I agreed with her, and we moved over to a less crowded side of the concourse. I then went off in search of an authoritative piece of information. I found a harassed Network Rail staff member, who was explaining that it was unlikely the fire would be under sufficient control for trains to leave the station that night. I fought my way back to where I had left June and relayed the message.

"Well, we can either spend the night in a hotel near here, or go back to Wandsworth," she said. "Having said goodbye, I really don't know how we can just turn up on their doorstep again."

I agreed and we were just wondering if we should try the Charing Cross Hotel, when June's mobile stared to chirp. It was Mary, who had just heard the news about the fire and was asking what we planned to do. When June said we were going to stay in a hotel overnight, Mary instantly overruled her mother-in-law and insisted that we return and stay another night with them. Apart from the saving in the cost of a central London hotel, she said, Alice was disappointed at not having said goodbye to her grandparents.

So, that apparently was settled. We turned around to leave, but when we saw the queue for taxis, we decided to have an early meal at a nearby Italian restaurant. As my stomach was now reminding me that it had missed lunch, I agreed that this was an excellent plan.

Two hours later, with dusk now heavily overshadowing London, we arrived back in Wandsworth.

Deciding not to unpack anything, we just took out our night clothes and washbags and I was about to take these upstairs when Noel called after me.

"Dad, your man Moule was on the phone about an hour ago. He sounded very upset that he had missed you."

I stopped on the stairs and asked over my shoulder, "Moule and I have said goodbye to each other. Did he say what he wanted to talk about?"

"No but I think you should call him back tonight. He made it sound as if it was urgent that he talks to you."

"I will but it's odd that he called here." I carried on up the stairs. "He has your mother's phone number."

Back downstairs, I borrowed June's mobile and pressed in Moule's number. He answered so quickly that I got the impression he had been hanging by, waiting for a reply. By then I was quite expecting some kind of apology for his terse send-off in the afternoon, so I was not surprised on hearing the semblance of contrition in his voice.

"Jarge, thank you for callin' me back. Look, it's important I talk to you again. There is something I have to tell you. It's burning a hole in me head, so I mus' get it out." He had slipped back into the strong patois.

"Okay but can't we talk about it over the phone?"

"No, no," he pleaded, "I have to look you in the eye when we talk. It's not something I can discuss on the telephone. I am jus' overjoyed that I caught you still in London an' I'm sorry at how we parted this afternoon. If I see you, I can explain."

I sighed but decided not to go into why we were still in London. I was wondering now how we would ever get away from the place. But at least visiting Moule again early the next day would give Charing Cross ample time to clear the line.

When I went to tell the family what I had committed myself to do, I deemed it no more than a minor nuisance.

I was wrong about that. If I had been given a thousand guesses, I still would not have been any nearer the mark.

CHAPTER 13

As I trudged off on the familiar route to Clapham High Street, I had no clue as to what was on Moule's troubled mind. No, not quite true. I had an inkling in that something in our parting words had suddenly and unexpectedly thrown him into a state of mental anguish. Or maybe a kind of panic. But what I was unable to do was to place that clue into the context of anything we had discussed over the past weeks.

So, when I rang his bell on that breezy late October morning, I had the feeling I was about to delve into the unknown. Moule greeted me solemnly at the top of the stairs and invited me in. I took off my coat and hung it on the back of the door.

"Please," he said, pointing to one of the armchairs. He sat in the other one facing me and for a few moments we stared at each other speculatively.

"Would you like a coffee, Jarge?"

He made to stand again but I declined the offer. I was keen for him to get to the point of this emergency visit.

"I must apologise again for being so... *dramatic*... but there is something I have to know for now and all time or I shall never have any peace of mind. I could not let you go home before I know the truth."

I felt for that moment as if I were a naughty schoolboy, summoned to the Head's study to be reprimanded for some perceived misdemeanour. As a result, I didn't quite know where to put my hands. In the end I linked my fingers, placed them across my stomach and then leant back in the chair.

"Well, I hope I can help, Moule," I said tentatively. "The train was cancelled yesterday, so you were lucky to catch me."

He nodded several times, as if taking in my simple statement. He then launched straight into his.

"As you left here yesterday, you said you had attended de Carteret School in Mandeville." I grunted in agreement. "Well, this might seem a funny question for you, Jarge but were there other boys at the school at that time by the name of Grant?"

I was expecting a fast ball from him but this one just looped across to me so benignly, that I was able to play it with ease.

"Yes, there were three of us. Why do you ask?"

"Three of you? You were related?" He had ignored my question.

"In my last year at DC, I was there with my younger brother and a cousin. My cousin was about my age."

"But your brother was younger," he said, and I noted that he was breathing slowly and deeply, as if trying to keep control in a potentially difficult situation.

"He's a couple of years younger. He'd been sent to DC when he was eight. When we came to England in fifty-six, he went to primary school for a year before moving on to the same boarding school as me. After university, he qualified as a doctor and then he emigrated to Canada. He's still there today. Where's this leading?"

Moule wasn't listening. He appeared to have no interest in my younger brother and his progress. Instead, he seemed to be making some kind of mental calculation.

"How about your cousin?" His voice sounded strained.

"We were very close, not only in age but in temperament. He was a far better sportsman than me though and was really good at cricket. If things had turned out differently, I think he could have played for the West Indies."

"You mean if he had been black?" Moule asked in the same quiet voice.

"Well, maybe that would have helped but I actually meant if he had lived."

It still pained me that my favourite cousin had died so young, and I looked down at my hands for just a second. If I had been distracted any longer than that I would have missed Moule's expression. From one of anxiety, it had now taken on the hue of someone in deep despair. He had the look of a man whose worst fears had all been bundled together and dumped on his doorstep.

If I had been puzzled when I arrived at Moule's flat that morning, I was now in an entirely different state of mind. I was completely disorientated. I sensed a catastrophic revelation coming from the man but at the same time, I was defenceless in my unpreparedness. All I could do was wait for the dam to burst.

I didn't have long to wait.

"For the past sixty-two years I have lived with the memory of a great wrong that I have committed," he began sombrely. "There are not many days that I do not think about it. It continues to haunt me day and night. It don't matter how many layers of pretence or of camouflage that I cover myself in, the pain remains deep inside. I live with this because it changed the course of my life and made me prisoner in my own being."

Moule had begun talking to me slowly and quietly but gradually, he began slipping away from his audience. I could sense it. He was beginning to talk to himself, about his former self. It was clear that the man was about to prise open a wound that, by his own acceptance, had barely healed over more than sixty years. He was beginning the process of stripping away the persona he had created in order to recondition his life. I was mesmerised.

"I have spoken of the times that I strayed as a young boy into places where I should not have been. It was trespassing but as I was doing no harm to people or property; it was not a crime. Once I picked up a little toy car, but the owner of that toy would not have missed it. His parents could have bought him a dozen more like that and not felt any loss of money. To me though, it was the only store-bought toy I ever owned. I also stole mangos from other people's trees that they would not have missed and sometimes went onto Kirkvine land. But even on that day, when I went up to de Carteret's shooting range and dug out the bullets from the wood, I was doing no harm."

At that point he did look up at me for a second. I simply stared back at him, unblinking.

"That man didn't have to set the dog on me. I ran like a thief runs from the scene of his crime, even though no crime had been committed. When the dog bit me I went down on the red earth, but I did not cry out. When I shook the dog off and saw the man running towards me with a big stick, I got up and ran again. The dog had a piece of my pants in its mouth and was shaking it like a rat, while the man cursed him and told him to go on after me. I jumped over the stone wall and did not stop until I reached home. Blood was flowing and the pain was bad but still I did not cry. But all the while my mother was cleaning up around the teeth marks and stopping the blood, another kind of pain overcame me. It was a pain of shame and — I didn't know the word then — indignation - at the humiliation of what had happened to me. A man had set a fierce dog on me because I had strayed onto land that was the territory of the sons of rich people. Even when the dog let go of me that man was urging it to go and kill me like the rat it thought it was shaking. It was only then that I cried but it was tears of humiliation that I was shedding and not from physical pain.

"So, when a young boy is driven to those lengths of resentment, all he can think about is revenge." He suddenly looked up again and focused on my face. "Revenge is a powerful emotion, Jarge, especially when it seizes the mind of an ignorant, twelve-year-old, black boy. I had been treated like a piece of bagasse that comes out of the sugar mill when all the juice is crushed out of the cane and not as a human being. So, yes, I was seeking vengeance."

I tried to swallow but found that there was no saliva in my mouth. It was slowly beginning to dawn on me that Moule was about to reveal what I had always sensed was a missing slice of the early life he had recounted to Sonia. It gave me the strange sensation of being a voyeur, peering in at someone's private grief and inner torment but still, I could not imagine what might come next.

"You might be right about my father deciding to go to England because he thought he was in danger from the drug dealers, but you were not right that it was the only reason. I have said that he used me and my future as the reason, but I never said why, and I never intended to tell anyone… until last night. Until you told me where you went to school. I might have told you some story about my education and a better life in England for all of us but that was just a cover-up. No, the real reason was that he was protecting me from the forces of Jamaican law. Or so he told me and Mavis and, at that age, I had no reason to doubt the genuineness of what he was telling me. He convinced me that I would be locked up or worse if we stayed."

Although I sat several feet away from Moule, it was quite clear to me that his eyes were misting. He put his head back and stared at the ceiling, perhaps in an attempt to hide it but behind the dark, heavy eyelids he was crying. The big man was silently weeping.

He moved his mouth several times as if attempting to form the next words he had to say. Then at last they came.

"The fact is that I killed someone," he announced through a voice cracked with pent-up emotion.

I stopped breathing for what seemed like several seconds. Moule had not looked at me when he made the fateful statement, but he now pulled out his large, red handkerchief and wiped his eyes.

I didn't even think about what I was doing. I just got out of the chair, went into the kitchen and turned on the cold tap. I splashed water on my face and then drank from my cupped hand. I dried my face and filled a glass with water. Going back into the sitting room I handed it to him. He silently mouthed his thanks and then drank. He lowered the glass very gently to the floor and took a few more seconds to compose himself.

"I did not know how to express my feelings or how to extract vengeance for what had happened at the school grounds but a couple of days after the dog bite, I went back there in the daytime. I didn't know what I was going to do but I just knew that if I was there, then something would happen to give me a chance for revenge.

"I had come across country through the bush and now I was at the bottom of the long, stony driveway that led up to the headmaster's house. The drive had a boundary wall with a lot of loose rocks and at the end there was and maybe still is, a very tall tree. I can see the scene now as if it was yesterday. As I stood by the wall, just waiting and watching, three boys came down the hill path from the school. When they reached the tree, they saw me and stopped."

Moule covered his face in his brown, wrinkled hands and I could see perspiration glistening between his splayed fingers.

I found myself staring at him with such an intensity that my eyes began to ache. My heart was beginning to beat so fast and hard that I thought I could hear it. It was not that warm in the room, but I could also feel a line of sweat pulsing from my brow. I believe there are times in one's life when a situation is so excruciatingly traumatic that one loses a sense of the present: of what one might call the *here and now*. I have never fainted but twice come close to it. The place where you are situated begins to rotate, the pulse beats faster, and head and hands perspire for no rational reason. You want to grip onto something, anything, to stop from falling over. This suddenly was one of those occasions. I felt I was surely going to faint, because suddenly I knew what was coming. I knew it as surely as if I were telling the story myself.

But I didn't faint. I couldn't. I had to concentrate on what Moule was saying.

"I did the only thing I could do to express my anger. I started to shout at them. I used all the cuss words I knew and I could not stop. Then one of the boys, the one in the middle of the three, shouted something back at me and so it developed, until… until the boy in the middle of the three bent down, and picked up a stone. I called him a bad word and then… and then he threw the stone.

"It was a good throw from about ten yards, maybe less and it hit me on the arm. It pained me, so without any hesitation or thought, I picked up the same stone and pitched it back at him. But even as I let go of that small rock, I knew I had done wrong, and in that instant, I willed him to dive out of the way. He had to move. The boys to the left and the right shifted like lightning, but the thrower never budged." Moule's voice had reduced to a hoarse whisper. "*He never budged.* The boy never moved an inch. He stood still as a statue and took the stone right in the middle of his forehead. If I was throwing down a mango, I could not have made a straighter or stronger throw."

I watched Moule in open-mouthed awe and mopped the dampness from my forehead with a handkerchief. He did not appear to have noticed my state of distress, maybe because he was too absorbed in his own. And in any event, at that point he would not have understood my reaction.

"The boy fell to the ground like a ripe breadfruit and blood was pumping from his head. I just had time to see his friends go over to pick him up before I turned and ran. I should have been at school, so I couldn't run home. Instead, I just ran and ran until I dropped into a gully with all my breath gone. When I looked up after a while, a jackass was standing over me and chewing grass."

I wanted to say something but could not find any words.

Moule was visibly shaking now and it took a few seconds

for him to bring himself under control before continuing.

"A couple of days later my father told me that people from the school were out looking for the boy who threw the stone. I don't know how but I could tell that he knew it was me. Maybe he had checked on the school attendance." Moule stopped and gave me a haunted stare. "Later the same day he said to me that the boy I had hit had died. He said the head wound had caused a bleed on the brain. From that moment he was telling me that he knew it was me and that, as a murderer, the police would be after me. If I was to escape justice the only thing to do was for him to take me away from Jamaica."

At last, I found my voice.

"But your mother..." I managed to say. "I thought she worked at the school. She would have known that..."

"No, she had given up that job some months before. But she had a good friend up at the sanatorium and that person confirmed that the boy had died." He stared at me with a blazing intensity. "Mr Grant, I have never told anyone about this but you... you deserve to know. It is right that I tell you."

I blinked at him in an uncontrolled manner and my mouth gaped, because even though my brain was in turmoil at that moment, I was suddenly fully aware of what had really happened.

It came like the turning on of a light switch. I had been slow, because of the stunning effect of Moule's previous revelations. But now I knew. My God, the poor man had lived all these years under a monstrous misapprehension. Moule had just opened his mouth to continue, when I cut him short.

"Moule, you must know the name of the boy who died."

"Yes, it's the same as you. His name was Grant." He swallowed and closed his eyes. "I killed your cousin and have lived with that sin for all these years. I can never ever expect forgiveness for this crime. But neither could I let you go away without telling you what I had done. I could not die with such a sin untold."

The tide had now passed over me and the flood waters were rapidly receding. The drama of his long-held secret and the painful confession had hit me like a bullet, but I now felt completely calm, as I replied to the distressed man in front of me.

"No, Moule, you didn't kill my cousin." I waited for his reaction, but he didn't seem to have heard me. "You didn't kill Ralph. Do you understand?"

He looked up slowly and focused on my face.

"My cousin died of encephalitis in the DC sanatorium. He died on the day before you threw that stone."

There was silence and for several seconds all that could be heard was the sound of passing traffic below. Then, slowly, he shook his head in incomprehension.

"How can you know this?" His brain was coming slowly into sync and adapting to the sudden and extraordinary reversal of the narrative. "I saw the stone hit him. I saw him go down. I saw the blood. How can you tell me that he died the day before?"

"I was as angry as you were on that day," I said, "but for a very different reason. If they had got Ralph to Mandeville hospital sooner his life might have been saved. I didn't know that until much later but at the time I was simply angry and resentful that he had died. He was only twelve and should have had a long and rewarding life ahead of him. He was my cousin and my best friend."

Moule was peering at me in a puzzled way, as if seeing

me for the first time, or perhaps suddenly seeing me as a different person altogether.

I stood up slowly and looked towards the window, where a weak ray of sunshine was oozing through the leafless trees opposite and penetrating the unwashed panes and then into Moule's flat. I turned my gaze to the deflated man slumped on the chair opposite.

"Moule, put on your glasses and come over here." I walked over to the window but at first, he did not react. "Come here and bring your glasses. I want to show you something."

He did as he was told, mechanically picking his spectacles from the table as he shuffled over on his bare feet. When he was about three feet from me, I asked him to come closer. I think he believed I was going to ask him to observe something outside, so I told him to put the glasses on and look at me.

"When I was younger," I began, "my hair line was lower and very often the hair flopped forward over my brow. Now the hair has receded and turned grey with age and in certain lights there is a feature that can easily be seen when you look closely. Look closely now."

I bent forward and turned my head slightly to one side so that the sun might cast a shadow.

"Do you see it?" I asked, as I adjusted my eyes to watch for his reaction. "Do you see the indentation on my forehead?"

Moule leaned forward slowly and his eyes narrowed as they focused on my face.

The reaction was dramatic. His eyes flew open wide and, as if not believing what he was seeing, he tentatively placed a long finger against the mark on my forehead: the dent that I see every morning when I look in the shaving mirror.

"No!" he exclaimed and then jumped back like a man who

270

has suffered an electric shock. "No, it cannot be. Not you?"

He staggered backwards until his body came to rest against the window frame. There is no doubt that at that moment, Moule believed he was looking at a ghost.

"I told you, I was deeply upset by my cousin's death, so when you started shouting at us, I simply reacted and yelled back. Then, the instant it got out of hand and I threw the stone, like you, I knew I had done a terrible wrong. So, I simply stood and took my punishment. That might sound crazy but it's true. You saw it. Like a statue, you said. Maybe it's as well that I didn't move, because if I had then I might have lost an eye. But you certainly didn't kill me, Moule. I'm still here. I'm still alive.

"When the headmaster heard what had happened, he was about to send out a search party to catch the boy who did it, but I owned up and said I threw the stone first. He would have beaten me but then he said I had been punished enough. The head wound soon healed but the scar remained as a shameful reminder of what I had done. And it's still there to remind me today."

We stared at each other for several seconds, perhaps both taking in the enormity of what had happened between us. Not sixty-two years ago but just in the past few minutes.

"So, Moule, we have both born our scars all these years," I said.

I don't think he heard much of my speech, because he appeared stunned all the time I was talking, but when I had finished, something extraordinary happened. He suddenly lurched away from the window frame and stumbled forward at me and, for an instant, I thought he was going to strike me.

But, no, he did quite the opposite. I was suddenly engulfed

in those long arms and as his tear-stained cheek pressed against mine, I smelled the musky odour of whatever he treated his hair with. The big former Rastafarian was sobbing and murmuring something unintelligible. It sounded like a prayer.

After a while I gently eased him away, saying a few meaningless consoling words. The sobbing ceased and the big, red handkerchief came out again. He stood back, proud and erect now, staring at me and nodding gently with a beatifical smile across his full lips. He didn't say anything, because I think just then he had lost the power of speech.

"Moule," I said, swallowing hard and returning his smile, "Sonia tells me that there is a bottle of twelve-year-old Appleton in a cupboard somewhere here."

He stuffed the handkerchief into a pocket and licked his dry lips slowly before replying.

"Jarge," he replied hoarsely, "there surely is. There surely is."

For the second day in succession, I missed having a solid lunch.

EPILOGUE

I last spoke with Moule two weeks before Christmas. With his release, as he put it, he had applied for a passport and this had arrived, with no questions asked, in time for him to arrange a trip to Jamaica. He had contacted his sister in Oracabessa and she had appeared delighted at the prospect of a reunion. He was due to fly two days after we spoke. He also planned to try to trace his daughter, Selma, when he returned from Jamaica.

I was about to end the call when he said that he had to confess something to me. Something he called a *foolishness* on his part. Amongst the pile of unopened junk mail inside his front door, was a flyer from a local office equipment and furnishing company. Printed on the front of the envelope was the company's name: *The Home Office*. It was easy to smile about that now.

Noel had received a response to his enquiry regarding Moule senior but the only positive data still on record was that the man had been on the Jamaican police force's radar for some while up to 1956. However, there was no hard evidence to hold him and maybe they had been quite happy for him to leave the island when he did. There was also a footnote that a police informer had reported that Moule's father's name was on a drug gang hit list, but no reason was given. I saw no benefit in passing this on to Moule, unless of course he asked a specific question. I also accepted that we would never know if Moule senior had lied to his son about him killing a boy from DC, or if it was simply a tragic misunderstanding about the identity of the boy who died. It no longer mattered. The important thing was that Moule was now free of the burden of guilt.

Noel also told me that the youths who had attacked Sonia and me on the Common had been found guilty of causing actual bodily harm and given suspended sentences and an order to carry out unpaid community work. More importantly, he told June and me that Lavender Hill police station had been reprieved after a concerted campaign opposing the mayor's proposal to close it. Shortly after that, Noel was promoted to Inspector but that probably had little connection with the station's reprieve. Then, about five weeks after that there was some more good news, which might not have been wholly unconnected with the promotion. Mary was expecting a baby in July next year.

At the end of the Christmas term, I phoned Sonia to ask how her Moule story had been received. To my joy and relief, she told me proudly that it had not only been given high marks, but she had also won the school's English prize. I mentally patted myself on the back for my not inconsiderable contribution.

When she asked me what I would call Moule's story, if ever I were to publish it as a book, I said I hadn't given it that much thought to date. I reminded her that there was no question of using the story commercially without Moule's full consent. But if I could use it, she persisted, what title did I think I would give it? Then, with little hesitation I said, *The Grand Moule of Clapham*.

Sonia laughed and said she would call it *The Mango Hand*.

I agreed that that would also be a very appropriate title, but little did she know the reason why.

OTHER NOVELS BY NIGEL MILLINER

Edge of a Long Shadow
Cow Barn, Sleeps Six
A Door Marked Hawker
and writing as Nigel Horne:
Only God and the Swagmen
All About Face